John Llewelyn Davies

The Christian calling

John Llewelyn Davies

The Christian calling

ISBN/EAN: 9783337025076

Printed in Europe, USA, Canada, Australia, Japan

Cover: Foto ©Andreas Hilbeck / pixelio.de

More available books at **www.hansebooks.com**

THE

CHRISTIAN CALLING

BY THE

REV. J. LLEWELYN DAVIES, M.A.

RECTOR OF CHRIST CHURCH, ST MARYLEBONE.

𝕷𝔬𝔫𝔡𝔬𝔫:

MACMILLAN AND CO.

1875.

[All Rights reserved.]

THE first ten Sermons in this volume were preached as a continuous course in All Saints' Church, Scarborough, in the August and September of this year. It will be observed that they aim at setting forth some leading features of the state of life to which Christians are called,—Peace, Liberty, Righteousness, Holiness, and Love,—in their twofold aspect, as towards God and as towards men. The desire of the Vicar of All Saints', the Rev. R. Brown Borthwick, that these Sermons should be printed has led to the publication of the volume, which will be a memorial of Sundays to which I look back with much pleasure and thankfulness. The other Sermons deal chiefly with difficulties which are felt as besetting a life according to the Christian calling at the present time.

December, 1874.

CONTENTS.

I.

PEACE WITH GOD.

2 CORINTHIANS V. 18.—"God hath reconciled us to himself by
Jesus Christ."

I CAN only allow myself a very few words of
introduction, in commencing the course of Sermons
which by the kindness of your Vicar I have been
invited to preach in this Church. You know, I
think, that my subjects are to be certain leading
features of the state or condition into which it has
pleased God to call us. By giving our attention to
these in the order in which I have arranged them,
and in their several aspects towards God and towards men, I hope that we may be led, God
helping us, into a surer knowledge of our Christian
privileges and duties. I desire that we should
throughout bear in mind that both privileges and
duties rest alike upon the calling of God. "All
things are of God;" let this be the general motto
or text of my course. What we know of God is
just so much as it pleases him to reveal of himself;

D. S. S.   I and he has revealed himself *in calling us*. That is why St Paul corrected himself when he had said "after that we have known God;" adding, "or rather, have been known by God." Our true attitude towards God is wholly a responsive one; he calls, we listen, and look, and answer. Those who thus hear the voice of God, let it speak to them in whatever way it will, begin to know something of God, at the same time that they are learning really to understand themselves.

And now I hasten to bring before you my first topic, Peace with God; by which I mean, the peace which God has made between himself and us. This, as you know, is the Scriptural and Apostolic account of peace with God. It originates with God; it is he who has reconciled us to himself by Jesus Christ. To declare this, was the office of Apostles and Evangelists.

And I think we shall understand better what their Gospel still continues to proclaim, if we first make an effort to think of their message as coming new and fresh to men who have not heard it before. In the Apostolic age, the Gospel had this genuine novelty; and therefore the original language concerning the Gospel, which we read in the history and the letters of the Apostles, assumes for the most part that its work is being newly done and its first impression produced. Let us trace then the working of the Gospel when it is "good news," news as well as good; when it is brought as a light to those who have hitherto been sitting in darkness.

You may think of heathens, or men who have not heard of Jesus Christ, in any age of the world —in the first century or in the nineteenth. There is no great difference between one age and another in respect of the essential qualities and conditions of human nature.

Suppose the Evangelist to present himself to such persons as a stranger. He lets it be known at once that he speaks in the name of *God.* Whatever his audience may be, he may always count upon some sort of acknowledgment of God in their hearts. There is that in the universal heart of man,—yes, I say it confidently, not forgetting the absurdities of idolatry, or the blindness of the lowest savages, or the scepticism which prides itself on being in the forefront of civilization,—which is ready at once to confess a just Power, ruling above, to whom men owe reverence. When a serious and forcible appeal to such a Power has elicited this acknowledgment, it will probably awaken at the same time two conflicting feelings. The thought of Supreme Righteousness can never be wholly unwelcome to men ; it may stir up a lively hope and joy in their souls. But it will also make them conscious of the wrong that is in them. Supreme Righteousness cannot appear friendly to human unrighteousness. So it is a matter of course that some sense of fear and estrangement should be awakened in all men who hear of a just God. "How can he regard *me ?*" says the voice of conscience in the sinner. "He must be my enemy. This stranger comes to tell me of one who may probably take vengeance upon me."

The Evangelist, we will suppose, goes on to speak of God as gracious. He knows there is need to overcome the repugnance to the thought of God created by the consciousness of wrong-doing. He assures his hearers that the God of heaven and earth is not a vengeful Destroyer; he points to proofs of his beneficence and of his longsuffering. His hearers listen not unmoved, not without some degree of assent. But the sinner in each man says, "What can there be in common between me and this good and gracious Being ? It is impossible that he should look with any satisfaction on me ; nor is it a pleasure to me to dwell in thought on him.

I wish to follow my own ways, and to be let alone. I should like to forget this gracious Lord of heaven, and to escape out of his sight. Still, he may be powerful, and I may not be too insignificant for his notice ; if I can learn any means by which I might ward off his hostile purpose, it will be safer to try to propitiate him."

The Evangelist never says that such apprehensions are idle. He never tells the sinner that he is sure to go unpunished. It is not his commission to proclaim that God does not care about men and their doings. He affirms earnestly that God is grieved by sin, and will punish it. But he is still more earnest in conveying the announcement which he is charged to deliver. He takes for granted that his hearers are sinners, alienated from God by their sins. It is no wonder to him that they do not like to retain God in their thoughts. But he brings them overtures of reconciliation from God himself. He calls sin their enemy; God he declares to be a Friend who is seeking to deliver them from their enemy. He assures them that while sin is and must be a barrier between them and God God himself removes the barrier by forgiveness. God is sending to them the message of a pardon which puts away their sins, and claims them as reconciled to him.   But the Evangelist is not the bearer of a merely verbal forgiveness.   He has the story of Jesus Christ to tell.   He says that he comes in the name of the Son of God, who has lived and died in Judea.   In accordance with ancient promise and expectation, God has sent his Son into the world. Jesus of Nazareth was the Christ, the Son of the living God.   He lived amongst his countrymen, and in the closest intimacy with a chosen few, but he spoke and acted as the Son whom the Father in heaven had sent.   He was the living embodiment of Divine forgiveness, seeking the lost that he might save them, shewing infinite sympathy with all who were unhappy, making common cause with the ignorant, the weak, and the helpless, trying to awaken faith in those amongst whom he taught, and then blessing with acts of healing and deliverance those who believed.   But this active unwearied grace is not all that the Evangelist has to tell of in the Son of God.   He adds, with wonder in his own heart springing up anew each time he tells the story, that the Son of God came to suffer and die, as well as to teach and to do good.   His own countrymen, enemies in their minds through wicked works, blindly rejected his grace and sought to destroy him.   Jesus went to meet their anger, not bending before it, but yielding himself willingly to all it could do against him. As he approached the death which he foresaw, the essential Divine glory revealed itself in him more and more perfectly to those who believed in him. Giving himself up with no reserve to his Father, he died, as the Son of man, the cruel death of the Cross. For the moment all hope and light seemed to perish with him. The cause of unhappy sin-laden men descended with him into the grave. But it was safe with him there, and could never again be parted from him. The Father, having given up his Son to death, raised him again from the dead. Jesus Christ rose, to live for ever at the right hand of God, not abandoning mankind, but carrying them with him to the Father. Thenceforth it is his glory to work out the Divine purpose of redemption. He has given his Spirit to be the life of all who come to the Father through him. He has commissioned those who were intimate with him on earth, and others after them, to go forth as his envoys, proclaiming everywhere the Divine reconciliation, and entreating men to receive the forgiveness of sins and to be at peace with their Father in heaven.

This is the substance of the Gospel of Christ, coming as good news to ignorant and sinful men.

It is a message of peace, a declaration of pardon, a pleading offer of reconciliation; and it points to Jesus Christ, Son of God and Son of man, the crucified and risen, as the Mediator—the Living Peace —between God and men. No one believing in him can doubt God's grace. No one can consider him, without being drawn and won by him. In him the enmity between God and man is done away. Where any longer is place for it? The man who believes in Christ is a rebel who lays down his arms, making no conditions, urging no excuses, overwhelmed with the love and grace which seek not his, but him.

It never happened, in the Apostolic age any more than in subsequent times, that when this word of God was spoken to a multitude, it was welcomed by all who heard it. No: to many it has seemed incredible, in many the enmity has been too strong to be overcome. Sometimes it has appeared to be spoken altogether in vain. The seed might be widely scattered, but it was not sure to find the good soil in which it could take root and grow. But those who have gladly received the word have always had this experience, in proportion to their faith,—that they have entered into peace. However deep their humiliation, however genuine their disgust with themselves might be, they have perceived and felt that, in Christ, God was making peace with them. The Death and Resurrection of the Son of God have been powerful to dispel all misgivings as to the insuperable nature of sin, all doubts as to God's willing and availing acceptance of the sinner. Christ has effectually proved himself to be Peace between God and men.

But we hereditary Christians are in a different position from non-Christian audiences, in Antioch or in Ephesus, in modern India or in Africa, hearing the good news concerning Christ for the first time. There is no question for us about becoming Christians and joining the Church; we are members of the Christian Church already.

Well, brethren, the Church of Christ to which we belong is built up upon the reconciliation or atonement which the first Evangelists proclaimed to an estranged world. Men asked to be joined to the Church, because they believed that in Christ they were reconciled to God. They came into it as pardoned sinners. Each one, in becoming a member, received a washing with water which assured him that he was a forgiven man, cleansed by the unbought grace of God. From the Day of Pentecost to this day, that Sacrament of Baptism which Christ ordained has stood forth in all its simplicity, the abiding witness of the remission of sins. The Christian profession rests upon reconciliation, freely given, humbly and gratefully accepted. No one that is a baptized Christian has a right to be anything else than reconciled to God.

Christians may be addressed in two ways.

This is one way :—a teacher may dwell upon the symptoms of worldliness and corruption in them, symptoms which their neighbours can easily discern, and of which they can hardly be unconscious themselves. He may expostulate with a man, " What are you, to claim to be a Christian, to profess to be pardoned and reconciled ! Don't you know that you are walking in the ways of carelessness and sin, with a heart too seldom turned towards God, caring for the things of this life, not setting your affections on things above ? What have you to do with peace ? Your Christianity is merely nominal ; beware how you in any way count upon it. Your place is with the outside heathen. Until your heart be changed, you have no part or lot in the matter." There may be too much truth in such warnings ; and it may seem both faithful and wholesome to utter them plainly.

There is another way, which to some might seem less safe. This is,—to urge upon Christians, not their own shortcomings, more or less grave and deplorable, but their vocation. Instead of telling them that they are *not* Christians and trying to prove it, the teacher might plead with them earnestly, "You are Christians. You are washed, —you have received the washing which typifies spiritual cleansing and bears witness of forgiveness ; you have been called, you have been consecrated ; your true condition is that of being reconciled to God, having comfort and assurance in approaching him, and walking in conformity with his will. If you call yourselves Christians, this is what Christianity is. Claim your privileges by all means. Assume that you are at peace with God through him who gave himself for you on the Cross."

This mode of address you will recognize as familiar to you in the Epistles of the New Testament. St Paul spoke in this way to the Corinthians and others. If it is objected that to become a Christian in those days required courage, involved many sacrifices and dangers, and therefore implied an earnestness of faith which we cannot count upon in an ordinary Christian now ; I admit it. But it is also true beyond dispute that the little societies which St Paul so confidently addressed as elect and holy, were deformed by disbelief, by immoralities, and by disorders, which we in these days can scarcely think of as compatible with any sort of Christian profession. Amongst the Christians of the New Testament were at all events some who denied a resurrection, some who required to be warned very solemnly against fornication, some who exhibited vulgar insolence and greediness in the Communion of the Lord's Supper.

But the real justification of this mode of address is not to be sought in the character of those who are addressed, but in its own proper tendency. So far from condoning sin and carelessness, it wages a relentless war against them. It does not say to a man, "You may be at your ease in cherishing enmity against God;" but "What manner of person ought you to be, you who by the blood of his Son are reconciled to God!" We cannot appeal thus to those who do not profess to be Christians; but in speaking to those who do, who have been baptized and have never cast off their Christianity, and who are to be found in Churches, may we not use their Christian calling with great force against their unfaithfulness and inconsistency?

After declaring without reserve, "God in Christ

reconciled you to himself," it was entirely natural to St Paul to go on, with pathetic entreaty, "I beseech you, in Christ's stead, be reconciled to God!" God has laid the foundation; each Christian might assume it and stand upon it,—the more he did so, the better; but then he had to build on it the superstructure of his conscious and progressive life.

What say you, my brethren? If the testimony, "God has reconciled you to himself," comes home to you with any reality, does it not make you conscious with shame and self-reproach of the estrangement which too surely mars your peace with God? Will you not ask the God of all grace to purge your hearts of the dispositions which are so dishonouring and so displeasing to him? Let me say—and may the Spirit of God put life and power into the words!—to him that is least a Christian amongst all the Christians who hear me, "My brother, believe me, God has made peace between you and himself. Do not look for the evidences of this reconciliation in your own soul. Tainted, distracted, perverse, desponding, all this your soul may be. You know partly in your own conscience what you are, and God knows still better. But it is not in yourself that you are to look for the grounds of reconciliation. See them in Christ, see them in his words of authority, see them still more clearly in his Passion. See what an eternal fountain of pardoning love has been opened in him! Suffer yourself to be touched and won. Break through the evil influences which keep you back from the Saviour who calls you. Know your true Friend, know your real enemies. The influences that flatter your self-will would be your ruin; God, who asks for your heart, will be your strength and salvation!" And you that have come out of estrangement into God's peace, let me entreat to value that peace more highly and to be more thankful for it. Never suppose that it depends on your goodness or on your faith. What you have to do is not to make it but to enjoy it. It is your blessedness to live the daily life of those whom Christ calls his friends.

II.

PEACE AMONGST MEN.

Colossians iii. 15.—"Let the peace of God rule in your hearts, to the which also ye are called in one body."

It is particularly required of Christians, as every one knows, that they should be at peace amongst themselves, and that they should endeavour, so far as lies in *them*, to live peaceably with all men. The common conscience of Christendom bears witness that this is a Christian duty; and those who do not profess to be Christians themselves, will often reproach professing Christians with their wars and schisms and private quarrels, as proving their reckless inconsistency. "How hollow and false modern Christianity must be," they say, "when it cannot even constrain Christian men and nations to be at peace!"

There is, we must admit, much that is hollow and false in our Christianity, and we ought to be thankful to any one who will make us aware and ashamed of it. Taunts like these are not, however, aimed in general with any discrimination. What they may most usefully do for us, is to awaken us to the consideration of our own principles. We shall best learn where we as Christians are wrong, by asking ourselves what it is to which we are called. Undoubtedly we ought to be at peace. Why then ought we? What is the foundation upon which external peace should be built up? To what kind of peace are we called?

When peace is mentioned in the New Testament, it is not always easy to determine whether peace with God is meant, or peace amongst men. In any such uncertainty, it can hardly be wrong to meet the difficulty by saying that both are meant. For it was a deeply rooted feeling in the minds of the Apostles, as it was the doctrine of their Master, that God, in reconciling men to himself, at the same time and by the same act reconciled them to one another. St Paul, for example, having in his eye the two divided and hostile sections of the world with which he was concerned, the Jewish and the Gentile, rejoiced to declare that God had reconciled both to himself in Jesus Christ, so making peace. If the Jews were drawn to the Father in Christ, and if the Gentiles were also drawn to the Father in Christ, they were of course drawn together. They were like two separated bars of iron attracted by the same magnet. If, instead of thinking of sections of the world, you think of two individual men, that had been enemies, both at the same time reconciled to God, you will feel that it is impossible they should remain enemies. It is not indeed a matter of course that two persons should become hearty friends by being attracted to the same person. You may remember that even amongst the loyal and affectionate followers of the Lord Jesus there were jealousies occasioned by the desire to receive distinguishing marks of his favour. But that was when Jesus was "known after the flesh," before he had gone up to his Father's right hand. Consider, brethren: he who is at peace with God has thankfully received the pardon of his sins, —of the sins which alienated him from God, and caused him to be troubled by the thought of God. He has repented of his sins; but what are they? All things that offend the just and gracious Father. Amongst the chief of them are all the dispositions which set man against man. Can he who hates his brother be on happy terms with the just and forgiving Father? It is in the nature of things impossible. Every Cain must feel his countenance fall when he brings an offering to the Lord; he drives himself out from the presence of the Lord, and must be hid from his face. It is only when God is not truly known that the man who harbours ill-will in his heart can come to the Being whom he mistakenly worships as God with prayers and offerings. He who has found in Jesus Christ the way to the Father has been made ashamed of jealousy and resentment. The Spirit of sonship is the Spirit of the family, the Spirit of brotherhood. The true Christian is moved to this kind of appeal to God,—"O our Father in heaven, forgive us our trespasses, as we forgive them that trespass against us."

When we ask ourselves therefore why it is that Christians are bound in some eminent and peculiar degree to be lovers and makers of peace, let us answer that it is because God whose Gospel we have received has called us to peace,—to a peace that is first with himself and then of necessity with all whom he names his children. This may not be the only reason, but it is the profoundest reason, and the most expressly Christian. It is the motive that ought to work in us most powerfully and abidingly, and that will guide our desires most surely into the practical way of peace. Taking our stand upon this ground, we shall recognize that our conceptions of peace must always be in the first place and essentially spiritual. We cannot begin from an outward or superficial peace. It is the rooting out of ill-will and its seeds from the heart that must be the Christian's primary object. And experience tells us that these feelings have private life for their chief sphere. Common daily efforts, such as all may make, are those which it would be most satisfactory to me to urge upon you; and I believe that in giving our minds chiefly to these, we shall be discharging most loyally our obligations as children of the Divine peace.

We have not much to do, we who are assembled here, and at this moment of nearly universal peace, with the question of wars between nations. But you are aware that it has been not uncommon to speak of open war between nations as the one great violation of God's peace, and the scandal by which Christendom is most deeply disgraced. To some it has seemed the natural and consistent inference from this view, that a nation ought not to go to war under any provocation. Others are ready enough to assume that this would indeed be the Christian mode of acting, but that it is incompatible with the honour and safety of a nation. Now I admit war to be shocking, and a cause of wide-spreading misery, but I do not allow that it is a necessarily unchristian act to go to war. Nor does it seem to me at all clear that war in general is accompanied by the ill-will, which is the real violation of God's peace, in anything like the degree in which it causes fighting and bloodshed. Fighting and bloodshed and devastation are miserable works for men to be engaged in ; but war, we may gladly acknowledge, can be carried on in a generous temper of mind and with none of the malignity or baseness of hatred. When we look at the matter from the specially Christian point of view, we must not begin from the measurement of outside evils. Our duty is to see that we remember the bonds by which God in heaven has knit together the nations of the earth ; that we do not give way to national vanity, cruelty, or vindictiveness, in time of war; and that in time of peace we cultivate the behaviour, of justice, courtesy, and good feeling, towards other nations, which may tend to prevent war. It is certain that when war is declared, some one has been in the wrong. A preacher of the Gospel should urge his countrymen to be just, generous, and self-restraining, not only as individuals, but as a nation. But I know of nothing in the Gospel which forbids na- tions to strike blows against injustice or greed, or which would stamp the prudence that prepares for war, the regard of the citizen for national honour, and the gallantry of the soldier, as unchristian.

There is another class of conflicts with which we are somewhat more closely concerned. Peace, in its outward aspect, is greatly marred by religious divisions and controversies, and by civil struggles between parties and interests. We cannot but see in the multiplied schisms of Christendom memorials of obstinate self-will, and hindrances to the ideal unity of the kingdom of God, which may well cause us to grieve. In the struggles between classes of society, especially between the richer and the poorer, when the privileged classes and those which have capital try to hold fast all their comparative advantages, whilst the industrial multitudes try to win for themselves a less meagre share of what is desirable in life,—there is much that Christians must lament. But here again, let me suggest, we should not begin from the outside. The essential violation of God's peace is not in controversy itself, but in the elements which embitter it, in rancour, in hardness, in unwillingness to recognize good on the opposite side, in making the support of a public cause minister to personal pride and interest. Every Christian has need to pray earnestly that zeal for the cause to which he is attached,—be it that of the

Church, or of Liberalism, or any other,—may not betray him into intolerance and spite, and into that sin against the Holy Ghost which attributes gracious and beneficent action to an evil origin. Wilful misconstruction of motives, to which controversy so often gives occasion, is a terrible sin against God's peace. We cannot tell how far, or how quickly, external divisions would disappear, if every one in contending for his communion or his party were enabled to feel kindly and justly towards those from whom he differed ; such results we may be content to leave in the hands of God ; but all Christians are assuredly pledged by their calling to cherish the just and kindly feeling, and we cannot doubt that its effect would be great and glorious. Meantime let us be thankful for the softening influences which have passed over both civil and ecclesiastical contests in our land, and which make it much easier than it was formerly for the private Christian to be moderate and charitable.

But it is in social and domestic life that the most important triumphs of God's peace are to be won.

I do not mean to underrate great causes and public affairs, the progress of mankind, the dignity and the duty of our country. Still less would I imply that the *Gospel* has nothing to do with these larger interests. Our Christianity, if it is that of the New Testament, ought to raise us out of the narrow egotism of our individual hopes and fears, and to nourish our humanity and public spirit. But it seems to me that it is in the more private sphere, of the home and of the neighbourhood, that it is most difficult to fulfil the duty of living peaceably with all men; and also that if the peace of God could govern our hearts in these our relations with those who are nearest to us, we should be sure to be made in all other respects followers and servants of peace.

And each of us, my brethren, has his neighbours, in contact with whom he must live. No one is so insignificant, no one is so solitary, that he has not some with whom he may either quarrel or be at peace. Nor is any one, I venture to affirm, so happy in his lot or in his temper as to be without his own trials in this matter.

Where the tie is closest, and human lives are most inseparably entwined together, there it is most blessed to be at peace, there the misery of discord is most intolerable, and there patience and sweetness of temper may be most severely tried. A preacher, when he speaks of the irritations of the home and of the houshold, may make sure that he is touching a responsive nerve, a responsive chord of the heart, in every one of his hearers. The peace which we have in view now is something more, you understand, than a decent veil of behaviour and good manners. You may vex and alienate, without openly breaking the peace. We know that explosions not unfrequently take place; but we cannot say in how many cases self-respect restrains the inward resentment from exploding. You can scarcely become intimately acquainted with any family circle without learning that there are members of it who find it hard to get on with other members. In local society, how inevitable is jealousy between those who aim at the same distinction, scorn exhibited by one who thinks himself—or herself—superior, angry defiance thrown back by those who regard themselves as insulted by the scorn, the unreasonable misunderstanding which sees an unintended slight, the long smouldering feud which a little good sense and placability might quickly extinguish!

My Christian brethren, amongst *us*, partakers of the heavenly calling, these things ought not so to be. "No, certainly they ought not," I think I hear some one answer, "but it is not *I* that am in fault! I do not wish to quarrel, I am a very reasonable person, but I am specially unfortunate in my circumstances. It may be that I have been born with a somewhat irritable temper, but I could control it, if I had not to deal with a companion or a neighbour with whom it is impossible to be on pleasant and easy terms." My brother, be assured of this, that there are scores of persons round you saying precisely the same thing. The instinct of us all is to excuse ourselves and throw the blame on others. Very likely others deserve the blame. But let us not wait to get the due share of responsibility accurately apportioned to each. That the Eternal Judge alone can determine. Let us think rather with more earnestness of the solemn fact, that God is calling us to peace. How are we ever to reach it, if we are severally bent on justifying ourselves? Look upon peace as a blessing which God holds out to us, a blessing to all and to each, a common good, a common glory, which is to be won, not by self-justification, but by self-suppression. If we must justify ourselves, let us try to do it, not before men, but before God. Let us not imagine ourselves, as we are so often apt to do, pleading our case in a human court, ingeniously putting forward everything that tends to excuse or to commend ourselves; but let us come at once into the presence of our God. See whether the steady recollection of God's grace and purpose does not brush away our pleas like cobwebs. What is it that we believe that God has done for us? Has he been extreme to mark what is done amiss? Has he exacted of us all that is due to him? Nay, because we had nothing to pay, he has frankly forgiven us all. When we were sinners, Christ died for us. The Father has reconciled offenders to himself in the Son of his love. His desire and end is Peace. He entreats us to receive his forgiveness. He says to us daily, "Be at peace."

If you go into the presence of this gracious Father, and allege, "My neighbour commits this or that trespass against me," the unmistakeable voice of God enjoins you, "Forgive him!" You ask, perhaps, "What, if he does not confess his fault in a proper manner and beg my forgiveness?" "Yes!" God replies to you, "Let there be no barter of your grace. Think only of extinguishing the unfriendly feeling, of healing the wounds and making the scars invisible, of bringing about peace, so long as it be genuine, in any way you can." The sense of our unworthiness in God's sight is the best ally of humility and forbearance and graciousness in our dealings with our fellow-creatures. But it is good also to realize that God's end in redemption was to establish amongst his children the living unity of one body in his Son. All discord is a rebellious violation of that unity; and every one who fails to do what in him lies to keep that unity, is setting himself against God's redemptive purpose.

It is a world in which the most true-hearted Christian could not hope to go through life without giving offence. We are not to let truth and justice suffer, in a vain attempt to preserve peace. Even the Prince of Peace was compelled to say, in anguish of heart, "Think not that I am come to send peace on earth! I am not come to send peace, but a sword!" There was something of the same sadness in the heart of his Apostle, when he said, "If it be possible,—as much as lies in *you*,—live peaceably with all men." That is all that each Christian can make the aim of his endeavour. But how much might thus be accomplished! Let us have faith in him who calls us. The Peace which is to be the crowning glory of him whom we follow is to be conquered gradually from the powers of strife. We have to be fighters for peace, soldiers in the army of the Divine peace-maker. It is only by long struggles with himself that an inheritor of human passions can hope to subdue those tendencies which would make him a promoter of strife rather than a peace-maker. But what reward can be more blessed than that which is granted to all such efforts? To possess a deep inward joy, to spread happiness around, to be an instrument in working out the great Divine purpose,—is it not worth while to make earnest and ever-renewed efforts for the sake of such privileges? And these are not distant, imagined, rewards. You have seen them, I trust, actually given by the God of peace to some of his favoured servants. He lets us all see in some measure with our own eyes how good and joyful a thing it is to dwell together in unity.

III.

THE FREEDOM OF SONSHIP.

ROMANS VIII. 15.—"Ye have not received the spirit of bondage again to fear; but ye have received the Spirit of adoption, whereby we cry, Abba, Father."

THERE is a danger against which we in these days have some special need to be put upon our guard, described by St Paul under the name of *bondage*, or a *servile* condition, in things relating to God. Our tendency at the present moment is to shrink from irreligion, and to rejoice in the spread of all religious feelings and practices. There are many, I believe, to whose thoughts it has scarcely occurred that there is such a thing as a spirit of bondage by which the most religious persons may be oppressed, and from which it is the glory of the Gospel to set men free. Such forgetfulness is not due to any lack of warnings and explanations in the New Testament. No doubt the kind of bondage most familiar to us, and of which none but the utterly careless can be unmindful,—that of lawless desire and a perverse will,—is constantly kept in view in the New Testament as opposite to Gospel liberty. But the Apostles, and especially St Paul, are often speaking of a bondage expressly associated with religion. And the two forms of bondage are in their view connected in kinship or close alliance. *Death, Sin, the Law,* are three oppressors in league together. There is a whole world of practical theology in these few words, " The sting of death is sin, and the strength of sin is the law ; but thanks be to God who gives us the victory through our Lord Jesus Christ !" Here "the law" might be explained as the religion which brings into bondage. It is impossible that the danger of such a bondage can have passed away from the world. I fear rather that we may have too little knowledge of that *liberty* of the Gospel which makes the bondage also known and felt.

You Christians, St Paul says, did not receive a spirit of slavery again unto fear, but what you received was a Spirit of sonship, in which we cry Abba, Father!

That they had received *some kind of spirit* was to the Christians of that age a fact of experience, which no one doubted. The entrance into the Church was marked, as a general rule, for every believer, by an access of new spiritual emotions prompting him to unwonted utterances. So that a Christian defined himself no less as a partaker of a Spirit from above, than as a believer in a risen Lord. St Paul therefore takes the receiving of a spirit for granted ; the question is what kind of a spirit it was. He tells his readers emphatically that it was not one suitable to slaves, generating a habit of fear ; they had not simply exchanged a heathen or a Jewish spirit of bondage for a Christian spirit of bondage; the Spirit received by the Church was —he does not here use the formally opposite phrase, one of *freedom*, but an equivalent and more instructive term—one of *sonship*. From the day of Pentecost onwards, the true Spirit of the Church had always prompted the believers to cry to God with trust and hope as to their Father. That impulse declared the nature of the Spirit ; it was evidently a *filial* Spirit ; if its cry was one which God inspired, then they in whom it moved *were* God's children. God was himself claiming them as his children, by teaching them to call him Father. "As many as are led by the Spirit of God, they are *sons* of God,"—otherwise, how could they call God Father? And the Spirit of *sonship* is essentially the Spirit of *freedom*. In no other way can men attain to the highest kind of freedom, and be permanently secure against every kind of bondage, than by living the inner life of children of God.

If you wish to see how much slavery there may be in religion, you have but to glance at some of the heathen religions. They have not been all equally oppressive; where nature has been bright and free from terrors, there religion has generally had its cheerful and joyous elements. But how frightfully have some races been tormented by their religions! Having experience of arbitrary rulers and cruel enemies in the visible world, they have peopled the invisible with principalities and powers far more cruel and capricious. Their worship has been *devil*-worship. Imagine how the fear of their false gods must have harassed the souls of a people, before they would make their sons and their daughters pass through the fire, to propitiate them! This seems the last extremity to which the spirit of bondage could drive human beings; but, short of that, the lives of men have been filled with misery and darkness in various degrees by the malevolent powers which they have placed in their heaven.

Whilst much of this dread, and of the servile temper nourished by it, prevailed in the world to which the first preachers of Christ offered their Gospel, there were some in that age who congratulated themselves on having found emancipation from superstitious terrors in *philosophy*. "Happy he," says the Roman poet, "who has been able to learn the causes of things, and who has put all fears and inexorable Fate and the noise of greedy Acheron under his feet!" We cannot forget how many in our own day are seeking freedom in the same path. It would be anything but Christian to fling reproaches at those who, whilst they persuade themselves that all the region which bounds this visible life of ours is an impenetrable blank, still hold by a high moral standard, and endeavour to live so as to serve their generation. Looking back to the time of the Roman Empire, we see the same experiment being tried. There were then also men who believed in no God, who despised the superstitions of the vulgar, who pursued knowledge so far as it was within their reach, and whose tone of mind was sustained by philosophical dignity. But we Christians of to-day are followers of men in the first century who did not pretend to be philosophers, but whose far higher pretension was that they had a calling of God. They also were lovers of liberty, though their doctrine of liberty was a different one from that of the philosophers who despised superstitions. They valued liberty even more, they longed for it more earnestly, they were enthusiastic—I do not say more so than the philosophers, for *they* hardly had this enthusiasm at all, —in desiring to make other men partakers of it. They held and taught that the God who sent them was offering freedom to men, and that every man who would come to the Father through Christ and accept the Spirit of sonship might become truly and consciously free.

Now in thus regarding spiritual liberty as a priceless gift from God to men, the Christian Evangelists were distinguished from mere propagators of a religion. They were raised above the passion of making proselytes. They quickly became aware that men might profess to be Christians without inheriting the liberty of the children of God. It must have been a very painful discovery. I am speaking now especially of St Paul, the greatest of the founders of the Church, in labours more abundant than all the others, but at the same time the one who made the lightest of a mere profession of Christianity, and the most watchful against influences which might mar the Divinely intended effects of the Gospel. It was the purpose of the

Gospel to make men free; the grace of God was therefore frustrated if men, instead of coming with open truthful hearts to God, put themselves under the tyranny of a law or a ceremonial or formal works of any kind. That was to regard God as an Exactor rather than as a Giver, as a hard Ruler rather than as a Deliverer, as one who was to be shunned and to be put off with the barest fulfilment of a bargain or task rather than as one who was to be trusted and appealed to for help. And St Paul saw with true spiritual insight the servile dispositions which grow naturally out of the servile relation, and which threatened to degrade the Church of Christ. To be a slave almost implies as a matter of course to be deceitful. What slave-owner ever felt that he could *trust* his slaves? Govern a child tyrannically, and you are responsible for breeding in him a reserved, suspicious, un-candid, temper of mind. So, those who cannot come to God in the Spirit of sonship, enjoying trustful access and freedom of speech before him, almost inevitably learn to lead a double life. Their aim is to close the secret recesses of their hearts for themselves, and to give a certain outward service to God. Formalism, legalism, asceticism, are always dangerous to the open, truth-loving disposition which the grace of God would cherish.   Nor are they really powerful against the dominion of the senses. The "Law," in Pauline language, is weak against the flesh, because it cannot give *life;* it cannot cleanse, brace, quicken the soul; that is the work of the Spirit, of the Spirit which is filial and makes free.

So that whilst there was the world to conquer for Christ, St Paul thought it worth while to spend a great part of his labour in contending for freedom against bondage in the little societies of baptized believers.   His doctrine is perfectly clear, but it needs to be insisted upon in every age of the Church as in the first.   The Gospel, he taught, is the story of the Son of God who revealed his Father as perfectly *fatherly* towards men. What is fatherliness?—It is made up, we may briefly say, of the two elements of justice and goodness.   To call God our Father is to say that he is altogether righteous and gracious towards us. Well, the Father through Christ invites men to come to him.   On their part, everything might keep them back, unworthiness, dread, want of de-sire.   But by his free grace and by spiritual help God removes these hindrances.   He appeals to faith, and shews himself to be such a one as may be trusted. The only way of going to God is with the inmost emotions of the soul. There must be confession without reserve, thankfulness for pain as well as for pleasure, the sense of dependence, the supplicating desire of the highest good. When the heart thus opens itself and allows itself to be drawn into the holy of holies which is the felt presence of the Eternal Father, there is freedom. No longer is there any constriction of the heart, no longer the pressure of any chain upon the soul, no longer a cowardly fear of the future, no longer a suspicion that the forces of nature may be wielded by a destroyer. This freedom, won and enjoyed, is what men want and what God desires for them; every thing else is comparatively unimportant. What pleasure can God who sees in secret find in any outward service, in any arbitrary self-infliction?

It is quite true that we creatures of flesh and blood have to live an outward as well as an inward life. This will not bear to be forgotten. The outward must serve the inward. But when the outward *separates* itself from the inward, when it ventures to come into *competition* with it, then it must be treated even with contumely. When the liberty of the children of God is in question, even Scriptures, sabbaths, almsgiving, denials of appetite, prayers, sacraments, may find themselves put aside with something like disrespect.

Christian brethren, it is not easy for us to rise to the high spiritual level of St Paul's teaching; but this, you surely know, is what he taught, and this doctrine, even if you have misgivings as to its being too lofty, your consciences must confess to be profoundly and gloriously Christian. Do not believe that it is in itself dangerous; only perversions of it are dangerous. Free thinking, free living, free love, have acquired bad associations; but the things which have become justly odious under these names have no right to connect themselves with St Paul's teaching. You cannot make too much of spiritual freedom, so long as you understand by it what St Paul did,—the free access of the soul, in the filial Spirit, to the righteous and gracious Father.

This kind of freedom is very far indeed from setting people at their ease to do what they like. It by no means tends to promote a free and easy, inconsiderate, habit of mind. Let any one try it, and see what the effect upon him is. Let him come to God with the utmost imaginable confidence, with the fullest assurance that there is nothing to debar him from intimate communion with God. But of course he must remember who and what God is, that he is true and just and loving, that he is the Father of the Lord Jesus Christ who died for us on the Cross. Our freedom is to know God as he has thus been revealed to us. And is such a Father to be approached without reverence, without awe? Judge, if you please, by what you know of the mind of the most spiritual Christians. Was St Paul a light, irreverent, kind of person? Did he take life easily? Or were those who had known the Lord Jesus as a companion and friend and who had believed what he told them of God's goodness and desire that they should be made free, distinguished by levity and unconcern? St Peter, in one of the most instructive passages of holy Scripture, urges that the consciousness of having been set free and of being admitted into filial communion with God will directly promote watchfulness and awe. " If ye call on the Father, who without respect of persons judges according to every man's work, pass the time of your sojourning here *in fear;* forasmuch as you know that you were not redeemed—or set free— with corruptible things, as silver and gold, from your vain conversation, or empty manner of life, handed down from your fathers, but with the precious blood of Christ...who was manifest in these last times for you who by him believe in God that raised him from the dead and gave him glory, that your faith and hope may be in God." *To put our trust and hope in God,* this is the condition of freedom bought for us by the sacrifice of Christ. As the redeemed or freedmen of Christ we are entitled to call upon the just God as our Father. But *therefore* it is not for us to live carelessly, without purpose or aim, doing the first thing that routine or desire suggests. This is the very *bondage* from which Christ came to rescue us. No, the children of him who is known to us through Jesus Christ must feel reverence in their hearts for the Heavenly Father in the first degree, and then for their brethren, for the world which he creates, for the work which he has put us into the world to do. St Paul says even more than this; "Work out your salvation with fear and trembling, for it is God who works in you both to will and to do of his good pleasure." You see that this extreme view, of God working in man both to will and to do, does not involve to St Paul the apparently logical consequence that man is irresponsible; on the contrary it produces a deeper sense of responsibility. Another of the Apostles, St John, does indeed say that perfect love casts out fear; but then by adding, "because fear hath torment," he shews that he means by fear that kind of it which has torment. He also would have commended the fear that is consistent with love, the awe of profound admiration, the sense of unworthiness, the anxiety not to displease or to forget such a Father.

Yes, my brethren, there must be seriousness in the mind and the life of a Christian, a seriousness tempered by trust and hope and joy, but often not unmixed with sadness. The little use we make of our true freedom, the small value we set upon it, are enough of themselves to fill us often with sorrowful self-reproach. It is the will of our Father that our path through the world should be beset with difficulties and trials; we often cannot see our way clearly; at the very best we cannot always stand upright. But let our sins and our perplexities not drive us away from God, and make him distant to us and persuade us to seek help and comfort in rules that we can observe and works which we can perform, but bring us nearer in confession and prayer to him. May he never be transformed in our eyes into a Being from whom we should reasonably desire to escape; may he be always to us our supreme helper and friend. Let us not approach him as those who have to deprecate his anger by grovelling before him. Even in the forms of our outward worship, Christian freedom, or in other words reverence for the true character of God, would disapprove of any acts appearing to symbolize the servility of a frightened offender. Let us ever keep our thoughts fixed on Eternal Righteousness shining upon us through Eternal Love. Let us bear in mind that the Sacrifice of the Son of God was intended to set us free, and that his glorious name is the Redeemer. Our deserts at God's hands are indeed as bad as we can imagine them to be. But God does not give us only what we deserve. He gives us his Son to be our Head; and with him he gives us the Spirit of his Son. It is due to God that we should welcome into our hearts the Spirit of Jesus Christ and suffer it to work in us all filial affections.

IV.

CIVIL FREEDOM.

GALATIANS V. 13.—"Ye have been called unto liberty: only use not liberty for an occasion to the flesh, but by love serve one another."

IT is a very common observation, that the word *freedom* has various senses, and that there is need of discrimination in using it; that a man may be perfectly free, for example, in the sense of being perfectly protected from injury by a just and equal law, and yet be a slave to an appetite like the love of drink, or be oppressed and fettered by ignorance. Every one who has to say anything about freedom will find a similar reflection occur to him. No sooner do we begin to speak about it, than a multitude of distinctions and qualifications have to be made. Whether freedom ought to be desired or not, whether it ought to be allowed or not, is entirely uncertain till we understand the kind of freedom which is meant and the circumstances in the midst of which it is to be exercised.

Nevertheless the idea of freedom must be a high and noble one, or it could not have excited so much enthusiasm as it has done in men's minds. There is a spell in the name of liberty, which we may be hardly able to account for. The true and only way, as I believe, of accounting for the inspiration which has moved men to suffer and die in the cause of liberty, is to understand that liberty in its highest form is essentially *spiritual*, and to regard all inferior forms of it as deriving their life and worth from the highest. My purpose to-night is to shew the vital connexion between the common forms of freedom as between man and man, and that freedom which we enjoy towards God through receiving the Spirit of Sonship.

How would you describe liberty? If you say that a man is *free* when *he is able to do what he pleases*, the definition is a natural and obvious one, and certainly has some truth in it; but you will never persuade yourselves that it is a great and glorious thing for a man to be able to do as he pleases. On the contrary, there could be nothing *worse* than to tell a number of foolish persons that there is no restraint upon their doing just what they like. That would end in license and anarchy; and these are names of confessedly evil meaning.

The state of things when each man "does what is right in his own eyes," is one which we do not desire to bring about. It is felt to be a blessing when license and anarchy are suppressed by the force of a superior authority. It is plain therefore that the freedom whose cause is a holy one cannot consist in the simple absence of restraint upon men's acts.

But add a qualification, such as every one is ready to suggest. Personal freedom, it will be said, must of course have its limits. It is a good thing to be able to do as one likes, *so long as one does not interfere with the corresponding liberty of others.* When men live in society, the freedom of each must be limited by what the rest may similarly demand. Social freedom will be perfected, when the individual spheres within which each may do as he likes without interfering with his neighbour are as large as possible. This view is a very intelligible and convenient one, but it surely does not account for our reverence for freedom. Again I repeat, there is nothing sacred in the idea of a man doing as he pleases. The restraints are better than the freedom. If it were a supremely good thing that the sphere within which a man may do what he likes should be as large as possible, then it would seem to follow that the less we enter into those relations which have the effect of restraining us, the better. An unmarried man has more liberty, in this sense, than a husband and a father. He is much more at liberty, as we say, to do as he pleases, to go where he would like to go, to adjust his habits to his private tastes. According to this view, the lover of liberty will regard with disfavour domestic ties, social ties, and the general complexity which belongs to advancing civilization. The boast of freedom will be that expressed in Dryden's lines,

> "I am as free as Nature first made man,
> Ere the base laws of servitude began,
> When wild in woods the noble savage ran."

But that is to reduce the idea of freedom to an absurdity. We do not need to argue in these days with any one who thinks that freedom is to be sought by reversing progress and by dissolving society into units.

According to the principle which I have undertaken to expound, our essential freedom *comes of God's calling.* We are free, when we are God's true spiritual children, as he would have us be; when we are in filial sympathy, of knowledge, affection, and will, with the gracious and righteous Father. Of this freedom I spoke this morning. The freedom of politics and social life may *appear* to be something quite different in kind from this, but I do not believe that it is. It is nothing less than this that stirs the enthusiasm with which liberty is honoured by the wise and good. Liberty, thus regarded, is voluntary self-conquest, not self-indulgence, a noble instead of a base thing : and the common recognized conditions of political and social freedom are felt to be good, because they minister to the essential liberty of God's children. Freedom is realized, when men are awakened to *a consciousness of their high destiny and responsibility.* There cannot be anything that deserves the name of freedom, except where there is the dignity, the elevation of character, arising from this consciousness. Whatever has a tendency to promote such a character in a nation is worth contending for.

We are all of one mind in holding *slavery*,—I mean the possession of a man as a piece of property by a fellow-man,—to be a hateful evil. We are proud of the old glory of this English soil, upon which a bondsman could not put his foot without becoming free. If we have to confess that our history is stained by the complicity of Englishmen in the slave-traffic and in slave-owning, it is some comfort to us to think of the solemn and costly act by which the nation abolished slavery throughout the British dominions. Now this our feeling about slavery is due perhaps mainly to our knowledge of the barbarities which have been so naturally associated with it. Moreover the thought of a man being bought and sold by another man is so contrary to our ingrained belief as to the relation between man and man, that it excites in us an instinctive repugnance. But take slavery at its best; suppose the slave to be never bought and sold, and always kindly treated ; slavery of this kind may be made by its apologists to appear a very tolerable condition. Still, in the absolute subjection to the will of another, which is implied in all slavery, there is an essential mischief. It excludes the slave from the dignity of responsibility. It keeps the man a child. It stunts and dwarfs his humanity. The cares of the husband and the father are not fully laid upon him, so as to train him in the higher qualities of the man. And this, let me remark by the way, is one of the worst evils of dependent pauperism. It encourages people to throw off their domestic responsibilities, to be careless and *servile* in their habits ; and so it wages a steady and insidious war against elevation of character. If it is represented, then, that the condition of the slave may be a very comfortable one, and that he has the advantage of having no cares, we should reply "No, not the *advantage*, but the degradation. Our point of view ought to be that of the spirit, not of the flesh. To be free is, for a spiritual being, to be tried, to be called upon to act, to be constrained to care for others and to provide for oneself. The flesh may look back with longing to the fleshpots of Egypt; but it is better for the spirit, for the man, to wander and to hunger in the temptation of the wilderness."

The freedom bestowed on the Israelites by the deliverance out of Egypt was *national,* even more than personal. The children of Israel were treated as a people, to whom the blessing of orderly legislation was given, and who were to take possession of a promised land. And the freedom which has inspired the trumpet-notes of song and nerved the patriot to effort and endurance and sent its bracing breath through human history has generally been the deliverance of a people from a foreign yoke. Why then is it glorious to fight and suffer and die for national independence? Because to be conquered and made tributary involves *moral* humiliation. The land that serves strangers is *spiritually* disinherited. The prosperity of the inhabitants may be reasonably cared for; they may not be subjected to constant galling insults, though these can hardly be absent : but the higher spirit in the nobler part of the population feels that it has not its just rights. The citizens of an independent country acquire elevation from the consciousness of a national calling. It may be a small country, a Switzerland or a Belgium ; but, so long as it is independent, it is able to reflect that it, too, like its neighbours, has its appointed place in the world. It has the duties, the responsibilities, of one of the family of nations. This is food for high thought, exercise for high faculties. When it has lost its self-respect, the heart of a people is smitten as if with a blight. The child is no longer born to an inheritance of noble traditions and solemnizing responsibilities. Ah, my brethren, think what it ought to be to us to be born to such an inheritance as ours ! God grant to us not to be unworthy of it.

Once more, there is a kind of freedom which we English know well, opposed to the condition of being governed, not by a foreign race, but by despotic authority at home. We hardly call it a free country, in which the citizens do not personally possess a share, in some form or other, of the powers of government. In this sense of the word, that country is the freest in which the greatest number of people are practically interested in the life and work of the nation. Our historical mode of enjoying this freedom is through representation. We vote for representatives; and our representatives, when assembled together, have a predominant voice in the supreme government of the country. In thinking about these things, we are compelled to admit that no form of government is ideally perfect. Voting for those who are to govern us is evidently not everything; for most of us very decidedly disapprove of what is a perfectly genuine form of it, that of electing by a plebiscitum a Ruler who is to exercise despotic power. It is not a vote, given now and then, that nourishes the free-man's responsibility and dignity; it is the fact of having, in one way or another, or in various ways, some living interest and influence in the national life. One nation cannot in this matter lay down laws for another. But we may say generally, that there are two points to be aimed at by those who would promote domestic political freedom. One is, that each citizen should have some link of contact with the sovereign power, so that he may feel that he has something to do, though it may be extremely little, with the greatest affairs of the nation. The other is, that he should have a more visible and realizable interest in the small affairs of his own neighbourhood and society. For that which freedom, in any genuine shape, has to do, is to call out the sense of responsibility and to mix a man up with larger than selfish interests. Despotism is adverse to true spiritual freedom, because it encourages a man to feel that public affairs are provided for without him, and that he may therefore give himself up without distraction to the promotion of his own interest.

Questions concerning political freedom and the way in which it may be most healthily diffused are sifted in the discussions and struggles of the day. I have only two or three observations to offer from the point of view of this sermon.

1.   First, as to religion and the Church. I am quite ready to admit that religion may be and often has been adverse to freedom. Here indeed we have one test of the better and the worse religion. But the method we have been following leads us to the conclusion that a national Church, apart from its direct work of bearing witness to the Gospel of grace, ought to serve the cause of freedom in an important degree by giving elevation and sacredness to the idea of *the country*. The national Church is the witness of the Divine Call-

ing of the nation. It should keep us in mind that it is God who gives us this beautiful land of ours with its golden harvests, and that we are placed and nourished here in order that this nation may be a servant of God in the world. I ask you, my brethren, whether you are not consciously lifted in the scale of spiritual freedom by thinking of our England as a Christian country, which accepts the election of God and confesses Christ as Lord.

But it is greatly to be desired, in this same interest of spiritual freedom, that the people generally should claim an active share in Church matters. Through Parliament and the Crown the nation generally has as much power in Church matters as it chooses to exercise. In these days in which we live, representatives should be made aware that it will not do to neglect matters so vitally affecting the welfare of the country as those of religion. And I cannot but believe that it would be a great gain to extend, through some such machinery as that of parochial Church Councils, the local and educating influence of responsibility.

2. Again: it is an important problem, what amount of legal regulation is desirable in the common life of a people, with a view to the promotion

of genuine freedom. It is absurd to assume that law is the opposite of freedom; but it is quite true that there may be an excess of government, that the machinery of law may interfere more than is desirable in private and social life. I believe that this problem is not to be settled by theory, but by experience. Political tact ought to feel its way towards the best limit of regulative interference. Such maxims as that you cannot make people virtuous by Act of Parliament, and such sayings as that of an eloquent orator, that he would rather see England free than sober, appear to me to confuse rather than to help the inquiry. We already, with universal assent and approval, do a great deal in the way of regulation. The question is whether we cannot do more, without defeating our highest object. That object is to train and help all English persons to *self*-government, and so to lift them to a higher exercise of genuine freedom. Whether a particular step will help or hinder this object is to be determined by practical wisdom rather than by theoretical maxims.

3. My own belief is, if I may venture to express it, that we do rightly in cautiously pressing interference in several directions. In some departments,—as for example, in the relations of capital

and labour,—the legislation required may be that of withdrawing special interference, rather than that of extending it. It is not to be denied that a great deal of the best legislation of this century has consisted in thus withdrawing regulation from interests and arranging that they shall be let alone. But on the other hand experience seems to have abundantly proved that much good may be done by putting a check upon occasions of temptation. The regulation of labour in factories is almost universally admitted to have been a great blessing. The regulation of the sale of intoxicating liquors is allowed as good by all up to some point or other; it is an important question whether further steps in the same direction may not be successfully made in the future. It is a good thing that gambling should be hindered as much as possible. In all such matters, it is a gain to do something when we cannot do everything. In one most important matter, I am confident that we may hopefully go forward,—I mean in compelling parents to send their children to school. To press this compulsion firmly, and to apply it universally, would be, I am persuaded, a great and almost unmixed benefit to the country.

These are lines in which a lover of freedom and

of his country may still find practical work to do. So much has been done in the way of removing injustices and abolishing privileges, that it is not easy now to discover a grievance. But we have always the higher aim before us, of promoting universal elevation of mind and character throughout the land. To labour in this cause is now the truest service of freedom.

I hope it does not appear to you an arbitrary connexion which I have endeavoured to bring out, between the liberty of the children of God and every inferior form of liberty which can claim our reverence and service. I do not see how the loyal Christian could really care for anything secular except through seeing its relation to the kingdom of God and the work of redemption. But if the Father of our Lord Jesus Christ is the Ruler of the world, this relation can nowhere fail. Let me not be supposed, however, to forget that the grace of God is able to bestow the transcendent freedom in the absence of every other. For the spiritual freedman of Jesus Christ,

> "Stone walls do not a prison make,
> Nor iron bars a cage."

Slaves, in the first Christian century and in all subsequent times, have been made truly free by the grace of God, and have been content to bear their lot without rebelling against it. You may trace in thought how the sense of responsibility, the consciousness of a calling, the feeling of self-respect and dignity, might be awakened in the breast of a slave, and be made to work in him far more powerfully, by the direct voice of the Gospel, than if he were trained from infancy and through manhood to the blessed cares of the family and of citizenship. So now, whilst we acknowledge with thankfulness what we have gained from the happy conditions of our English Christian lives, and whilst we long and strive that such advantages may be imparted to all our brethren as widely as possible, let us not think it enough to be free citizens, responsible parents. No; these relations point to a higher. We can only realize the most perfect freedom in these lower though still Divinely ordained conditions by being free in that condition to which God calls us all, in the filial Spirit of his Son. We are not free till the chains of sin by which we are tied and bound are loosed from us by God's accepted forgiveness. When we can come to God as our Father, remembering his righteousness, his holiness, his goodness, not afraid of him, but throwing ourselves upon his grace and help,—then we can stand upright amongst our fellow-men, then we can lead an inward life over which neither circumstance nor desire shall have dominion.

Seek then, dear brethren, the freedom which is to be found in the fellowship of the believer with his Lord. If the Son shall make you free, said Jesus himself, ye shall be free indeed. Aim always at the highest blessings, knowing that our God loves best to give us these; and there is nothing higher than a life of faith in the Son of God, a life fed by his Spirit, a life whose secret power is hid with Christ in God.

V.

THE RIGHTEOUSNESS OF FAITH.

ROMANS VI. 13.—"Yield yourselves unto God, as those that are alive from the dead, and your members as instruments of righteousness unto God."

MY endeavour this morning will be to press home to your reasonable convictions the great doctrine of justification by faith. The advance of knowledge has not, I believe, either falsified this doctrine, or made it obsolete. It needs to be guarded against perversion: but, rightly understood, it goes to the roots of our inward nature, and reveals to us both the way of our true life and a danger that will never cease to beset us.

St Paul's well-known phrase is, that faith is counted, reckoned, or imputed, unto us for righteousness. He borrowed it from the history of Abraham in the book of Genesis, where it is said, Abraham believed in the Lord, and he, the Lord, counted it to him for righteousness. The word *imputed*, I may observe, means precisely the same thing as *counted* or *reckoned;* and it would help to clear away some artificial notions from the doctrine of righteousness by faith, if we were to put aside the word *imputed*, and to use instead one of the plainer words, *counted* or *reckoned*. You will thus perceive that something of a false emphasis has been laid on *imputed*. "Imputed righteousness" is named, as if it were a particular sort of righteousness; but you could hardly give this significance to "counted righteousness" or "reckoned righteousness." St Paul's point is, not that righteousness is imputed or counted or reckoned, but that it is *of faith*. According to him, a man is righteous in God's sight when he believes ; that is to say, not when he has duly performed a certain set of required acts or observances, but when in his inmost soul he trusts God and surrenders himself to him. But, if a man is thus righteous, by trust and self-surrender, as Abraham was and as all true Christians have been, *whose* is the righteousness to be properly called ? St Paul gives the profoundly true answer. It is not the man's own righteousness; he does not originate what he does; he yields himself to God, and his members as instruments of righteousness unto God. It is *God's* righteousness therefore, disposing of him and working in him; and the man is righteous in so much as he does not claim to be righteous in himself, but rejoices to be clothed with the righteousness which is of God. I need hardly add, that when St Paul spoke of righteousness, it was the same thing whether he said that of *God* or that of *Christ:* he held that the Eternal Righteousness had been revealed in Christ, and that the form of it which had been seen in Christ was precisely the ideal form for man.

There is nothing arbitrary or artificial therefore in our receiving the righteousness which is of God by faith. All is as real as possible. A man is in his proper condition, is as right as he can be, when he believes in God; and this essential rightness of faith for man is verified by experience when it is proved that the more thoroughly he believes, the more easily and successfully does he lead a good life.

We need not trouble ourselves about "imputation"; what is most necessary for us is to understand as well as we can the nature of the Divine Righteousness, and the meaning of Faith in relation to it.

One way of regarding Righteousness, and the most helpful for our purpose, is to think of it as bringing forth order. Our understanding is always baffled when we attempt to arrive at ultimate ideas of what God is in himself. But the affirmation that God is righteous has a clear and adequate meaning, if we take it as declaring that God originates and maintains the living Order of the universe. For us, correspondingly, to be righteous will be to conform to this Divine order,—to take our place in it, and to go forward, without breaking loose from it, in its progress and development.

The order of the external world is a part of that which God, the Righteous Being, originates. The constancy and regularity of the material creation might be called God's physical righteousness. The inspired men of the Old Covenant were full of admiration and awe towards the order of Nature, and used to speak of it freely as illustrating the righteousness of the Eternal Maker. They did not indeed know the wonders which the inquiries of science have laid open to our view in these later days. But they were accustomed to meditate reverently upon the obvious phenomena of the visible world; and their profound appreciation of Righteousness in the higher sphere prepared them to see with pleasure the signs of Law in the lower sphere. The elements, they perceived, were ruled by the Maker's eternal statutes. His word ran swiftly through their changes. He had given them a law that was not to be broken. Modern science has enabled us to see in existing phenomena an almost infinite complexity, and has at the same time succeeded in tracing back the growth of things to simpler and simpler origins; but its very boast is that it discovers order and development every-where, in the remotest past as in the present. Here then, let us say, we have the physical aspect of the Divine Righteousness.

But there is another kind of order, more im-portant than that of the material universe, the order of the world in which spiritual beings and spiritual affections are the elements, and with reference to which we do not speak so much of what *must be* or *will be*, as of what *ought to be*. The will, con-science, responsibility, introduce entirely new con-ditions into our conceptions of order. Scientific men may delight to shew how—certain antecedents making certain consequences inevitable—the natural world could not have been other than it is. Organ-isms and their environments must, they tell us, act and react upon one another so as to bring about the results in which we fancy we trace de-sign. Their language, in expounding this universal necessity, tends to become grandiose and authori-tative, as if they had then reached the height of things. But when they come to real human life, they are themselves compelled to change their language. They then praise and blame, reprove, rebuke, exhort, like any unscientific person. They will say "If you do this, such a thing will happen; if you do that, such a thing will happen; you may do which you please, but you ought to do this, and you ought not to do that." There is plainly something more here than molecules and molecular attractions and repulsions. The mystery of *dis*-order has entered. Whilst we speak of the Divine Righteousness, originating and sustaining a certain order in the spiritual world, we are obliged to recognize *un*righteousness, which refuses to conform to that order. It is true that the two worlds, the physical and the spiritual, are so subtly interwoven that we know not how to separate matter and spirit. This need not surprise us, when we confess that both come of one Creator. But the most ordinary human being whose conscience is not dead may infer with certainty from the inward conflicts of which he is conscious, that he belongs to another world as well as to that of which he shares the conditions with the plants and the stones; and he cannot doubt that in the ideal order which suffers so many violations, we come nearer to the Creator himself than in the natural order which has received a law which cannot be broken.

Whilst then we Christians look up to an Eternal God who has ordained and constituted the services of men and of other spiritual beings in a wonderful order, we always take for granted that it is in our power to observe or to violate this order. Simple necessity, we affirm, belongs to the inferior kind of order, choice and voluntary action to the higher. The seed cast into the ground has no power to choose whether it will germinate or not; it is subject to what scientific men are fond of magnifying as inexorable law. But man, appealed to by Pleasure and Duty, has the consciousness of making a choice between them. If he chooses Duty, he conforms to the order of God's righteousness; if he chooses Pleasure, he fails from that order. We do not shut our eyes to the difficulty there is in holding that man may disarrange what God ordains; we confess the difficulty, and hold the belief in the face of it. It is the method of God's dealing with his spiritual creatures to let them know something of his spiritual order, and not to coerce them as involuntary atoms but to move them as thinking and willing persons to conform themselves to it.

But this word which I have been repeating so often will be more significant when we have considered what God's spiritual order actually is, and so have made the word a living one to our minds. St Paul's doctrine of righteousness by faith gives a simple and positive definition of it. God's order for men is that of a Family of his children. As the Righteous Being, this is the plan according to which he constitutes mankind. He does not set them in motion like whirling atoms, out of whose physical concourse indefinite combinations may proceed; he makes them his children, members of a family, having the two great primary and comprehensive relations of sonship to himself and brotherhood to each other. You can easily see that this is not a mechanical or stationary order. It admits of endless growth and development. It is good for us to think of God as gradually unfolding his Creation, the spiritual part as well as the physical. He is continually making it more complex and wonderful. There is always something more for men to learn, always something not quite the same for men to be. As the child grows into the man, so the human race has grown from the infantine stage to what it is now. And as we see in the child, so it is in the race; it is by living and trying and striving that men grow. They feel forward into the future, along the lines which the Maker has laid down for them, and after the objects which he more or less distinctly presents to their view and aspiration. But at no point do we see—or shall we ever see—the two great relations disappear from this advancing order, or cease to be primary in it. Still, the highest ideal for men is to be children towards the Eternal God, and to be to one another as children of the same heavenly Father.

And now, what is Faith, the Faith by which a man becomes righteous?—It is the act or movement which joyfully accepts these relations for the government of the heart and life. When God says to a man, as he does in the Gospel through Christ, "Thou art my son," justifying Faith replies, "I thank thee, O heavenly Father, this is what I rejoice to be and will be; I will trust in thee, will yield myself up to thy purposes, will find my joy in learning and doing thy will. I will be nothing in myself, be thou all to me, and in me, and through me!" Faith is the filial response to God's fatherliness. All believing has its secret and perfection in the filial attitude towards the true God.

By faith, or the filial mind, we may confidently say with St Paul, a man is justified. To accept without reserve the relation of sons and daughters to God, is the appointed and only righteousness for human beings. God requires nothing more of them than this. If they do this, they fall into the order of his spiritual righteousness. They yield themselves to be what he would have them and what by his persevering Providence and discipline he is making them.

By faith then a man is justified, and not by works.

Not by works. But let us give to "works" here the sense which St Paul has consistently in his mind. He means acts which can be separated from the inmost self, all that do not involve and express the real feeling of the doer, works which it is possible to do whilst the doer has some other mind and consciousness than what might be represented by his actions. Generally, it is enough to say that works are outward things. But this definition is not adequate or strictly accurate. For the works which do *not* justify may even be emotions, when the emotions are artificial. To submit the soul or nervous system to the thrills of a revival or a mission, in the belief that this emotion is something that God will receive as satisfactory, is, in essence, to seek justification by works. And on the other

hand, man is and must be a *doer*, not less in his condition as a believer and child of God than when he is
choosing to be independent of God. And the word
" work" is often used for that which is *not* separable
from the man himself—for what he really does, and
therefore for what he really *is*. In this case, "works"
are opposed to profession or person, as reality to
show. And as the word *faith* may very naturally be
used for religious profession, you may have this
curious result,—that one who says "a man is justified by works and not by faith" may be meaning
the very same thing as one who says "a man is
justified by faith and not by works." Actually the
same thing. For they both mean to affirm that God
accepts reality, not appearance ; the man himself,
not something separable from him ; the genuine
attitude of the heart, and not religious observances
or outside works.

Who could describe in their infinite variety all
the ways in which men have sought to manufacture
a righteousness of their own before God? My
brethren, there is an all but ineradicable desire in
the human heart to put God off with something
which is not really itself! The most plausible form
of this something is *religion*, I mean external religion. Sacrifices, confession and penance, Church-

going,—these are express attempts to offer to God what is supposed to be pleasing to him ; and surely, men say to themselves, if we abound in such offerings, God will be pleased with us and count us righteous ! But it is not difficult to see how hollow these observances may be ; and many, emancipating themselves from these, have sought a righteousness of their own in two other principal paths. In morality ; in the punctual performance of what men in general recognize as good works. And in spiritual religion, with its professions and phraseology and exclusiveness. These also, the morality and the so-called spiritual religion, though the doers may be flattering themselves that they are not as those formalists who hope to commend themselves to God by religious observances, may be just as truly *works*, by means of which men may be seeking to establish their own righteousness. Our human nature, like the garrison of a besieged fortress, tries every expedient to avoid unconditional surrender, the blessed humiliation which is really honour and deliverance and happiness !

The weakness of all these "works" is that they are ineffectual and betray us; they stand in the way of our becoming what God would have us be. The Gospel of God's grace, persuading us to believe, calls us to real living righteousness. Compare two men together,—the one keeping his eye upon some "law," and laboriously endeavouring in his own strength to make himself irreproachable by the perfect fulfilment of it, the other casting himself on the goodness of God, rejoicing in hope of God's glory, and surrendering himself to be the instrument of God's will. Can you doubt which of the two will be the best man, the most thoroughly righteous, by every test of righteousness? The preachers of Christ who have spoken most boldly of faith as the one thing needful have not been indifferent to practical goodness. No, indeed; it has been their love and longing for it that has made them fearless of misconstruction in denouncing the vain attempts of self-righteousness. They have desired to see men humble, self-forgetful, alive with a joy and strength given them from above, and thus *able* to do the good and acceptable and perfect will of God. We commonplace Christians are deeply indebted to those who, like St Paul and like Luther, have felt so keenly the obstinacy of self and the need of stripping it of every disguise and of driving it out of every stronghold, so that the Christian may live no longer in himself but in Christ. Life, as they knew, power of life, is what

we want; and that is to be had, not through perpetual miserable disappointments and condemna-
tions in vain efforts to keep the law, but through
the fellowship of faith with Christ the Risen Son
of God. In him we have the Divine forgiveness,
free and full; in him the unspeakable gift of sonship. If we realize him as raised from the dead on
our behalf by his Father and ours, then we may
have courage to call God Father with the full confession and surrender of the heart; then we may
feel that we are not our own, but his, bought with
a price which secures us to be his for ever. In
that consciousness we are righteous, and the Spirit
of the Son of God is able to flow into our hearts
and through our members, actuating and enabling
them for the service of God. Therefore, dear
brethren, if any one amongst you feels with inward
dissatisfaction that his life is at the best a poor one
for a Christian, sadly wanting in happiness and in
energy, let him ask himself whether he has entered
with any reality upon his inheritance of sonship.
Let him be assured that the filial state is the absolutely *right* one for him, that from this he must
take his start to run the race that is set before him,
that on this he must build up his practical life.
And that he may learn to be filial towards God,

let him contemplate Christ. It is the glory of Christ not only to have proved through suffering his own supremely perfect sonship, but to draw men his brethren to himself and to the Father that they may be sons of God in him.

VI.

RIGHTS AND DUTIES.

ROMANS XIII. 7.—"Render to all their dues."

I BELIEVE that a certain distinction has established itself in the general mind between Righteousness and Justice. The two words were both originally used in the same sense, the former being English or Teutonic, the latter its Latin equivalent. Thus when we want to say "make righteous" in one word, we say "justify." But, partly perhaps because Righteousness is a great Bible word and Justice the word of jurisprudence, we have come to think of Righteousness as a relation between men and God, and of Justice as a relation between man and man. It is of Justice, accordingly, that I am to speak to-night.

Justice is at once the support and the fruit of civic life. Men cannot live together without some degree of justice; and as they go on living together and their social life becomes richer and more complex, the action and experience of life breed the higher and more perfect forms of justice. But, secular as Justice truly is, we shall not find ourselves compelled to separate it from the Righteousness of faith. On the contrary, my hope is that by considering secular justice as it connects itself with the Christian calling, we may improve our conceptions of what is just. It ought always to be the ambition of theology, not merely to defend itself within an exclusive circle of its own, but to prove itself able to throw light upon all duties and interests.

Human righteousness towards God is *of faith;* that is to say, God has called men to be his children, and they will be right, and do the works which he has prepared for them, when they accept the condition of sonship with its proper feelings of trust and dependence and self-surrender. But God does not isolate his children from one another. It is a part of his calling that he places them together, and binds them with many ties, and calls upon them to feel and act towards one another as those who are children of the same Father. In making men his children, God makes them also a Family.

Here then we find the Christian account of Justice. The true *order* of mankind is that of spiritual persons living and advancing together as members of the one family of the. Heavenly Father. To be completely just is to behave towards each person according to his place in the family. To fill one's own place and to act towards all others in accordance with the tie by which God has bound us respectively to each,—this is what the Christian acknowledges to be his duty. The same law is described in Christian theology under the expressive figure of a Body. Each member or organ has its own function, and to discharge this is its proper business. The eye has to see, and the ear to hear. But the many members make one body; and each organ, if we imagine them conscious, has to respect the functions of the others, and to work with them for the purposes of the whole body. It is the natural action of *growth* to develop the number and the perfection of organs by a process which philosophers call *differentiation.* That is to say, at a low point in the scale of creation, there are fewer distinctions in a body; at a higher stage we find more organs, performing more offices, and we call the body more perfect. But the perfection of the body depends on the subordination of the parts and the harmony of the whole. A similar process of differentiation goes on in the growth of human society. Occupations, trades, offices, become more numerous and are more distinctly separated from each other. The relations of human beings to one another become indefinitely manifold and subtle and complex. And thus Justice *grows* with the growth of society. But it is at all times "a kind of harmony." It is most thoroughly realized when men fill their own places, serve the whole society, and are affected each towards each according to their mutual relations. This is the eternal and Divine ordinance. God, who has called men to be his children and to have his Son for their Head, binds them together in one body, and bids them live a harmonious life of mutual obligation and regard. The more entirely we live to God as his children, the more successfully shall we live together as brethren. Each relation that life develops we shall reverence as God's appointment, and it will be a part of the righteousness of faith to fulfil it.

No other maxim could better sum up the requirements of Justice than that of our text, " Render to all their dues." Of course we do not mean by dues only those which men are compelled by penalties to render. It is impossible for any one who takes a spiritual view of Justice to see in it what the law of the land enforces and nothing

more. It is the weakness and misfortune of thinkers who do not expressly acknowledge a spiritual
basis of human life, that they either seem to build
a moral structure on the air, or that they outrage
moral feeling by making *force* the origin and explanation of everything. There are those who
admit no conception of justice except the will of
the stronger, expressed in threats. A man's *duty*,
according to this doctrine, is what he is ordered by
a stronger than he to do, on pain of its being the
worse for him if he refuses to do it. You see at
once how different the Christian conception of
Justice is from this. When we Christians adopt
the maxim, which is not itself an exclusively Christian one, " Render to all their dues," we understand
by " dues," all that, according to the idea of mankind as the Family of a Heavenly Father, is due
from each to each. To some extent, the interpretation of " dues," thus understood, is variable and
progressive, because, as I have taken pains to
shew, society is developed as it advances, and we
learn through experience what corresponding action
or affection any new or modified relation demands.
Christian morality, therefore, ought not to be stationary. We are pledged by our Christian calling
to study with reverence the circumstances in which

we find ourselves and to watch with a pious hopefulness for improvements. A faithful willingness to be led onward by the Heavenly Hand ought to characterize the Christian mind in dealing with mutual obligations. At the same time no one doubts that the main requirements of Justice are thoroughly ascertained. Our need is not to find them out, but to be persuaded to comply with them. Our natural selfishness is always putting us in the way of thinking what is due from others to us, and not what we owe to others. And Justice will never flourish as beneficently as it might do, so long as each of us thinks earnestly and with spirit of his rights, languidly and as if under compulsion of his duties.

The sentiment of Justice is, thank God, a powerful one in the English mind. The more flagrant forms of injustice excite in us a healthy indignation which refuses to tolerate them. The appeal to Justice, when it is a well-grounded one, never finds dull ears in an English audience. Often, it is scarcely necessary to say, we are embarrassed by conflicting obligations. Those who see a case from one point of view only may think there is an injustice where those who look at it from another will reply that there is none. Conflicting obligations are means of spiritual discipline evidently intended to train us in discernment and faithfulness; and the experience of the difficulties and perplexities which they create ought to make us considerate in judging each other. But on the whole, it could not, I think, be fairly charged against us that we are indifferent to justice.

But the maxim, "Render to all their dues," if we enter thoroughly into the feeling of it, will make us aware of a certain divergence of our habitual standard of justice from the Christian rule, to which I desire to call your particular attention this evening. We are too much biassed by the fact of possession. It is not to be denied that possession is entitled to great consideration. The course of our history in this favoured land, which has been so happy in its freedom from violent changes, has tended to give to possession an unexampled tenacity. The maxim "Let each keep what he has" might be alleged with some reason to be more characteristic of the English conception of justice than that of St Paul, "Render to all their dues."

"Let each keep what he has." I readily admit that in a country where a matured system of law is administered with punctilious integrity in the penetrating light of public knowledge, this principle will go a long way in maintaining justice. And it is very natural that here, more than anywhere, the legal form of justice should encroach too much upon its moral or spiritual form. But, not the less, the ideal of justice will be very poorly satisfied in a Christian community by the defence of existing possession.

I may illustrate what I mean by our extraordinary reverence for property, for vested interests, and for bequests. Now, it would be a very bad thing for us if no one could call what he had his own, if life had no stability, and industry no secure reward. All that is patent. It would be a downfall, indeed, if we were to lose the protection of a settled law of rights and ownership. But what I am noting, from the Christian point of view, is this,—that we have given ourselves up to a kind of worship of property and vested interests and bequests. Our regard for these things, instead of being cool and moderate and conditional, has been touched with the imaginative emotion which turns it into a religion. The very phrase, "the sacredness of property," discloses the feeling with which we regard it. We are inclined to exalt possessions, as objects of worship, above the irreverent discussions of reason. When we hear of speculations which question how deeply the right of an individual to what he has inherited or received goes down into the nature of things, and by what conditions it should be limited, we are not content with putting ourselves temperately upon our guard, which would be reasonable enough, but we look upon the speculators as profane and cry out upon them with a kind of horror. Who is not familiar with these symptoms of a worship which the Christian can hardly call anything but an idolatry?

The Christian who takes his principles from the New Testament learns there no reverence for the rights of the individual possessor as against the claims of the community. To put it thus, seems almost ironically moderate, when we think of the history of the Christian Church and of the teaching of our Lord and of his Apostles. The Holy Spirit coming down on the day of Pentecost to create the Church of Christ, persuaded every believer to give up his rights of ownership and to throw what he had into the common stock. Throughout the New Testament, possessions are studiously disenchanted of prestige and sacredness. The believer is to consider them as a trust, for the management of which he will be held responsible. Everything is done in the earliest Christian teaching that could be done, to prevent men from setting an undue value on property and from regarding it as what the possessor might do what he liked with. The assumption throughout is that there was no need at all to lead men to reverence property, but a great deal of need to guard them against making too much of it. It was the common interest, not the individual, which needed the sanction of religion to sustain its claim.

The Scriptural doctrine of private rights agrees exactly with its doctrine of justice. We are to render to all their dues ; and in estimating dues, we are to remember that society is a *whole*, one body, and that it is a Divine *family*. Now it stands to reason that a single member, a single organ, cannot set up its rights against those of the body. The habitual feeling of every member must be that the interest of the body is incomparably more important and more to be considered than that of any part of it. I can understand the theory that would subordinate society to the individual, and maintain that all social arrangements have for their chief purpose to secure each single person in the enjoyment of his exclusive rights ; but this is demonstrably not the Christian theory, and the mind into which the Christian idea of the body and its members has been thoroughly wrought must find such a view wholly uncongenial to it. A sensitively Christian instinct ought to shrink with more repugnance from the assumption that private ownership is sacred and above discussion, than from protestations on behalf of the interest of the community. But the Christian hears God telling him that society is not only a living whole, but also a Divine family. And I think no one will contend that exclusive ownership is congenial to the family feeling. You who are parents know that your children are ready enough by nature to appropriate what they can, and to exclaim defiantly, " This is mine !" But it is not your delight to cherish and exalt this feeling, nor would you be distressed if your children learnt to say with pleasure of many things, " This belongs to the family." I do not say that you can abolish private rights, either under the domestic roof, or in society ; what I urge is that to consecrate private rights and give them predominance, is uncongenial to the properly Christian sentiment of justice.

The secular justice that is rooted in the soil of Christian theology is of a nobler and a finer kind, believe me, than that which watches over private ownership and vested interest and the grasp of the dead hand on property. It teaches us to throw our sympathies on the side of the poor when their interests seem to come into competition with those of the rich, on the side of the weak more willingly than on that of the strong. To do this is not mere condescending benevolence ; it is justice, the justice that renders to all their dues. "Giving *honour* unto the wife, *as unto the weaker vessel,*"—*there* speaks the Divine instinct, dropping as it were by the way a thought quite natural to one who had the mind of Christ, but one which could not have proceeded, at least with the same significant unconsciousness, from any other morality than that of the New Testament. What is *due* to the weak and defenceless? Protection. What is due to the ignorant? Enlightenment. What is due to the misunderstood? Endeavours to enter into their thoughts and feelings. What is due to those that are down? Efforts to lift them up. Your Christian hearts, I hope, brethren, have given these answers freely. Once more, What is due to the rich and great? An answer does not, I imagine, rise so readily to the lips. Shall we say, Honour, flattery, gaping admiration, sedulous anxiety to take out of their way any hindrance that would restrain them from doing what they like with their own, not only while they live,

but down to the twentieth generation after them ?
Are *these* due from their brethren in the Divine
Family to the rich and great ?   It is hardly the
Christian in any one that will give this answer, in
the life any more than with the lips.   Pause, if you
please, before you pronounce definitely what is due
to the rich and great.   But you could hardly help
including amongst their dues such as these,—that
the arrogance to which their position tempts them
should *not* be fostered, that occasions of falling
should not be put officiously in their way, that it
should be urged upon them by importunate re-
minders that the true glory of a man is not in
having or enjoying but in serving, and that they
should be rigorously made to understand that the
community does not exist for their sake, but they
for the sake of the community.   Such dues we have
no clear right to withhold from those that have
wealth and rank and privilege amongst us.

The spirit of Christian justice has, you will see,
to fight against the immense power of selfishness in
human nature and those influences and habits
which make up "the world."   The strong are always tempted to abuse their strength, the rich to
fancy that the earth is made for their enjoyment,
the multitudes to domineer over the few.   Chris-

tian justice appeals to the ordinances of a just and
gracious God ; it declares that he has made men
and classes for one another ; it demands a more
considerate care for all who are not able to take care
of themselves ; it stands up for the rights of slaves, of
the poor, of women, of unpopular sects and schools.
Above all and over all rights it proclaims incessantly
the dignity of the whole community, of the human
race itself. The order, the harmony, the well-being,
the growth, of the body, are ends for the sake of
which individuals are sent into the world and unto
which it is their happiness to serve. It is an ordained limitation of the deference to be rendered
to the weak, that it must not endanger the general
welfare. Authority must not be sacrificed to sympathy. Those who have money must not give it
away mischievously. Demands for equality ought
not to be allowed to outweigh the general good.

It may be a comfort to us to remember, when
we think of the work which justice has to do and of
the adversaries against which it has to contend,
that, for the Christian, justice is the same thing as
the righteousness which is of faith. We want to be
guided by light from above, to be helped with
strength from above. If we all bore in mind habitually that we are righteous *by faith,* and therefore

sought more and more earnestly with prayer and effort to be men of faith, simple, humble, fearless, setting the will of our Father above every earthly interest and power,—what a reinforcement we should bring to the cause of harmony and happiness, what services might we not hope to render to our country and our kind! Let me plead with you, my Christian brethren, not to be indifferent to the perfect fulfilment of justice, that is, of righteousness, that is, of the righteousness and Kingdom of God. Our Saviour exhorts us to be indifferent to everything else, in comparison of the Kingdom of God and his righteousness. And there is no conceivable way in which these can triumph, except through the prevalence of the living spirit which renders to all the dues which God assigns. If you see, as you may, an honourable devotion to the cause of justice in men who do not profess to be Christians, render honour to the men, for it is their due, and beware of undervaluing their cause as a merely secular one. The way to serve your Christian profession is to shew how considerate, how delicately just, how courageous, how devoted to the common good, Christians can be. This is what Christ asks of us. This is the way to honour him, because it is to walk in his own steps.

VII.

HOLINESS TO THE LORD.

THIS word "saints" has practically fallen out of
use in our modern religious language. If we were in
the habit of using it as it is used in the New Testament, we should call ourselves here "saints." We
should not need to make any distinction between
those who are truly religious and those who are
only nominal Christians; our proper title, taken as
we are, would be, the "saints" assembled in this
Church. But we do not, and could not, thus
describe ourselves. We have long dropped this
title, and we use another in its stead. Where the
Apostles would say "saints," we say "Christians."
The Church owes this latter title to the heathen by
whom the believers in Christ were surrounded in
Antioch and other Gentile cities. Amongst themselves they were not "Christians" in the New
Testament age, but sometimes the *brethren*, some-

times the *faithful* or the *believers*, sometimes the *saints.* You may find these names in the addresses at the beginning of the Epistles, as well as incidentally elsewhere. Thus Paul an Apostle and Timotheus a brother write to the "*saints* and *faithful brethren* in Christ at Colossæ,"—or, as it might have been rendered, "to the holy and faithful brethren." And St Paul asks, "Dare any of you, having a matter against another, go to law before the unjust, and not before the *saints ?*" By this name all the members of the Church, all the Christians, are comprehensively described.

I said not only that we do not, as a matter of usage, call ourselves saints, but that we could not. The name has come to have associations in our minds which prevent us from giving it this general application. We do not now understand by "saints" ordinary Christians doing the work of the world. (1) One class which the word denotes to us is that of eminent Christians of the early ages of the Church, who have had days in the Calendar assigned to their memory. Our separation from the Church of Rome, by leading us to reject the commemoration of the great multitude of middle-age saints, has helped to clothe the word with this peculiarly primitive character. (2) If by chance we describe any one of our own time as a saint, we mean to denote by the name excellence of a peculiar type, not such as ought to characterize Christians universally, but such as belongs to an exceptional nature and an exceptional lot in life. The saintly virtue, as we conceive of it, is retiring and contemplative rather than active and energetic, ascetical rather than joyous, feminine rather than masculine. The odour of sanctity is blown away, as it were, by the breezes of the world. (3) It is in accordance with this feeling that we more willingly think of saints as inhabitants of heaven than as living on this earth. This habit of associating the saints with the unseen world has created some important differences between us and those to whom the saints were primarily the members of the Church on earth. Thus, when we profess our belief in the " Communion of saints," we naturally suppose it to mean some kind of intercourse between saints in heaven and believers here below. But its more natural primitive sense would be " the partnership or fellowship of Christians." And the faith in it would be a belief that Christians, as such, are united to one another by bonds which give them common hopes, common interests, common affections, mutual obligations. This view is in agreement with the doctrinal part of our Collect for All Saints' Day, which calls to memory that God has knit together his elect in one communion and fellowship in the mystical body of his Son Christ our Lord. And so the dedication-name of an All Saints' Church, like this, bears witness to the idea of the Catholic or universal Church, as a body of consecrated members.

It is no loss on the whole, perhaps, to drop the title "saints" as a designation of members of the Church of Christ, in order that we may replace it by that of Christians, which appeals with so much power to our hearts. But if the word in falling out of use, has abstracted with it from the general Christian calling any of the *holiness* which was at first considered an essential feature of it, that, assuredly, is a serious loss.

The word "saint," which is borrowed from the Latin, is exactly equivalent to the word " holy." But it has the convenience of having been made a substantive, whilst holy remains an adjective, so that "a saint" can be said for a holy person, and "saints" for "the holy" or holy persons. In the passage I quoted just now, it is doubtful whether it is best to read " the saints and faithful brethren" or "the holy and faithful brethren." Similarly, we might read with equal accuracy, "called to be saints," or "called to be holy." To sanctify is, as you know, to make holy.

Let us now endeavour to recover distinctly the original and guiding sense of these words, at least so far as their usage in Scripture is concerned.

That sense stands out more obviously, perhaps, in the Old Testament than in the New. The idea of holiness pervades all the institutions of the Jewish people. Places, times, offices, things of all sorts, were made holy to the Lord. That is, they were separated from other common uses, that they might belong to the express service of God. To be holy was to be set apart for God. You will do well to hold fast to this, brethren, as the essential and permanent idea of holiness. It is the condition of being consecrated to God.

The Jewish people were frequently reminded in their sacred books of the reason why there was so much setting apart of things for Jehovah in their appointed customs. Their elaborate ritual service, with its multitudinous consecrations, and the distinctions of clean and unclean by which their life was burdened, were all intended to bear witness to them and keep them in mind, that they were themselves a people holy to the Lord. By word and by symbol alike it was pressed upon them that their God Jehovah had called and chosen them for his own people. They belonged to him ; he had made them his own from amongst the surrounding nations; by his voice of calling, by signal deliverances, by guidance, and by promises, he taught them his purpose of election. But they were slow and careless to remember him to whom they belonged. The principle of separation or setting apart was therefore wrought into their life, private and public, from morning to night, that they might feel their God Jehovah to be a calling and separating God. "I gave them my sabbaths, to be a sign between me and them, that they might know that I am the Lord that sanctify them,"—this may serve as a key of all the ordinances of consecration amongst the Jews ; they were symbols and witnesses of the holiness of the people,—that is to say, of the fact that Jehovah had called and chosen them, that he might dwell among them and they might be his. "I am Jehovah your God, and you are my people,"—this is the assurance which with incessant iteration runs through the Scriptures of the Old Covenant, and in being thus appropriated to Jehovah consisted the holiness of the Jewish people.

In passing from the Old Covenant to the New, we do not observe any change of the essential principle of holiness. Still the calling of God is the cause of holiness, separation unto God who chooses is the meaning of it. Christians are holy in that they belong to the Father who chooses them for his own in his Son.

In the instructions which our Lord gave to the Eleven before his Passion, he was careful to impress upon them that they had received this holiness. "Ye have not chosen me, but I have chosen you:" thus he reminded them of their special calling. Through this calling and the continuous personal discipline by which he had attached them to himself they were to regard themselves as having been made holy and clean. The Apostles were in the most solemn sense consecrated persons; and this meant that they were chosen out of the world and set apart for the special service of Christ and the Father.

The task assigned to the Apostles as founders of the Church was a special one, but their consecration was not exclusive. Every believer taken into the Church was taught that he too was a "saint." The faith to which he was invited was that God had chosen him and was calling him, and that he was henceforth to consider himself as separated and holy to the Lord. The Apostles were not in the habit of making distinctions between the members of the Church. It would have been entirely contrary to their feeling and conviction to use for example such language as this,—" Some of you, who shew by your lives that you are truly devoted to Christ, we shall gladly recognize as saints, the rest we must sorrowfully regard as unholy and profane." Speaking to a mixed multitude of Christians, St Peter says freely, "Ye are a chosen generation, a royal priesthood, an holy nation, a peculiar people; that ye should shew forth the praises of him who has called you out of darkness into his marvellous light: which in time past were not a people, but are now the people of God; which had not obtained mercy, but now have obtained mercy." And if any one urges that though the Apostle does not in word discriminate, yet he must have had in his mind an implied distinction, between those who were truly religious and those who were only nominal Christians, I answer that the distinctions of personal character were not one but many, but that St Peter was not thinking of personal character in the Christians whom he was addressing, but of God's calling. From this point of view it is certain that any distinction between some members of the Church and others was foreign to the Apostolic mind. The first teachers of the Church wished every Christian to believe that he was chosen and called. To those who were still outside the Church the preachers of Christ said, " God has sent us to you, and to every one whom the offer of salvation can reach, to assure you that he forgives you and calls you into reconciliation." As many as consented to believe, they washed with water in sign of cleansing through forgiveness; and then to the baptized they addressed their appeals on the ground that they had been chosen, called, washed, consecrated, and were therefore no longer their own.

It is most true, however, that there is a distinction between the consecration of unconscious things and that of the conscious spiritual creatures of God. A building can be set apart for Divine worship; and a living soul can also be set apart for Divine worship: but a living soul is a very different thing from a building. In the conscious being, *consent* is required; and until the consent of the heart is won, the consecration remains in a manner frustrated. So that there is profound reason in the twofold Apostolic exhortation, though it may sound illogical, "You *are* holy; therefore *be* holy." These two clauses sum up the New Testament teaching as to sanctification. Each clause, the affirmative and the imperative, was spoken with solemn earnestness; but I am inclined to believe that the former was then felt to be the more important of the two. The former declared the foundation, laid by God, the latter pointed to the superstructure, to be built by the Christian. And it was through knowing and feeling what God had done, that men were drawn and enabled to contribute their part to the accomplishment of God's purpose.

To say with inward thankfulness and joy, "Thou hast chosen me and made me thine own,— let me be thine!" is the instinctive utterance of Christian holiness. Our Lord himself is the Holy One for us to imitate, in that he perfectly surrendered himself to his Father's will. "They are not of the world," he says to his Father, of those whom the Father had given to him, "even as I am not of the world...As thou hast sent me into the world, even so have I also sent them into the world. And for their sakes I sanctify myself, that they also might be sanctified through the truth." The Lord Jesus *sanctified himself.* It is usual, I think, and right, to regard this as meaning, "I devote myself, in my approaching sacrifice." It was in his Passion and Death, most completely, though not only, that our Lord offered himself to his Father. But this self-consecration or sacrifice of Christ did not originate in himself. As he so often said, the Father sent him, commissioned him, sealed him, anointed him. It was his glory, his meat, his life, to fulfil the will of the Father who had sent him. This was the sanctification of the Holy One. And the same kind of consent to be taken and used for God's service is the holiness of Christians. Holiness is not—any more than righteousness—the laborious discharge of a ceremonial; it is, let me repeat it inward consent to God's election. If we would be holy, the sense that God calls us to be entirely his must master us, so that we shall desire and strive to be in all things and effectually his.

Look at the things that men do, good and bad, right and wrong, from the point of view of this principle of holiness. They do them from various motives, or from almost no motive; from some inward prompting and preference, or because others have done the same things before. The principle of holiness will constrain us to discriminate between these in a certain manner. We are in the world, immersed in the general human life, conscious of the influence of custom and desire; but we are not of the world, we belong to God.   Our question will be, Which of these things fall in with our resolve to yield ourselves to God's service?   Which of them do we know by instinct or learn by experience to be contrary and destructive to it?   These latter we call unholy, profane, and they ought to become thoroughly repulsive to us.   The right feeling will be that they defile, as dirt does the clean body, a spirit that is pledged to entire dedication to God.

One word here, to meet a difficulty which the conception of holiness as meaning separation to God's service may suggest.   If we mean by "holy" that which is set apart, unconsciously and consciously, to God's service, how can we speak of God himself as holy?—What we imply, I think, when we call God holy, is that he *disapproves and repels* these human acts and affections which we learn to be inconsistent with our devotion to God. God's holiness is not another element or attribute of his nature, it is another *aspect* of it.   It expresses the repugnance that there must be between the perfect nature of the just and loving God, and the things which in us are unholy and produce defilement.   It is wholesome for us to remember with awe that we have to do with a jealous and a holy God.

There can surely be no doubt, dear brethren, as to the powerful influence which the consciousness of having been made and claimed for God's service, of having been chosen in Christ to be holy and blameless before him, would have upon our lives. There would issue from it a perpetual condemnation of the cruelty, disregard of ties, and sensuality, by which this world which Christ redeemed is still defiled. And therefore it is well that we should cherish all recollections and habits which may impress upon us our sanctity as Christians. We, like the Jews, have holy seasons, holy places, holy things; and of late years there has been a considerable revival amongst us of reverence for all things that minister to the worship of God. Sacraments, Churches, holy days, have been rescued from comparative neglect, and are the objects of pious and increasing consideration throughout all classes in the land. This revival of reverence is good, upon one condition,—that we do not look upon external things as inherently sacred, but as witnesses that we ourselves who live and work are sanctified by the Lord our God. God, we ought to know, does not want holy *things*, but holy *persons*, minds and hearts and members given up in rational sacrifice to him. Our holiness is essentially spiritual; and God, who knows our weakness and does not blame us for it, gives us a Spirit which the Church has always called the holy and sanctifying Spirit. Without his inspirations, how would it be possible for us to live for God? God is invisible, and we are creatures of flesh and blood, upon whom the visible world is always crowding its impressions. It is so natural for us to live as children of the world! Yes, if it were not that we are subject to other impressions also; that our heavenly Father is continually appealing to us by higher influences, and making himself known to us, and stirring up in us the consciousness in which we may know that we are not of the world, even as our Saviour and Master was not of the world. Do not believe that there is anything arbitrary, unmanly, or obsolete, in true Christian sanctity. Christ as our Head, and the Holy Spirit moving in us, make it natural for every one who professes and calls himself a Christian to be holy. We are not bound to any strained asceticism, to any desertion of our appointed industry, to any gloomy religious fears. The ideal we shall aim at in giving ourselves to

God will be to become guileless and pure and gentle and courageous and diligent as well as devout and prayerful. We are to desire, as followers of Christ, to be innocent as little children, not in their mere ignorance and inexperience, but through the power of those affections of the children of God which lift us above the world, and give us a hearty distaste for all that is base and vile. He that in these things serveth Christ is acceptable to God, and though he does not seek their approbation, he ends by being also approved of men.

VIII.

THE CHURCH AND THE WORLD.

St John xvii. 16.—"They are not of the world, even as I am not of the world."

I ENDEAVOURED to make it clear this morning that the proper idea of holiness is that of dedication to the exclusive service of God. Holy things are those which are set apart for the use of worship; holy persons or saints are those whom God has made his own by election and calling, and who consent to be his. Holiness therefore implies separation; and those who are to be in any sense *holy* must in some way be *separate.* What kind of separation is rightly involved in, or required by, Christian holiness in the present age, is the question which we are to consider this evening.

The most obvious way of being separate is that of refusing to have fellowship with other people who do not think or feel as we do. "Come out from among them, and be ye separate," is an exhortation addressed by St Paul to the Christians

of Corinth. And when we look back to the beginnings of the Church, we see small societies of
persons who have come out very decidedly from
the world surrounding them. The Christians were
separated in religion, in morals, and in social life,
from their neighbours. Their Christian profession
imperatively required them to be thus separated.
Their holiness was endangered by free association
with the heathen. And it was necessary that they
should draw together closely and seek support for
their faith in mutual encouragement and in the
common atmosphere of a Christian society. We
can understand easily enough this state of things,
when we recall the circumstances of the first age
of the Church. Within the Church there is a close
communion or fellowship of the saints with one
another; on the outside there is a marked separation between the few saints and the unholy world
surrounding them.

But the scene changes when we pass from the
first century to the nineteenth. What is to be said
about separation when the whole society is professedly Christian? From whom are we, the Christians of this country, to separate ourselves? Christians are not a select few in England; nor is
England a little Christian land surrounded by

heathen nations. How far can we use, in what way can we reasonably and honestly apply to our own case, the Scriptural doctrine concerning the separation of Christians from the world? What is for us the holy fellowship, and what is the world?

The true and thorough answer to be given to these questions is this,—that the primary and essential separation of the holy is *from all that defiles*. This is to be insisted upon now as much as ever and in all possible circumstances. But the social separation from persons or classes is altogether a secondary and variable matter. It may be that the only way of avoiding defilement is by separation from certain persons ; then such separation becomes a duty of holiness. But otherwise all refusal of fellowship between human beings is undesirable and to be regretted. There ought never to be separation for separation's sake, between Christians and non-Christians, or between some Christians and others. And to trust to such separation for the promotion of holiness, is a fatal error. It is the more fatal, because it is also a very natural and seductive error.

There are two conspicuous forms of this perversion of the idea of holiness in these later ages.

In both, men start from the notion that it is a fundamental necessity of Christianity to cut out some portion of the world for God, and to leave the rest of it as *not God's*. The one kind of separation we may call *religious*, the other *ecclesiastical*.

1. When Christians have been most in earnest, great stress has been laid upon the difference between being really, and being only nominally, Christian. The Bible speaks of regeneration, of conversion, of the absorbing faith of the believer, of the required renunciation of all earthly things. A great number of baptized and professing Christians have been very unlike what Christians according to the Bible standard ought to be, some shamelessly profligate, many conspicuously followers of fashion and pleasure, still more, cold and heartless believers in the crucified and risen Christ. How was it possible to assume that such Christians as these had undergone the new birth and were living a life in Christ? It was a natural conclusion that there must be an inner circle of true believers as well as the larger body of nominal Christians. The believers, it was held, had undergone the inward change which transformed them from being children of the world into children of God. The line of separation, it then appeared evident, was to be

drawn between the regenerate and the unregenerate. The genuine Christians would know one another by having the same tastes and interests, the same preferences and the same aversions; they would feel also the vital difference between themselves and the unconverted. There would thus be a living communion or fellowship of the holy, and a more than formal separation between them and the rest of the world. And it would then be regarded as highly important for the true believers not to make light of their separation from the world, but —while they longed to persuade their perishing brethren to submit to the inner change which would enable them to cross the line,—to take care that the line was not obliterated. It became a duty of charity to the unconverted themselves, to warn them by protests and by repulsion of the danger of remaining children of the world.

There is something pathetic in the distress and perplexity which have been occasioned by this theory of the difference between converted and merely nominal Christians. There is so much that is true in it, so much that is high and self-denying in the life that it enjoins. To many and many a humble Christian it has seemed absolutely necessary, at any cost of feeling, to hold it and act upon it.

And yet nothing, I think, can be more clear and certain than that the kind of distinction assumed does not exist in fact. When the Gospel is suddenly preached with warmth in the midst of an utterly dead and careless generation, the real difference between those who accept it and those who turn their backs upon it may for a time be nearly as great as the theory assumes. But in the families and the households of the converted, and generally in an age like our own and in such a society as that represented, for example, by this present congregation, the line comes to be more and more evidently an arbitrary one. It is difficult,—is it not impossible?—to say that a select number of this congregation have undergone a change which makes them utterly different from the rest. Your mind refuses to effect the separation practically, which is the way in which, if made at all, it ought to be made. The most thoroughly honest will be the most unable to decide in their own case whether they belong to the regenerate or the unregenerate. I have heard it said, "The test may be a very simple and Catholic one; a person can surely tell whether he *loves Christ* or not." But no: this test fails, the moment you begin to apply it. Every one here, I may hope, loves Christ a little; no one here loves

Christ in the degree in which it is reasonable that saved sinners should love their Saviour. In brief, you have not two sets of persons, one set of one nature, the other set of a totally different nature. The two natures are struggling together in each person; and the degrees of difference between Christian and Christian are so various as to be indeterminable by any measurement.

I have alluded to the distress which the attempt to make a separation of the converted from the unconverted has occasioned to multitudes of earnest souls. But the pain thus given is not the worst result of it. A graver evil is that it tends to make religion unreal and artificial. Religious people have been led to cling to arbitrary forms of outward habit as if they were identical with the deepest spiritual characteristics. To dance or not to dance has been made the test of a Christian. Consciences have been miserably confused. And along with artificiality a very genuine worldliness has stolen into the most exclusive Christian society. The strictly religious have not been more kind, more frank, more magnanimous, than others: and people of the world have had too much excuse for justifying themselves on moral grounds in not desiring to be religious.

Happily, as members of the Church of England, we are under no constraint or even temptation to bisect Christian society into the two classes of the converted and unconverted. The necessity of doing this is a tradition of the religious world, but not of the Church of England. Our Church treats all its members as the Apostles treated the members of their Churches. It throws the broad mantle of the Christian calling over them all; and beneath this, it assumes that there may be every kind and degree of unworthiness. It is our own fault if we allow this comprehension to seduce us into indifference to holiness. There are none here who have a right to think of their condition as other than a holy one. You are all holy brethren, partakers of the heavenly calling, called to be saints. The same standard is placed before all, and each will have to answer to himself and to God for the manner in which he conforms himself to it.

2. I turn now to another mistaken mode of effecting the separation implied in holiness,—that which I have called the *ecclesiastical.* According to this, the Church is holy, and the world in its civil form and organization is not holy. It is very important in these days that we should set this

view distinctly before our minds and ask ourselves whether we assent to it.

It is not so easy, however, to make the theory a satisfactorily distinct one. The "Church" is a word which is notoriously difficult to define. So is the "World." The case is simplest in modern Romanism. There the Church means ultimately the Pope. The portion of mankind which adheres to the Pope is holy, and holiness is bound up with hearty and unqualified submission to the Pope. Civil governments, so long as they are obedient to the Holy Father, partake of his holiness; as soon as they set themselves in any opposition to Rome, they become unholy and profane. That is intelligible enough as a theory. But the holiness of the Church, thus understood, proves itself to be only a matter of definition and theory, when we find civil governments more righteous, more observant of the will of God, as they often have been, than the Pope and the Church. In the long struggles of history between the Papal See and national governments, it is impossible for any fair inquirer to refuse to admit that the policy of Rome has been continually marked by falsehood, intrigue, and violence. The Court of the Pope has often been as profligate as any other Court. The title of "His

Holiness" seems one of bitter irony, when given to some of the occupants of the Papal See. But in our own Church, which does not acknowledge the Pope, there is a strong tendency to make out that the Church, as clerically organized, appropriates God's calling and is alone holy, and that the world, as organized under civil government, is altogether outside of that calling which makes holy. Ecclesiastical assemblies are held to have the Spirit of God pledged to them exclusively. Men quote our Lord's saying, " Render to Cæsar the things that are Cæsar's, and to God the things that are God's," as if Cæsar meant civil government and God ecclesiastical government, and as if Cæsar and God had separate jurisdictions, each limiting the other. But Cæsar did not mean the national government as distinct from the ecclesiastical, and most certainly God did not mean the ecclesiastical government, and it is even absurd to imagine that God's authority does not interfere with that of secular government. There is nothing in the New Testament to suggest that ecclesiastical organization has God with it any more than the civil system of society. The Lord Jesus did not come as a priest, but as the son of a carpenter; the Apostles were not Jewish priests, they were all drawn from the ranks of the laity.   Pilate, the representative of a secular foreign dominion, did indeed put our Lord to death: but our Lord himself said, " He that delivered me unto thee hath the greater sin."   The priests were those who really caused Jesus to be put to death; he was sentenced to death for blasphemy by the Church Court of the Sanhedrim. When the Apostles were addressing and teaching the believers in Christ, they used abundantly, as I have shewn, the terms expressing holiness;   but these terms were invariably applied to the whole body, and to the body not as organized under overseers and elders, but as doing the work of God in the world.   I am not contending for a general confusion of functions; I do not say that ecclesiastics have not their own place and honour; but I confidently deny that the holiness of the Church is intended to belong to its ecclesiastical functions only. Because the Church is holy to the Lord, therefore all the business of life, including the high and sacred work of civil government, is to be discharged as to the Lord, and may claim the assistance of the Divine Spirit.

The simple truth is that any theory of holiness which would cut out a portion of the world for God, leaving the rest as not God's—whether the selected portion be the inner circle of true believers or the outward ecclesiastical organization—is altogether a wrong one. The Scriptural doctrine of holiness claims all the world for God. It does reject and excommunicate, indeed; but not willingly any portion of society or any person, assuredly not civil government; but all tempers and habits displeasing to the just and gracious God.

My brethren, when you have been repelled by some erroneous notions of exclusive sanctity, when you have turned away from the sainthood of men who thought they gave themselves up to God by deserting the world and by outraging the senses, or from the Pharisaism of narrow religious cliques, or from ecclesiastical fanaticism, the easiest course may seem to be to throw aside all ideas of holiness, and to content yourselves with what society may determine to be sensible and moderate and practical in morals and religion. Let me entreat you to beware of this bias, and to resist it as a temptation. Be not persuaded to take a worldly view of life and to make respectability your standard. We cannot afford to lose the elevating influence of the consciousness of sanctity. You know what the sense of honour has done for the privileged classes of society, how it has made men regard it as an intolerable insult to be charged with lying, cowardice, or meanness, and has thus been in some degree a real safeguard to them against the faults deemed unworthy of a gentleman. Well, holiness is the Christian's honour. The sense of holiness is a much better thing than the sense of honour. It is the heritage of the poorest and most despised, as well as of the highly bred. It does not threaten an accuser with sword-point or pistol-ball, whether the accusation be well-founded or not; but it shrinks with disgust from the sin itself. It cherishes the instinct which feels shame not in being thought to be defiled, but in being defiled. I know not how the place of this instinct of holiness could be supplied.

Let it not be lost from amongst us, Christian brethren. Let us not have to cast about for new influences to be furnished by philosophy to do the purifying work of Christian sanctity. Begin from God, and seek his effectual aid. Study to think of yourselves, not only here and on Sundays, but on week days and in your appointed industry, as dedicated to God. Has he not called you to be his own? How come you to be Christians? You have not chosen Christ, but he has chosen you. He took you for his members before you could have an opinion or make a choice. So far as your Christianity has any honest meaning at all, it means that you have been introduced by God into a holy state, made members of Christ, children of God, and inheritors of the Kingdom of heaven. "What? know you not that your body is the temple of the Holy Ghost which is in you, which you have of God, and you are not your own? For you are bought with a price; therefore glorify God in your body, and in your spirit, which are God's." Bear in mind God's character, as well as the calling and gifts you have received from him; remember with what an abiding anger he hates sin; try to imagine with what feelings the perfect Heavenly Father must behold his children corrupting and defiling themselves. And do not think of yourselves as if you were alone in the world. Look not every man on his own things, but every man also on the things of others. Respect those around you as also holy like yourselves with a Divine consecration. God has put into our hands the awful power of edifying or corrupting one another. Therefore beware that no corrupt communication proceed out of your mouth, but that which is good to the use of edifying, that it may minister grace to the hearers. These are the incomparable exhortations of Chris-

tian duty.   They are not the precepts of a worldly
and secular morality; they require the Christian
to emancipate himself absolutely from the dominion
of the world.   But they are good for the world.
They are in no respect unpractical, or opposed to
the welfare of the world.   The world is better for
all denials of its authority over the children of God.
Let us therefore come out of it, that we may the
more effectually serve it.   Let us refuse to be
governed by custom, to be awed by fashion, to
follow a multitude to do evil.   Whatever the cost
may be of a life regulated from heaven, it is wise
to look to God for guidance, for support, and for
reward.   Having the Eternal God for our Father,
let us cleanse ourselves earnestly from all filthiness
of flesh and spirit, perfecting holiness in the fear
of God.

IX.

LOVE TOWARDS GOD.

2 THESSALONIANS III. 5.—"The Lord direct your hearts into the love of God."

THE first and great commandment, said our Lord Jesus Christ, is this, "Thou shalt love thy God with all thy heart, and with all thy soul, and with all thy mind, and with all thy strength."

This commandment does not impose upon us onerous labours; it does not require us to perform services which would eat out a large part of our life. It was not this commandment to which St Peter referred, when he described the yoke of Judaism as one "which neither our fathers nor we were able to bear." To love is the happiest exercise of our human nature, not incompatible with other employment, not a burden superadded to life, but the sovereign lightener of its load. But is the command therefore an easy and a light one? There are many, I am sure, to whom such an account of it would at times seem ironical and a mockery. "Thou shalt love." Do we then love at command and by compulsion? If we are bidden to do a thing within our power, we can do it, whether we like it or not; but if we are bidden to like it, the very dictate is more calculated to provoke aversion than to create the liking. And what kind of affection is it that is thus imperatively demanded of us? Nothing languid or neutral, but a feeling of the utmost conceivable energy. We are called upon to love God with all the heart and soul and mind and strength. He who is to be the object of this love is a Being whom we have never seen, and whom, however near us he may be, it is certainly possible to forget. Add the further consideration, that our affections are being at all times powerfully solicited by quite different objects. It is no wonder if this commandment, when it is understood and acknowledged as calling for a real obedience, instead of being regarded as a light thing, often excites in our minds a feeling of helplessness and despondency. "There is nothing like such love in our hearts," we say, when we look within. And when, as we always do, we look at others to compare ourselves with them, we may reassure ourselves a little by seeing too plainly that our fellow-Christians in general are almost as far from keeping this commandment as we are.

I am not speaking now to persons who have made up their minds that there is no God who can be known, and that all who have believed in a God have been merely crouching before an enlarged shadow of themselves projected upon the obscure curtain of the surrounding world. I am addressing Christians, not altogether ignorant of the happiness of loving God, willing to believe that if it were only possible, there would be joy as well as safety in loving God with entire devotion, and even now, loving God more than they have given themselves credit for doing. But we are all troubled in some measure by the difficulties which weigh heavily at this time upon many ingenuous minds. Far as we may be from holding the creed that God is unknowable, we do not find him easy to know. We are aware that conceptions about God have varied greatly amongst religious persons and nations. Many opinions concerning the Divine nature have been abandoned, not—it would seem—because men have observed God more closely, but because the advance of scientific and social knowledge has made those opinions untenable. Each, in his own experience as a believer in God, has had to put away childish things. If we desire to make our knowledge of God more sure and defined, we are much at a loss how to do it. We cannot employ our senses upon the Divine nature, we cannot subject it to tests, we cannot go round it and survey it. We have no means of demonstration by which we can compel all rational minds to assent even to the most fundamental conclusions about God, and it is at first a shock and always a discouragement to find that there are able thinkers who do not share the convictions which to us are sacred. It may seem to us, moreover, that the high and lofty One inhabiting eternity, filling the immeasurable universe, needing nothing from us, with a range of government to which our life is so microscopically insignificant, is not such a Being as to draw forth emotions in us which we should naturally call *love*. We do not render the warmth of our hearts to an unsearchable mystery. And when we have confessed that the God of our worship is really entitled to our love, and our consciences have witnessed that we ought to love him, there is always the hardness of our hearts to deplore. We are wayward and selfish and sinful, and bestow our love wrongly, and either give way to evil influences or struggle against them with constant ill-success.

How poor and fitful, at the very best, must any human love of God be!

I am speaking, I say, to those who know that they are called to love God, but who are painfully conscious of the immense difference between the demand made on them by their calling, and the fulfilment of it by themselves and their fellow-Christians, and who are inclined to plead in excuse the difficulties which beset the human soul with regard to the knowledge and love of God. In what I have to say this morning, my endeavour will be to suggest to you some few thoughts, in the light of which those difficulties may appear, perhaps, less depressing and insurmountable.

1. Let us not take pleasure in fixing our thoughts upon the inevitable imperfection of our knowledge and the inadequacy of our faculties, so as to forget or underrate what we can and do know of God. Rather let us admit and take for granted whatever can be said as to the incomprehensibility of God, and then—putting this admission aside—let us consider whether God does not in fact in some manner and with whatever qualifications make himself known to us.

It is a first principle of the Christian belief in God, that he has revealed himself as a Father to us in his Son Jesus Christ. We have no higher or more essential or more trustworthy knowledge of God than that which we receive by studying Jesus Christ. Now when we think of this, we have before our minds much that need not be affected by the weakness of our faculties or the variableness of our mental conceptions and acquirements.

Go to the heart of what the Son of God declared by word and life concerning his Father. If Jesus Christ was true, God the maker and controller of all things is essentially *good*. Christ does not directly tell us much of the modes of God's relation to created things; he passes by metaphysics and ontology. But he gives us to understand that goodness is higher than power, and moral creativeness more Divine than physical. He shews the Father to us as having a gracious will, and purposes of blessing, and an orderly and trustworthy moral government. The degree of Divine Love which he declares is very difficult for us to believe; the way in which that Love acted through Christ may strike us at first as strange and incongruous. The Love shewed itself not by a mastering and overpowering benevolence, but in self-humiliation and sympathy and appeal, seeking not to make all men happy by arrangement, but to win human hearts into spiritual fellowship with itself. The former method might have seemed to us the more likely: but compare the two, both as to essential quality and as to the value of the effects produced,—Love speaking to human hearts in sacrifice and appeal, and Love arranging things so that there may be no suffering. Which is the better? This is perhaps the most absolutely vital of all possible questions. All other questions of belief seem to me to mount up ultimately into this. If our hearts confess that Love is more Divine than Power, and that Love manifested in Sacrifice surpasses Love in any other form, then the fact that we should not have expected to behold the Eternal Father giving up his Son, or the Lord of Glory consenting to be crucified, becomes to us a strong additional argument for believing that in this act of Sacrifice we do indeed see the essential Divine Nature revealing itself. And no difficulties of the understanding, which, as we are agreed, is quite incompetent to comprehend God, ought to be allowed to overthrow this testimony in which spirit recognizes Spirit.

When we have caught a glimpse of this highest thing, Love appealing through sacrifice and thus working out a living spiritual order, we may say that we have a knowledge of God which is not liable to be affected by the conditions which make so many of our apprehensions temporary and unstable. St Paul saw that faith and hope and love *abide;* compared with imagination, understanding, and exposition, which have to do with things in a perpetual condition of development, and which experience shews to be variable, faith and hope and love are permanent; they are substantially the same in the child and in the man, in the primitive and in the civilized stage of culture. To these faculties of the spirit God reveals that which is eternal. So far as we apprehend his gracious and righteous will, drawing out our trust and hope and love, we have been permitted to penetrate to that which is essentially Divine.

Whilst, however, the revelation of God made to us through Christ is the supreme one, it is not isolated or exclusive. The Father of our Lord Jesus Christ is to be looked for in the glorious framework of Nature, in the gradually developed institutions of human society, and in the inspirations by which our individual life is visited and guided. Not embarrassing ourselves with attempts to form systems by which we may account for the whole world and all that we see in it, attempts which may very likely be unsuccessful and disappointing, we may hold fast in all inquiries and contemplations our belief in Supreme Love and Righteousness, and watch devoutly for the signs by which they may manifest themselves. Other revelations of God will not supersede that which has been given in Christ, and brought to us through the Bible and the tradition and development of the Church, but they will illustrate it, and bring it home to our minds at multiplied points of contact, and help us to feel its reality and power.

2. God then, let us be sure, is not a Being whom we cannot possibly love for want of knowing him. But what is the kind of affection with which we can regard the Being thus genuinely revealed to us? Must we not say that he is too mysterious, too much above us, to be *loved?*

Now, in Holy Scripture, the great test of love is *devotion.* What will a man *do* for one whom he loves? is the question. And it is from this point of view that we may most wisely regard the command that we should love God. The first and great commandment ought not, indeed, to be relaxed and toned down to suit human infirmity. The Righteous Judge will make due allowance for our frailty, but his commandments remain unchanged. They represent what is right and best for man. God has made it good and right for us to love him with all the energy of which our hearts are capable. That is an eternal law, expressed for our benefit in the form of an imperative demand. But if we wished to examine ourselves about the keeping of this commandment, it would probably not be the wisest course to look back upon our inward experiences, and to try to estimate the warmth of emotion of which we have been conscious towards God. Our emotions are not directly under our control; and, of the various kinds of feeling comprehended under the name of love, we might not perhaps understand accurately what is best suited to our relation to God; and we might therefore judge ourselves wrongly. It might be best to ask ourselves, not so much how we have *felt*, as how far we have been *loyal* to God in our outward and inward acts. Such loyalty will be the safest proof of our love.

We have examples, it is true, in all ages, of language of intense emotion uttering in words of undoubted sincerity the desire of the human heart towards God. Such is that of the Psalmist, " Like as the hart desireth the water-brooks, so longeth my soul after thee, O God. My soul is athirst for

God, yea, even for the living God." And I doubt not that the most fervent and passionate utterances of this kind of love will often awaken a sympathetic response in the Christian hearts of our own day. Where there is the sensibility that thrills easily into unsatisfied yearning, it is certain that the contemplation of God as he reveals himself to us, in the blended tenderness and mysteriousness of his nature, will touch it and draw forth the longing desire of love. But the love required by the commandment may be rendered in other forms than that of a brooding emotion. Let me suggest what the ordinary type of the Christian's love towards God would be. It ought to be grounded in *awe*. The *fear* of the Lord is the beginning, not only of wisdom, but of love. All increase of the knowledge of God must tend to deepen our *reverence*. Whether we dwell upon the vastness and subtlety of his creative operations, or enter into the secrets of his redeeming work and purpose, a spirit of reverence that will hush all mere familiarity of intercourse cannot fail to take possession of us. But our fear of God will be such as to dwell in entire harmony with *a grateful sense of his goodness*. The consciousness that we are unworthy in ourselves of the least of God's mercies will feed our reverential gratitude.   All the delightfulness of nature, all the bounty of the fruitful seasons, all the charities of domestic and social life, will form a scale of blessing leading up to the redeeming and fatherly love of God in Christ ; and the privations and crosses which give us pain, instead of being an account on the other side to be deducted from the goodness, will undergo a marvellous conversion when we learn that by these means God is making us more truly his children, and thus, with more power than any happiness untouched by sorrow, will teach our hearts to be thankful.   A very ordinary Christian, moved by influences which come to all alike, may well be expected to feel habitually a desire rising at times into intensity, to cast himself at the feet of God and to give himself up utterly to his service and pleasure.   But, above all, the Christian's love of God should imply earnest and deliberate *choice of the will of God* in preference to anything that goes counter to that will.   Loyalty, I repeat, will be taken as the essential proof of our love.   Without loyalty, emotions would have no worth in God's sight, but rather would be distasteful to him.   And the inwardly loyal Christian will assuredly grow according to his endowments and capacity in the filial love of God.

3.   And now let me refer in a few words to the hindrances which our sinful and worldly dispositions put in the way of our loving God.   Ah, brethren, it is here, as you know too well, that we find our chief difficulty.   Whilst the spirit within us, moved by the Divine Spirit, is crying Abba, Father, the flesh is lusting against the spirit.   We love the world, and if any man love the world, the love of the Father is not in him.   God is too *good* for our foolish and sinful hearts to love.

Well, we must lead a life of continual conflict. As the Eternal Father has made us to love him and claims our love, and on the other side enslaving and corrupting influences are always soliciting us, we cannot live as those who yield to a current which carries them along.   We must keep ourselves in an attitude of watchful resistance, ready to unmask disguised forms of evil, and exercising ourselves in the love of God.   And let us be sure that in all preference of good to evil God recognizes love towards himself.   Never accustom yourselves to associate God with technical religion only.   No habit, believe me, can be more fatal to the honest and manly love of God.   No, let me read in your ears once more those invaluable words of St Paul, " Whatsoever things are true, whatsoever things are honest, whatsoever things are just, whatsoever things are pure, whatsoever things are lovely, whatsoever things are of good report; if there be any virtue, and if there be any praise, think on these things." Remember, brethren, these are the words not of a modern thinker who sets morality above religion, but of him who declared in the same letter that he counted all precious things but dung that he might win Christ and be found in him. That love of all good things is in living harmony with the most intense devotion to Christ. To Christ;—yes, it is through him that we are most effectually bound to the Father and to all things in the world that are of the Father. As we consider Christ, we bring ourselves under the influence of the full stream of the Divine Love; and it is God's love, shed abroad in our hearts, which teaches us to love. We love God, because he first loved us. No human heart can really love God, except responsively, except through becoming conscious of being loved by God. So it is that sin and worldliness are most effectually shamed. If we knew nothing of the redeeming and adopting love of God, we might perhaps excuse ourselves in our running after vanities and our many insincerities and our degrading bondage to ease or luxury or excitement. But what sort of tastes are these for souls for which Christ died? O we must sometimes hate ourselves for the answer that we render back to the Divine Love! Cling, dear brethren, as for life, to the glorious Sacrifice which provokes in us this salutary shame. We do not want to be reconciled to our worse selves, we want to be reinforced against them. And the Cross that bears witness of the mingling of Divine Love and Sorrow will nerve our strength for conflict as well as soften our hearts in contrition. Under that ensign we shall be more than conquerors through him that loved us.

X.

LOVE TOWARDS MEN.

1 ST JOHN IV. 21. "This commandment have we from him, that he who loveth God love his brother also."

IF the voice of Christian doctrine were entirely silenced, it cannot be alleged that there would be any lack in these days of teachers to enjoin *benevolence* and *philanthropy*. *Love to man* is earnestly enforced by some moralists who either affirm or imply that there is no *God* for us to love. They delight to draw a contrast between Religion, which they suppose to be occupied with vain guesses about the unseen world and with the selfish hopes and fears of men as to what may be awaiting them after death, and the purely human morality which studies the happiness of mankind in this present world and the means which may most effectually promote it. The central principle of this morality is that the world is evidently the better when human beings seek to promote the general welfare. What is good for the whole is good for the members. Therefore

they say, let each control his selfish propensities;
let him keep in view the greatest happiness of the
greatest number, or the true progress of society;
and let him cultivate the benevolent affections
with skilful care. They urge that society should
use all its influence, especially through the education of the young, to train individual men and
women in unselfish benevolence; and they believe
that benevolence may thus be *bred* to any point
of perfection, as we see courage and other qualities
to be bred.

I have no wish to deny that much may be
accomplished by the steady cultivation of benevolence. A child may be so taught from infancy
to consider the feelings of others, that a habit
of kindness may become a part of the permanent
texture of his character. Reverence for goodness
and self-sacrifice may be cherished in boys and
girls by holding up these qualities before them
as ideals, and by treating with honour the more
signal examples of generous devotion. The experiment of promoting love for humankind without
that love of God and Christ which is the basis
of it for Christians, when tried with enthusiasm
by persons eagerly desiring it to succeed, has had
some undeniable success. Do not wonder at it.

The second of the two great commandments is this, Thou shalt love thy neighbour as thyself: and those who set themselves earnestly to fulfil one of the greatest of the Maker's laws are not likely to go unrewarded. The moralists of whom I am speaking are teaching an integral part of what we Christians are bound to teach. Put the doctrine of the Christian Calling by the side of an exclusively human morality, and what do we see? All that can really commend and establish itself in the latter has a place and a welcome in the former. The human morality says, Thou shalt prefer the promotion of the general well-being to the seeking of thine own pleasure. Well, that is what the Christian doctrine also says. It is evidently impossible for any morality to assert principles of benevolence wider or higher than those of the Christian Faith. But on the other hand the merely human morality does not even pretend to give an ultimate reason or authority for what it enjoins. It may say as emphatically or enthusiastically as it pleases to a man, "Prefer the general good to thy own pleasure;" and the man is likely enough to listen with deference, taking the command as being really, what it is, the voice of the Maker: but if he is assured at the same time that there is no invisible Power to which he owes loyalty, he may have the courage to ask, "*Why* should I prefer the pleasure of others to my own? Who are you that dictate to me?" And no satisfying answer can be given to him. He may be told that the voice of the wisest and best of mankind is to be heard in this command, but it may occur to him to reply, "Yes, but those wisest and best men thought they were only echoing the voice of the Supreme Maker," or he may simply refuse to submit his will to a tradition. Christianity gives the same command, and claims at the same time to surround it with authority and warmth and light drawn from the invisible world.

1. The first and greater commandment is, Thou shalt love the Lord thy God. "That means," some have said, "that Religion is to take precedence of the service of mankind and to form the larger half of human duty. The service of mankind will therefore evidently be the gainer if we can get rid of Religion." But that is a too hasty conclusion. The truer statement would be this: "He to whom as our Maker and Spiritual Father we owe absolute allegiance tells us that he has made men to be his family, and that it is his will that we should love one another. The

Eternal God has placed us here and given us the work and probation of life, that each may learn to subordinate himself and to live for his brethren." Do you not feel that the command to love one another, when it is thus received as from God, instead of encountering a formidable rival, has on the contrary been reinforced by the most impressive authority imaginable? You might as well want to get rid of the steam-engine from the train, as to divorce duty to man from loyalty towards God. The belief that duty to man is a command of God brings to the aid of human goodwill and service all those feelings of reverence and awe and obligation which we know to be the most powerful by which the human soul is moved.

2. The Gospel, moreover, presenting Christ, the Divine Son of man, to men, offers to their homage a worthy and ideal human object. It makes *man sacred*, with a sanctity in which the meanest share. A point, surely, of incalculable importance. If you look at men as mere earthly creatures, knowing them after the flesh only, you may with much reason have a very poor opinion of them. In your own circle you may have much fault to find with most of those with whom you

have to do. But how differently do men look when they are *seen in Christ!* The habit of confessing Christ as Lord, and the feelings of reverence and love drawn out towards him, cause us in some degree to assume and act upon the relation of our fellow-men to Christ even when we do not distinctly or consciously realize it. Most certainly, to a true Christian, no man is entirely dissociated from his Lord. Our fellow-men are those for whom Christ died ; their flesh and blood have been worn by the Son of God. If we know anything at all of him, we know that it was his glory to humble himself for the sake of his brethren, not separating himself from the weak or the defiled, but rather striving to raise them by sympathy and fellowship. In the lowest, Jesus Christ saw children of his Father, to be loved and sought and saved. It was his earnest desire and effort to persuade his followers to see men in him and him in men. Remember those words of judgment, " Inasmuch as ye have done it unto one of the least of these my brethren, ye have done it unto me. Inasmuch as ye did it not to one of the least of these my brethren, ye did it not unto me." What a violently strange notion it would have seemed to a St Paul or a St John, that the following of Christ should turn any man away

VIII.

THE CHURCH AND THE WORLD.

St John xvii. 16.—"They are not of the world, even as I am
not of the world."

I ENDEAVOURED to make it clear this morning
that the proper idea of holiness is that of dedication to the exclusive service of God. Holy things
are those which are set apart for the use of worship;
holy persons or saints are those whom God has
made his own by election and calling, and who
consent to be his. Holiness therefore implies
separation; and those who are to be in any sense
holy must in some way be *separate*. What kind
of separation is rightly involved in, or required
by, Christian holiness in the present age, is the
question which we are to consider this evening.

The most obvious way of being separate is that
of refusing to have fellowship with other people
who do not think or feel as we do. "Come out
from among them, and be ye separate," is an exhortation addressed by St Paul to the Christians

of Corinth. And when we look back to the beginnings of the Church, we see small societies of persons who have come out very decidedly from the world surrounding them. The Christians were separated in religion, in morals, and in social life, from their neighbours. Their Christian profession imperatively required them to be thus separated. Their holiness was endangered by free association with the heathen. And it was necessary that they should draw together closely and seek support for their faith in mutual encouragement and in the common atmosphere of a Christian society. We can understand easily enough this state of things, when we recall the circumstances of the first age of the Church. Within the Church there is a close communion or fellowship of the saints with one another; on the outside there is a marked separation between the few saints and the unholy world surrounding them.

But the scene changes when we pass from the first century to the nineteenth. What is to be said about separation when the whole society is professedly Christian? From whom are we, the Christians of this country, to separate ourselves? Christians are not a select few in England; nor is England a little Christian land surrounded by best sense of the proverb, "Charity begins at home." It is in the home that love has its first place. The child's primary love is due to the parent; and as the infant grows into the man, he finds other bonds which claim according to their degree the feeling appropriate to each. In accepting our various domestic and social relations as having Divine authority, we learn through experience what is the best form for our love in each case to take. Children are to honour their parents, parents to govern their children; the husband is to be as the stronger partner, the wife as the weaker, in the closest of all unions; there is an ideal affection of brothers and sisters, friend and friend, of fellow-citizens, and of fellow-Christians. Love begins in the home; and from thence it spreads, as in the water-circles which become gradually larger and less strongly marked, till it embraces all mankind.

There is one form of love to man, which is at the same time thrown out into prominence by natural causes, and specially characteristic of Christianity—I mean kindness towards the unprosperous and the afflicted. I have desired that this should be considered as one form of that love due from man to man which has its more important life in the closer relations of human beings. It is most undesirable that we should fall into a habit of thinking the second great commandment to be fulfilled in compassion towards the poor. But there is no claim more conspicuous and undeniable than that which the condition of the miserable makes upon the goodwill of the prosperous. On the one side there is need, on the other side there is power to relieve. The law of Christ takes note of these differences in the external lot of those whom Christ calls his brethren, and imperatively requires the happy to sympathize with and help those who suffer. " Whoso hath this world's good, and seeth his brother have need, and shutteth up his heart from him, how dwelleth the love of God in him ?" When the Son of man sits on his throne of glory and judges the nations, he dispenses blessing to those who have given meat to the hungry and drink to the thirsty, who have taken the stranger in and clothed the naked and visited the sick and imprisoned, whilst a terrible curse is pronounced on those who have done none of these things. There is nothing peculiar to Christianity in its commendation of this simple kindness towards the unfortunate. Every religion, every system of morality, has some maxims of pity and philanthropy. What Christ has done is to build up practical compassion upon the foundation of sonship to God. He, the Son of God, makes the cause of the afflicted his own. "If you would please the Father," he says to us, "see that you do not harden yourselves against your brothers who are in need." The teaching of Christ and of his Apostles has not been without fruits. It has been the glory of Christendom that those who have cared for their Christian calling and profession, amidst all differences and errors of belief have never been callous to the cry of distress. Hospitals, orphanages, almshouses, countless agencies for the relief of suffering and destitution, spring up like flowers over all ground which the Gospel has conquered for the name of Christ.

Experience has taught us that there is another need, besides that of urging the claim of the hungry and the naked upon Christian charity. Every precept of the Gospel requires to be understood spiritually, and to be applied with reasonable regard to the conditions of particular cases. We are under a dispensation, not of letter, but of spirit. This being a principle of supreme importance for all Christian life, the neglect of it is visited by a Nemesis which often seems hard to comprehend. The very best and most characteristic precepts, when they are followed literally, are smitten as it were with disease, of paralysis or of corruption. There are two alternative forms of legislation, either of which it was open—so to speak—to Christ to choose. He might have laid down nothing about the spirit, but have given every command surrounded with qualifications relating to all possible circumstances, so that his disciples might have found in the books handed down to them an immense directory of conduct. This method Christ did *not* choose, but preferred the other. He impressed upon his hearers that they were, first of all, subjects of the Spirit. This was their essential and characteristic privilege; their difficulty, it might prove to be, but a glory of which they could not divest themselves. To disciples who were thus pledged to think and live and act in the spirit, Christ delivered precepts in bold and trenchant form. He threw aside qualifying conditions; these were needless for those who would use spiritual discernment; the absence of them would be an abiding witness against unspiritual and literal discipleship. But the one comprehensive perversion of Christianity and all its maxims and practices is the materializing, which is also the literalizing, tendency. Christians have always been forgetting and refusing to live in the

Spirit. And what does Gospel teaching become to those who take it and judge it "after the flesh"? It cannot, thank God, altogether lose its virtue; but it does become in a very considerable degree unintelligible and unpractical, and in a very painful degree misleading. The subject is too large a one to illustrate now, except by the single instance of the New Testament precepts of almsgiving. These are very direct. "Give to him that asketh thee, and from him that would borrow of thee turn thou not away." "He that hath two coats, let him impart to him that hath none; and he that hath meat, let him do likewise." Precepts like these ought to have protected themselves against a merely literal interpretation. But most unfortunately, instead of seeing that they were to be understood in the spirit, people have assumed that they were expressed hyperbolically, and were to be discounted. They have said, "I will not go so far as to keep to myself but one coat, or to lend to any one who would like a loan; but if I see any one who has not a sixpence, I cannot as a Christian refuse to give him something." And so all the way down the course of Christianity, people have given away money, bread, coals, blankets, tickets, *without regard to consequences*, as a Christian duty. But it is never a Christian duty to act without regard to consequences. And it has been found out that a great deal of moral and social and physical mischief has been done by alms-giving; and some cry out that Christianity has been proved to be wrong, and others retort that political economy is hard and unfeeling, and tell themselves that they have at any rate to save their souls by obedience and charity, and that God who gave the precepts must take care of the consequences. But the only mistake is that the precepts have not been understood as they were intended to be, in the spirit. It may easily happen that a precept can only be fulfilled in the spirit by doing the opposite of it in the letter. Our hearts, my Christian brethren, ought to be such as would gladly share our superfluities with those who are less fortunate. Do not think that there is anything hyperbolical or extravagant in this principle. If there is a rich man in this land who would not willingly give up his wealth to make many of the poor in city or country less wretched, he is not fulfilling the law of Christ. This needs still to be proclaimed unflinchingly, as Christ proclaimed it. But would he then fulfil the law of Christ by selling all that he has and dividing it amongst the needy refuse of some great population? No, he would not; and for this simple reason, that we know with absolute certainty that such an act would do more harm than good to the very persons who were made partakers of the gift. As to the careless giving of doles to those who ask for them, so as to maintain a certain number of persons in idle and degraded mendicancy, that is not only a social mischief, but it is so *easy* that it has been not undeservingly stigmatized as a culpable form of self-indulgence. I suppose there is no one here who has not learnt that it will cost him more under certain circumstances to refuse aid than to give it. It is beyond all question that the law of Christian charity often requires us to incur for our brother's sake the pain of refusing what he asks. It is plain to the eye of the most moderate intelligence that to give relief is often and often to place a stumbling-block or occasion of falling in the way of a weak brother. And our Saviour has said with the gravest solemnity, "Woe unto him through whom stumbling-blocks come!"

Let me exhort you then, brethren, to give earnest rational heed to what our Lord and his

Apostles have enjoined concerning brotherly kindness. Do not think that there is anything extravagant, obsolete, or unpractical, in these injunctions. They tell us, in the simplest possible manner, what the mind of the true Christian should be. You will never fulfil them as thoroughly as we ought to do. In striving to be utterly unselfish and compassionate according to the mind of Christ, you will be on your guard against acts which, however they may be prompted by pity, have a proved injurious tendency. You will interpret the obligations of those who have this world's good, not with more laxity, but with more severity. Whatever can be done with money, whether by restriction or by expenditure, to lessen effectually the more painful inequalities between Christian and Christian, *that* the law of Christ requires to be done. Christ points to the miseries of the wretched, and says to those who care to listen to his voice, not " Bestow in charity and offerings some fiftieth or twentieth part of your income," but, " Give thought, give effort, give considerate and respectful kindness, give things more precious than money, but do not spare money, to heal these sorrows. Those toiling multitudes, those ignorant and reckless creatures, are children of your heavenly Father. Say not, Am I my brother's keeper? for the Father has made all responsible, according to their opportunities, for their brethren. You will lay up treasure in heaven, treasure to which all the gold of earth is dross, if you can minister light and hope to any that are down and draw them with a helping hand into the freedom and blessedness of sonship."

And now, dear brethren, I bring to a close the course of sermons which I have been permitted to deliver in this place. I have preached to you, not as I could have wished, but as I have been able, upon great and inspiring subjects. I have endeavoured to shew you how glorious is the calling with which we Christians are called, how solid the foundation on which we stand, how various and fruitful the works which God has prepared for us to walk in. God grant to you to feel, with some quickened energy of conviction and hope, that the promise of the future still belongs to the Christian faith. We have entered into a time of sifting, a time, to many, of perplexity and discouragement. Such a time has been necessary, in order that we may be freed from some things that were temporary in our religion, from some that were dishonouring to the name of the heavenly Father, from a general artificiality and dependence on tradition. Let us be thankful if through any discipline we are thrown back on the centre of our faith, and brought nearer to him who not only was, but is, and is to be. It is a time to be cautious and discriminating, but not to give up hope. Be careful how you pledge the heart of your faith to the more secondary and outward traditions of our religion. Your safety is with Christ and the Father. Pray that God will uphold you with his free Spirit. Let your inward life be one of faith, nourished by the invisible dews and rains of heaven, and your outward life will grow in strength and usefulness and dignity. In one word, be Christians; you may well be content to be nothing more; resolve that with God's help you will be nothing less. And may he who has called and is calling you sustain and reward your endeavour!

XI.

THE PRIMARY BONDS OF HUMAN LIFE.

Ephesians VI. 7.—"As to the Lord, and not to men."

HUMAN Society, as we see it wherever it can be said to exist, is made up of certain primary relations. These relations are represented to us most simply by the correlative terms, husband and wife, parents and children, master and servant. The relations thus denoted may be variously modified in different countries and in different ages, as regards the reciprocal claims and duties implied in them; but the fact of their subsisting as they do so tenaciously under various modifications, only shews more impressively their permanent and universal character. Look at early stages of society, and you see in primitive forms the ties of husbands and wives, parents and children, masters and servants. Look at society as it is now in civilized countries, after undergoing gradual developments which have made it more complex, and you find these relations still holding their place of importance. The most vital questions for us in these days are still apt to attach themselves to the mutual claims of husband and wife, of parent and child, of master and servant.

Now when we consider these relations with the instinctive desire to explain them, asking their why and wherefore, and trying whether they can be brought together under some common principle, we have a choice of three different methods of interpretation, which I will call the utilitarian, the historical, and the Christian. The two former are comparatively modern, the last is set forth in the New Testament.

1. According to the first, the one true object of action for men is happiness. All men desire pleasure ; and the one universal rational rule is that life should be so arranged, and that men should so act, as to secure the greatest amount of general happiness. The reason why man and woman come together is that they may be the happier ; the reason why any pair is marked off from other pairs is that all the pairs may be the happier. The justification of a life-long marriage tie is in its tendency to promote happiness. If there were

reason to believe that human society would on the whole be made the happier by an easily dissoluble bond, that would make it not only allowable but a duty to introduce divorce at discretion. Similarly, it is found to conduce to happiness that parents should protect and rear their young children, and that the children whilst young should be under the control of their parents, and after a certain time should become independent. Again, the relation of master and servant is to be explained as promoting under certain circumstances the general happiness. It may be the better,—it often has been the better,—for the ruled as well as the ruler that subordination should be established. But this relation ought to be sharply looked into and watched; for as soon as ever and in whatever degree it ceases to be for the benefit of the subordinate as well as for that of the ruler, it ought to be brought to an end or modified.

This explanation of human life and morality, as I need not tell you, has charmed and satisfied many minds by its simplicity and comprehensiveness and rationality.

2. But the great tendency of recent speculation has been towards the *historical* method of inquiry, which has been so strikingly fruitful in

many departments of knowledge. Men look to
see how things have come to pass, and they perceive everywhere the indisputable signs of natural
growth. All things were once rudimentary, and
through various strivings and pushings they have
come to be as developed and complex as they are
now. There is an extreme interest in thus discovering the mode of growth, and inquirers are
apt to be absorbed by it, and to be impatient of
theories for explaining any thing that exists, other
than the actual historical causes of which they can
trace the working. Human society as it is now,
in families and communities, is according to this
view nothing more than the result of the struggle
for existence. This and that arrangement are
found to be necessary, chiefly as protecting against
dangers by which life has always been beset.
Each custom which has prevailed in any race
and in any age is traced to some want or difficulty
or peril which it has helped men to meet. The
most familiar examples of this law are in the
physical world. It has been shewn very wonderfully, how the forms and clothing of animals have
been gradually rendered, through what has been
called the principle of the "survival of the fittest,"
such as would best enable them to thrive in the

particular circumstances in which they are found existing. But the manners and customs and laws of human society may also to a considerable extent be similarly explained. There has been no fixed rule, for example, about marriage in primitive communities. Customs of marriage have been found to be very much those which helped particular bodies of men to survive or to be strong. Many singular customs relating to marriage or other human institutions have been accounted for as being relics, preserved by the force of habit, of arrangements which were needed in a former stage but the reason for which has died out.

This historical explanation of social institutions is very interesting, and in great part novel. It cannot be denied that there is much truth in it. But it is defective in suggesting no principles of morality. So far indeed as it suggests anything at all as to the regulation of action, it seems to sanction the principle of selfishness. If society has been moulded into its present form by the struggle for existence, we may be supposed to fulfil the law of our destiny by continuing to struggle. On the other hand, it might certainly be urged that through self-defence and self-aggrandisement men have been led into the firm establishment of those relations by which peace and mutual help are inevitably fostered.

3. We do not find the utilitarian theory, or the historical method of accounting for things, in the Bible. The doctrine of the Bible is that human society is ordered by statutes of God. It is the Divine Lawgiver who joins pairs together, who sets men in families and in communities, who authorizes some to rule, and bids others to obey.

This doctrine is certainly not identical with the principle that society arranges itself with a view to happiness, or with the principle that the forms of society are due to the struggle for existence. And when the ordinances of God are so described that they can only be regarded as artificial, and cannot be understood as working through the order of Nature, the Bible doctrine of the regulation of all things by the will of God may be made to contradict and exclude the two other theories. But this is not necessary. It is quite open to us to believe that the commandments of God are to be discerned in what looks purely natural. But unquestionably the Bible teaches us to connect these permanent institutions of human society most closely with the mind and the working of God.

The devout worshipper of God cannot think

of the world as going on without him. To the Christian, the laws of the universe are always and necessarily, in whatever way they may manifest themselves, with whatever matter they may deal, the laws of God.

It is our God "who covereth the heaven with clouds, and prepareth rain for the earth, and maketh the grass to grow upon the mountains, and herb for the use of men." "Fear ye not me? saith the Lord: will ye not tremble at my presence, which have placed the sand for the bound of the sea, by a perpetual decree, that it cannot pass it; and though the waves thereof toss themselves, yet can they not prevail; though they roar, yet can they not pass over it?" Yes, the laws of nature are firm and unchanging, because they are the laws of the Eternal God. Does the earth nevertheless change and advance? That is because the "Father is *working* hitherto;" because "the everlasting God, the Lord, the Creator of the ends of the earth, fainteth not, neither is weary; there is no searching of his understanding." It is our privilege to see the mind of God in all fixed law, the working of God in all advance towards perfection.

But *man's* nature is nearer to God's than that

of the hills and the clouds, than that of the beasts and the feathered fowls. Our spiritual endowments join us in closer affinity to the Divine Spirit. The qualities and the relations which belong to the perfection of our race,—so we have been taught to believe,—grow out of the Divine nature, and rest upon the Divine power and will. This therefore is our faith about those primary and enduring institutions of human society, the relations of husband and wife, parents and children, master and servant, that the everlasting God ordained them, that the Divine life is in them. We need not be expected to deny that these ordinances promote human happiness: how could it fail to be so, when they are the ordinances of our Father? Nor need we deny whatever the researches of inquirers may appear to tell us, as to the gradual growth, under natural influences, of the more perfected forms of these relations. We shall conclude that God intended human society to grow as we may learn that it *has* grown. The two facts, that the essential forms of social life promote happiness, and that they have passed through stages of natural growth, will be in harmony with, but secondary to, the greater fact that they are the expression of the Divine will.

It is to St Paul that we owe the most striking *theological* interpretations of marriage, family bonds, and subordination.

He has taught us to see in the union of the wedded pair an image of the union between Christ and the Church. This idea did not however originate with St Paul. It was an old Jewish idea. In the prophets the Lord is spoken of as a husband to whom the daughter of Zion, the Jewish people, is married. And amongst the Jewish imagery of the Apocalypse we read of the marriage supper of the Lamb, and of his bride arrayed in fine linen, white and clean, which is the righteousness of the Saints. But St Paul, dwelling with his devout insight upon this poetical language, and putting together the two facts, of the common union between man and wife and the union between God and humanity, which have been seen by the prophet's eye to resemble each other, perceives that the analogy cannot be a mere fanciful one. The God who takes humanity to be his bride is the creator of the union between man and wife. When we look upon a married pair, we see a piece of the handwriting of God. We may learn by means of this to know something of the union between Christ and the Church ; and

wonderful order. The ordinance of rule and service amongst men is both a part and an illustration of that subordination. The ruler, in the eye of the Christian, rules not for his own pleasure but for the good of those whom he rules and for the glory of God. His authority is a burden, his government a ministry. It is the glory of those placed in higher positions, not to refuse to rule, but to serve by ruling. The best ruler is he who is most conscious of being a servant; who knows that he, as well as those whom he directs, has a master in heaven.

Now let me ask you to think, dear brethren, how the common life which we live is affected by this Christian interpretation of it. You see that it is made genuinely *sacramental*. The universal ordinances of social life exist in part for the shewing forth of mysteries. When we see the visible things, we may look through them to the invisible. The married pair may speak to us of Christ and the Church. The family may make us think of the gracious Fatherhood of God, of the submissive sonship of Christ. The voice of command and the act of obedience may remind us of the orderly subjection of all created things and persons to the one Lord. How wonderfully is our common life thus èxalted, dignified, consecrated! God is in it all! We are moving in a world, nay we are parts of a world, through which God is always manifesting himself, in which God is always putting forth his energy! Our own life, instead of being a limited vulgar thing made by ourselves, is in the closest contact with Divine mysteries, with the Divine infinity! Our feeling therefore ought to be one of reverence for our mutual obligations and affections, for ourselves and our doings!

And this mystical mode of regarding life, instead of being dreamy and unwholesome, has an immediate and most salutary bearing on practical morality. In order that we may do our duty faithfully, we greatly need, not only a persuasion that certain rules are for the best, but a constraining sense of obligation, a deep feeling of reverence. And it was with this that St Paul reinforced the accepted teaching of morality. Others could say, Let the husband treat his wife with the love of the stronger, and let the wife pay back to her husband the love of the weaker. Or they could say, Let parents bring up their children kindly and wisely, and let children obey and honour their parents. Or, Let masters be just and considerate, and let servants be loyal and honest. But then we know what terrible difficulties hinder us in the discharge of our duties, how much irritation is apt to be engendered between those who are thrown most closely together, how men are plagued by arrogance, obstinacy, jealousy, indolence, perverse or passionate desire. Against such influences, with the ready sophistry of excuses which they command, maxims based upon calculations about the general happiness are apt to prove weak. The Christian teacher says, Remember the Lord your God. You have to do with the Father, with Christ, with the Holy Spirit. The secrets of the heart are naked and open to the eyes of him with whom we have to do. Remember that God has brought you, *man and wife*, together. You were indeed mutually attracted, but this was a part of God's instrumentality for making you man and wife. And this relation into which you have been brought is, depend upon it, a very solemn one. It is not one of pleasure only; it is one of blessed heavenly discipline. Don't imagine you are free to do as you please. Your faithfulness is due not only to each other but to the Lord. You who are *parents*, be sure that it is God who has given you your children. You are to bring them up for him. They are not to be your playthings, or objects for your pride to feed on; they are God's children as well as yours. It will be no trifling matter for you, if you by neglect or selfishness manage to alienate them from God. *Children,* respect the parents whom God has set over you. He is your heavenly Father, they are parents through whom he teaches you what his fatherhood is. See in them not only such earthly creatures as they may happen to be, but representatives and ministers of God. *Masters,* bear in mind that you are God's commissioners, appointed to see that some of his work is done. Beware of selfish arrogance. Expel it by the remembrance of *your* Master in Heaven. *Servants,* the just commands which come to you are not the wilfulness of one whose better fortune you may envy and resent, but the commands of the heavenly Master who makes the universal order. Obey, not only for the sake of the earthly superior under whom you are placed, or in proportion to his worthiness, but with the devout and loyal submission of the heart to God.

Brethren, when you hear this Christian enforcement of your common duties, let not fear alone enter into your hearts, though you may well revere with trembling. Surely in these views of life there is light and hope also. We have the privilege of looking up to the Source of health and strength. Our affections may be refined, purified, made heavenly. Our prospects are not buried in the grave. If we let Christ unite us according to his law to those around us, we may know Christ the better through them, we may know and love them the better through Christ.

XII.

RICHES AND THE KINGDOM OF GOD.

St Mark x. 23.—"How hardly shall they that have riches enter into the kingdom of God!"

WHENEVER the New Testament is looked into with any fresh spirit of inquiry, a contrast is revealed which can hardly fail to produce some strong effect on the mind of a modern reader.

The contrast I mean is between the doctrine of the New Testament about poverty and riches, on the one hand, and the circumstances and habits of a wealthy industrial community, on the other.

This contrast may be misunderstood and misrepresented; various inferences, more or less erroneous, may be drawn from it: but that the contrast does exist in a startling degree ought not to be denied. It is real, and demands our constant and most serious attention.

Let me revive your recollection of what the New Testament teaches about poverty and riches by two or three illustrations which happen to be brought before us to-day.

It is St Matthew's day; and we read of a man named Matthew, or Levi, whose business it was to receive the customs or dues which the Romans exacted from the subject Jewish population. It was a gainful occupation; partly, because it was so odious a one that no one would undertake it without the chance of being able to make a good deal of money by it. But there was nothing necessarily immoral in it. Matthew was sitting at his official place on the beach of the Lake of Galilee, when Jesus of Nazareth passed by, and said to him, Follow me. And Matthew arose and followed him.

That is to say, he abandoned his occupation of publican or collector. We are not to suppose that the incidents recorded in the New Testament took place generally in the abrupt way in which the narrative relates them. The process reported in two brief phrases may have been a gradual and deliberate one. Matthew no doubt resigned his post in an orderly manner. But he *did* resign it at the call of Jesus, and became one of his followers.

He thus became associated with a remarkable band. Jesus had come forth from the family of a carpenter, probably a well-to-do family, and had begun the life and work of a prophet. He proclaimed the nearness of the kingdom of God, and taught, and did works of healing. He drew followers after him, from whom he chose twelve, naming them his envoys or apostles. These were mostly fishermen,—not particularly poor men, for they owned fishing boats,—but they all left their trades to go with Jesus and to do his bidding. We do not exactly know how they all lived; they may have received money from their respective families in consideration of what they had given up. But it is certain that they lived very hardly, having a common purse, and giving out of that to the relief of the poor.

Matthew, who was one of the Apostles, became also in after years the compiler of one of the Lives of Jesus. In his Gospel we find the longest and most characteristic example of the moral teaching of his Master, commonly called the Sermon on the Mount. From this discourse is taken the Gospel for this Sunday after Trinity; and we learn from it that Jesus spoke to his disciples as to poor men, that he did not urge upon them the duties of industry and providence, but bade them rely upon the bounty of the heavenly Father who fed the birds and adorned the flowers. He warned them, poor as they were, against care, and against the desire of riches.

Matthew was also, as an Apostle, one of those who had the charge of organizing the Church of Christ in its first days. It was done, as they believed, under a special impulse of the Divine Spirit. The most characteristic feature of the social life of the Church was that its members had all things common. They were mostly from the poor class, and when any one who had possessions was converted, he threw what he had into the common stock. This actual community of possessions did not last long; but its *principle* survived as of absolute authority in the Church. It was a part of the Gospel carried with them into the world by the Apostles, that in the Kingdom of God as they founded it upon the earth no one was to count what he had as his own, that private riches were dangerous to the soul, that the brother of low degree was to rejoice in that he was exalted, but the rich in that he was made low. As was natural, those who came into the Kingdom of God were not in general the rich; God called the poor of this world to be rich in faith and heirs of the promised kingdom. And the great enemy of the Gospel of

Christ was worldliness. The Cross and the World were in opposition the one to the other. When men could not recognize the glory of the Cross, which was the glory of sympathy, the glory of the high making common cause with the low, it was because the god of this world blinded their eyes.

Such is the doctrine of the New Testament. Critics need not pervert it very much,—though they must pervert it somewhat,—to make out that it is utterly opposed to the maxims upon which the life of a modern industrial community is built up. Certainly, the New Testament ideal looks strangely by the side of the Christian England of to-day. Here, it might seem, the one universal aim is to become rich. The modes of acquiring riches have been digested into a science. Community of goods is so far from being an accepted institution, that it is regarded by Christians with something like horror. Wealth has increased, and is increasing, in an unprecedented degree; and the rich rejoice more in being exalted than in being made low. It is not indeed true to allege, as some do, that whilst the rich are becoming richer, the poor are becoming poorer. On the contrary it is evident enough that the poor of this country, and of the rest of the world, are becoming less poor. Still, the social differences between the rich and the poor are very great; and whilst there are some persons enormously rich, there are many miserably poor. And there are two circumstances especially remarkable. One is that those who study the interests of the poor most earnestly and sympathetically do not urge them to live like the birds, but to look forward to the morrow, and to lay up treasure on the earth. They would have them, it might be said, practise providence rather than trust to Providence. The other is that, according to appearances, it is now easier for the rich to enter into the Kingdom of God than for the poor. The upper classes are, superficially at least, more religious than the lower. The Churches in which the New Testament doctrine as I have just illustrated it is read and proclaimed with authority are better attended by those who have possessions than by those who are without them.

Will you not allow, my Christian brethren, that the contrast of which I have spoken is a real one, and óne which should naturally cause us some perplexity and uneasiness? For my part, I cannot imagine a Christian of these days reading the New Testament in any other than a dead mechanical way, without having this problem presented over and over again to his mind,—How is the teaching of Christ and of his Apostles to be reconciled with the modern industrial and accumulating spirit? In what way ought an honest Christian in these times to act with reference to the questions of riches and poverty?

Suppose that we desired to be quite uncompromising and to follow the right without reckoning what it might cost us.

We take the side of the New Testament. We call Christ our Master; we confess him to be the Son of God who died for us. We are sure that it is not only right, but also safe in the long run, to follow him. What alternative indeed have we, so long as we profess to be Christians and disciples of Jesus Christ, but to follow him?

Shall we then set ourselves against the whole modern constitution of society? Shall we denounce property, however it may plead that it is an essential condition of social well-being, as the unrighteous mammon? Shall we maintain that it is the duty of every one who awakes to the obligations of his Christian calling, to give all that he has to the poor? Shall we teach that all true Christians, instead of providing for the morrow, ought to cast the care of their support upon their heavenly

Father? Shall we protest against all distinctions of society, and proclaim that in Christ there is no master and no servant, no employer and no work-people, no buyer and no seller, but that all are equal and everything is common?

These views, it will be said, are unpractical, revolutionary, Utopian. But the uncompromising New Testament Christian might reply that he quite expected to hear them so described by the world. It is nothing to him what the wise of this world may think of his views; he is the disciple of a faith which began by being esteemed as foolishness. He is quite willing to bear the reproach of being unpractical and Utopian, so long as he bears it with Christ and the Apostles.

Let us avoid then offering anything that might seem like a worldly objection to the course of conduct I have supposed to be suggested. Let us refuse, if we will, to let political economy over-ride our Christianity.

But our Christianity itself will interpose with a decided veto to check any such application of the doctrine of the Gospel. Suppose it were announced that a score of our richest men, penetrated by a desire to be thorough and not merely nominal Christians, had resolved to give all their goods to the poor. How would you receive such an announcement? With admiration and delight? The feeling which could prompt such a resolution would be indeed admirable; but the act would be one which, as Christians, we should reasonably contemplate with grave alarm. I do not see how it could fail to do moral *evil.* As Christians, we long that our brethren should grow into the true Christian character; *i.e.,* that they should become, amongst other things, temperate, self-denying, contented, peaceable, helpful. But what would be the effect of an announcement that fifty millions were to be distributed with the purpose of realizing equality amongst men, upon the moral character of those whom it affected? It could not fail to be disastrous. You know that it would generate idleness, covetousness, discord, disappointment. It would feed the fleshly tempers, instead of fostering the spiritual, in hundreds of thousands of our brethren. Ought a Christian to do an act which is sure to make his neighbours worse Christians rather than better?

If any one therefore were to ask me, Why don't you, as a believer in Jesus Christ and in the Sermon on the Mount, make common cause in the things of this world with the most destitute around you, and trust for the needful food and raiment to him who feeds the fowls and clothes the lilies? I should not answer that such an act would be fanatical or enthusiastic, or that political economy forbids it, but that, whatever else I ought or ought not to do, I believe in my conscience that to give away all I have to the poor would *not* be the best way to serve them as a brother in Christ. I know with undoubting conviction that we all need, for our spiritual benefit as children of God, the discipline of forethought and voluntary self-denial, of family responsibilities, of measured and considerate helpfulness. And therefore to turn the orderly arrangements of industrial life into a medley of equal enjoyments would seem to me to be committing an outrage upon New Testament Christianity at least as much as upon worldly wisdom.

There is another alternative. Does uncompromising honesty require us then to adopt the lamentable course of rejecting the earliest Christian teaching on this great question of riches and poverty as mistaken and visionary? Must we say, we hold by the order of modern industrial life, and *therefore* we put aside the Sermon on the Mount and the example of the Day of Pentecost as having no authority over us?

Let us pause before we do this. Let us consider whether we do not need that that very teaching should become instinct with living power over us.

We have been justifying industry and accumulation as instruments for making us truer children of God. St Paul does virtually the same thing, when he exhorts, "Inasmuch as you have put on the new man in Christ, let every one labour, working with his hands the thing which is good, that he may have to give to him that needeth." But do we mean therefore to approve all that devotion to the pursuit of wealth by which this age is characterized? Very far from it. There is, in fact, no thoughtful person amongst us who is not sometimes filled with shame and disgust and dismay at the predominance which wealth has gained over the motives of modern Englishmen. We are, beyond denial, idolaters in the serving of Mammon. Riches, to us, cover the multitude of sins. People are ashamed of being poor. We make a necessity of the most superfluous luxuries. All this is complained of by the poets, by satirists, by moralists, by political economists themselves. Those who profess no allegiance to Christ denounce the sway of the moneymaking spirit as dwarfing and vulgarising to the character, as lowering the dignity of human nature, as spoiling the quality of genuine enjoyment, as tempting men to dishonesty, as occasioning widespread disasters. The evil is a real one, the disease dangerous.

Now what cure, I ask, for the serving of Mammon is to be compared with the simple uncompromising service *of God?* This is the real point of all the teaching of Christ. "Break absolutely and finally," he insists, "the dominion of Mammon, of riches and the pleasures which riches can buy, over your hearts. Do this at any cost, by whatever means is the most likely to be effectual. Give yourselves wholly, with no reserve, to God. Give yourselves and whatever you have to God. And, inasmuch as God is the Father of your brethren, and desires more than anything else that is known to you the high well-being of you all, to give yourselves and all that you have to him will become, in its practical application, nearly the same thing as to give yourselves and all that you have to your brethren."

By what particular acts we may do the most good is to be learnt, according to the plainest teaching of Scripture, by experience and honest study. I do not doubt that it was right for Matthew the publican to leave his gainful seat. I do not doubt that it would have been better for the rich young man if he had consented to sell all that he had and to give to the poor and to go and follow Jesus. But it is not to be inferred that every collector of tolls or taxes ought to give up his occupation, or that every rich man ought to divest himself of his possessions.

The teaching of the New Testament, carried out to its ideal length, lays upon us the responsibility of using our means for the good of others as completely, as unselfishly, *as if* we parted with them and left ourselves with nothing. Is this easy, in a world like this? Nay, my brethren, it is difficult, most difficult. It seems to me, and I dare say you would think so too, that it might be easier to make a great sacrifice once for all, than habitually through a lifetime to hold all that one has as a trust for the service of God and for the benefit of others. It would be churlish to refuse to join in the chorus of admiration awakened by the liberality of that good man, Mr Peabody; but it may be permitted to say that, for an old man without wife or children to give away to the poor a great slice out of enormous wealth makes less demand upon Christian charity than for the parents of a family to manage unselfishly and liberally an income of a few hundreds a year or less. To be completely unselfish in the laying out of money is supremely difficult; and it is another difficulty, to lay out *wisely*. Where is the book, who is the sage, that will inform us how we ought to spend, how much we ought to give, by what giving we may do most good? If it is so *difficult* to use money according to Christian perfection in the present social order, let me at least be acquitted of recommending any low compromise between the spirit of this world and the spirit of Christianity. I recommend no compromise; I do not suggest the easiest course. I point out how, amidst many difficulties, it is conceivable that the highest Christian ideal might be realized without subverting the industrial order of society. And I say, if you would do your part faithfully in the place in which you find yourselves, if you would seek protection from snares which are constantly threatening to beguile and to master you, then keep your minds on the New Testament teaching about the things of this world. Study it reverently, teachably. See without misgivings in the joy and self-sacrifice and concord of the Pentecostal community the workings of the Spirit of God. Look with admiration on the company of those who left all and followed the Master who knew not where to lay his head. The more we are entangled in a rich society, the more we need the warning and bracing influence of these examples. No less than the Apostles, than the first Christians, ought *we* to be superior to the things of this world, free masters of our money, be it much or little, and not its servants. There are better things, let us be sure, than those which money can purchase. There is treasure in heaven. There are virtues, graces, joys, denied to those who care much about money, the heritage of the true children of God. If others are not prizing the real jewels, let that be no excuse to us for childishly preferring the showy counterfeit to the genuine treasure. Let us bear in mind the men in all ages who have shewn a lofty spirit about money, refusing to be bribed by it, not sacrificing the true interests of life to the pursuit of it, bearing with equanimity the loss of it.

Above all, let us consider Jesus Christ, the Son of God, who though he was rich, for our sakes became poor, that we by his poverty might be enriched. He is not the kind of master to be rejected by such a generation as this. He is the Saviour we need the more, precisely because the hold of the world is so strong upon us. God intends us, let us believe, to be members of a prosperous community, with distributed functions, with increasing command over the products of the earth. But he intends us to rule these earthly things as instruments of the spirit, and as a means for knitting mankind happily in one. And that we may be able to do this, he gives us not only this earthly prosperity, but also fellowship with Christ. He makes us citizens of the Kingdom of heaven. He pours into our hearts his own Spirit, to raise us up, and exalt us to the place whither our Saviour Christ is gone before. Brethren, let not these best gifts of our Father be thrown away upon us. If we value these according to their worth, he will provide that we shall have such enjoyment as is good for us of his lower gifts also.

XIII.

THE DIVINE RIGHT TO RULE.

St John x. 2.—"He that entereth in by the door is the shepherd
of the sheep."

In the passage in which our Lord declares himself
to be the Good Shepherd, he is not speaking of
himself only. He begins with a denunciation of
bad shepherds. Shepherds here mean rulers, men
who have any control or power over other men.
The name was commonly used in ancient times to
denote the governing part of a country or society,
the superiors who stand above inferiors. It is of
the qualities which ought to characterize rulers or
superiors that our Lord is speaking.

The passage, when thus considered, acquires a
new interest to many readers. The quality which
our Lord ascribes to himself becomes in him more
real when it is recognized as the fountain and highest example of that which should be shewn by all
men in their relation as superiors. And his teaching on this subject is perceived to be a lesson not

only of what we are to him as his flock, but also of what we ought to be, as his followers, to those who are put in any way under us.

A chapter of the prophet Ezekiel, which was probably in our Lord's mind, begins thus: "The word of the Lord came unto me, saying, Son of man, prophesy against the shepherds of Israel." And he proceeds to prophesy, accordingly, with astonishing directness and vigour, against the ruling classes of his country, telling them that the Lord God says, "Behold I am against the shepherds; and I will require my flock at their hand, and cause them to cease from feeding the flock." Now, a greater prophet than Ezekiel, he who was not merely *a* son of man but *the* Son of man, was again moved to prophesy against the shepherds of Israel. Jesus of Nazareth was in declared opposition to those who then exercised the chief power amongst his countrymen. St. John, in giving illustrations of the conflict, sometimes calls them "the chief priests and Pharisees," sometimes "the Pharisees," sometimes simply "the Jews." The following passage indicates what the state of affairs then was. "The Pharisees heard that the people murmured such things concerning him,"—that is, that the common people were beginning to think

that Jesus must be the Messiah. "And the Pharisees and the chief priests sent officers to take him."
The officers returned without him to the chief priests
and Pharisees; "and they said unto them, Why
have ye not brought him? The officers answered,
Never man spake like this man. Then answered
them the Pharisees, Are ye also deceived? Have
any of the rulers or of the Pharisees believed in
him? But this people, who knoweth not the law,
are cursed." There we learn the temper of the
shepherds of Israel both towards their flock and
towards the prophet who was calling them to account. A little later, after the cure of a blind man,
Jesus spoke some words significantly asserting the
authority which lays bare imposture and de-
nounces usurpation. "For judgment I am come into
this world; that they which see not might see, and
that they which see might be made blind." It
was sufficiently understood for whom such allusions
were intended, and some of the Pharisees who
were near him could not keep silence, but broke
out, "Are we blind also?" Thus challenged,
Jesus was ready to tell them what he thought of
them. "If ye were blind, ye should have no sin;
but now ye say, We see; therefore your sin remain-
eth. Verily, verily, I say unto you, He that

entereth not by the door into the sheepfold, but climbeth up some other way, the same is a thief and a robber. But he that entereth in by the door is the shepherd of the sheep."

It is plain that our Lord is denouncing the shepherds of Israel as being not true shepherds but rather thieves and robbers. But what is the particular fault he finds with them? This is not quite on the surface, and his hearers, we are told, did not exactly understand him. The fault, in one word, was this,—that *the rulers did not identify themselves with the people.*

Besides that chapter of Ezekiel, there is another much older passage, which may well have been at the same moment in our Lord's mind. It is in Numbers xxvii. We read that Moses, desiring the appointment of one who might be his successor, spoke thus unto the Lord (ver. 16), "Let the Lord, the God of the spirits of all flesh, set a man over the congregation, which may go out before them, and which may go in before them, and which may lead them out, and which may bring them in; that the congregation of the Lord be not as sheep which have no shepherd." In answer to which prayer, Joshua the son of Nun was selected and consecrated to be the leader of the children of

Israel. You observe the curious emphasis of repetition with which the relation of the leader to the people,—that he goes before them and they follow him,—is here insisted upon. This relation is equally the prominent point in our Lord's account of the genuine shepherd. You must bear in mind the mode of tending sheep in that Eastern country. The pasture lands are wide and open ; the fold is an enclosed place, protected by a sufficient wall. The shepherd does not drive the sheep before him, but he leads them, going out with them from the fold in the morning, returning with them into the fold at night. He is in the front, to encounter any danger, to find the best pasture, and to encourage the flock with his voice. The sheep know his voice, trust to his guidance and protection, and follow him.

This, says our Lord, is the type of the true leader of men. A man is not set over his fellow-men that he may make them tools of his ambition, food to his vanity, ministers of his pleasure, foils of his splendour. He has his superiority as a charge, that he may *serve* those put under him by *leading* them. The real test of the genuine ruler is this, Does he separate himself from his people, or does he associate them with himself? The good ruler goes in and out at the head of his followers by the same door with them ; the bad one tries to separate and exalt himself, *climbs up some other way.*

This is a central and a universal principle, the divine key to all lordship and superiority amongst men. Let men talk of the divine right of kings, or of the rights of property, or of the deference due to rank and station, as they please ; according to the law of the eternal Maker, as illustrated by the history of mankind, as vividly declared by the Son of God, and—what is more than all—as embodied in the life of the Son of man, a man has no real divine right to his higher position except as he makes it useful to those beside him in the lower. This is true in Church and in State, of the savage chief, of the imperial autocrat, of the constitutional ruler,—Sovereign, President, or Minister,—of the commander of an army, of the employer of labour, of the mistress of a household, of the master of a school, of the parent of a family. Our Lord's teaching about the good and the false shepherd, familiar and sacred as it is to our ears, fails to reach our minds and consciences unless it reminds us that the divine right to rule is in serving. To apply this test resolutely to all who have power, is not dangerous to a community; it is the true safety.

In the eyes of a Christian, the example of Christ must settle the question. Do we call him Master and Lord? Yes, and we say well, for so he is. What Christian does not acknowledge *his* Lordship? He is not Lord of the clergy and Sunday school children only, but of all sorts and conditions of men. And how did he reveal himself? He came not to be ministered unto, but to minister. "I am among you," he said to his obedient followers, "as he that serveth." He did not abolish command and obedience, ruling and serving, superiority and inferiority. No, but he insisted, that as he who was the Master of all gave himself to be the servant of all, so amongst them who should call themselves by his name, he should be held chief who did the most service. As regards human laws, it may no doubt be found expedient that privilege and power and authority should be secured against attack, however unworthy and unserviceable the person in whom they are vested may be: but by the law of the kingdom of heaven no man can claim to be a ruler of others except by proving that he can serve them.

And if we consider the rulers who have distinguished themselves in history, it may be seen that, on the whole, those have been felt to be the best shepherds who have most thoroughly made common cause with the sheep, not climbing up by some exclusive way, but going in and out before the sheep through the door of the fold. There have been selfish and ambitious conquerors who have been very successful although their chief motive was to aggrandise themselves, a class of whom the first Napoleon is the most conspicuous example: but even these have generally had the instinct or the skill of identifying themselves with their armies or populations, and have really led by sympathy and endurance men who willingly followed them. But the best rulers have been those who have consciously lived for their subjects, men like the Moses and the David of sacred history, who felt that they were called and appointed to a charge of great responsibility, not that they might lord it over God's heritage, but that they might lead the people onward in the path of safety and prosperity. Wherever rule has been justified to the common conscience, so that men have rejoiced in their rulers and been grateful to them, whether the power was nominally despotic or limited by law, the secret has been that the rulers cared not for themselves but for the people. But there is a natural and Divinely inspired discontent felt against those who have power, when they shew that they have forgotten the essential reason of authority and subordination, and that they fancy that, because they were born in a certain station or have in some way got power into their hands, the Maker and Father of all has put some of his children under their feet to pamper their luxury or their pride. You might be sure that if the Father of our Lord Jesus Christ has ordained government and subjection, the end of such ordination must be the good not of the few but of the many; and this truth, which Christ has taught, the instincts and experience of mankind have abundantly illustrated.

Yet the tendency of vulgar greatness is always to *dis*sociate itself from the common herd; to be exclusive rather than sympathetic, in interest, in taste, in enjoyment. We in England, my brethren, know perfectly well what this danger is. We know too well the secret of what made the false shepherds of Ezekiel's time and of the days of our Lord. There is not one of us here, I venture to say, who may not be the better for being reminded that the true shepherd is one who walks with his sheep and gives his life for them. There is not one of us who has not been tempted to draw off from other persons, to look down on them, to find satisfaction in claiming to belong to a superior class, or to have a more cultivated taste. That impulse, to make the burdens of others our own, is so rare, so difficult to cherish! That desire, to help and encourage others with any advantage that we possess, has so weak and occasional a hold upon our hearts! The simple and natural fellow-feeling, which joins hands with the true man in each neighbour in spite of any vulgarities and faults, and would help him unconsciously against the vulgarities and the faults, the fellow-feeling which draws and binds human beings together, and builds up a living society,—has so hard a fight against our stupid vanity and self-love!

It is good, then, that we should be led to honour a character and a career like those of the heroic traveller and missionary, whose mortal remains were laid yesterday in the most sacred soil of this our English land. We reasonably pay a tribute to Livingstone's energy and unconquerable resolution; these are qualities we cannot afford to make light of. But it is not by these chiefly, I think, that the national heart has been drawn to Dr. Livingstone. We have all learnt something of his goodness, his generosity, his gentleness, his enthusiastic and yet patient desire to serve the natives of Africa, his willingness to lay down his life for them in contending against the wolfish slave-trade which has been devouring them. Hardly any one has known so much of the native races of Africa as Livingstone, no one has spoken of them with more respect, no one has behaved towards them with a more hearty and simple good-will. And I suppose no European has been so successful in winning their confidence and affection.

This career, of long and successful fellowship with men of inferior races, is one of great interest for us to contemplate. It is evidently not easy for Englishmen, when they come into contact with inferior races, to be mindful at all times of their Christianity or even of their civilization. English settlers and soldiers, finding the Oriental or the African to be generally untrustworthy, sometimes treacherous, sometimes filthy, always difficult to understand and appreciate, have too often fancied themselves to be justified in treating these dark-coloured subjects or neighbours as if they were wild beasts. They have allowed themselves to beat and shoot and burn, in Africa and the East, with a freedom which would be considered shocking if the objects of these wild severities had been white men. It is difficult for us in England to judge fairly those who are tried by difficulties and exposed to dangers of which we have no experience; and we most of us feel a natural and not ungenerous desire to stand by our countrymen and justify them in any proceedings they may think necessary against savages. I hope it was unwillingness to say a word which should appear to reflect on the conduct of the handful of gallant men who vindicated the honour of our country on the pestilent shores of the Gold Coast, which kept almost every English tongue from uttering even an expression of regret at the burning of Coomassie. And yet it is scarcely possible, surely, to think without misgivings as well as pain of the deliberate destruction by fire in cold blood of all the houses of a populous city, as a punishment of the faithlessness of its ruler. If such a thing were done, even in hot blood, in Europe, it would excite, as we well know, a cry of execration against its perpetrators. The excuse is that the men, women, and children, whose every home was made a ruin in Coomassie, were African savages, and that the town had been defiled by atrocities which seemed to cry to heaven for vengeance. Well, I am as unwilling as others to judge the humane and honourable men who set that unhappy city on fire. But, when it is assumed that savages, or people of Oriental civilization like the Chinese, are not to have the benefit of the laws which mitigate the horrors of war between European nations, but that we may give their cities and their palaces to the flames without mercy, it is timely, I think, that we should ask ourselves why we are proud of Livingstone. Is it not, in a great degree, because he treated Africans—let those who will scoff at the phrase—as men and brothers? Is it not because he would have shrunk with repugnance from doing to an African what would have been an act of brutality if done to a European? From his grave in Westminster Abbey the single-minded friend of the Africans yet speaks to us; a more tried friend than any other, because he lived so long alone amongst them, bearing alone whatever was repugnant to European taste in their customs, and not turning from them in disgust; a friend who, the more intimately he knew them, felt for them not only the more pity but also the more respect. He appeals to us most earnestly to do whatever we can to help his Africans, and especially to drive away that desolating scourge of the slave-trade from their shores. But he appeals to us also to cherish in all our dealings that spirit of large and tender humanity which he had himself received from heaven, and to be in this respect followers of him, even as he was of Christ.

It has been my chief desire this morning, brethren, to commend to you this spirit of the true Shepherd as one which, if we admit it into our hearts, will pervade and Christianize all our actions and manner of life. But before I conclude, let me remind you of the more familiar lesson, that we are the sheep of the Good Shepherd. Our Lord did not shrink from declaring "I am the Good Shepherd." He was referring, no doubt, primarily to his Galilean followers. They knew him as the perfect Shepherd, going before them, leading them with his voice, prepared to suffer death for their deliverance. But he had other sheep than them; other followers who in other times and places were to learn the tones of his attracting voice, and to find safety and joy in going where he leads. His voice is that of the Father's love, entreating *us* also to come to God and to be at one with him. It calls us to the labour and pain of self-conquest, perhaps to the patience of suffering. But it bids us go nowhere but where Christ has gone before. As we follow that voice, we keep near to him, and he will lead us to refreshing pastures and sweet waters. Let us not choose to stray from his guidance. If we do we shall lose ourselves, and one day we shall repent of our wilfulness. If we are straying now, the Good Shepherd is seeking us, and calling us by name with that voice of mercy. He desires to save us from ourselves and from our enemies. He promises us rest in obedience. "Take my yoke upon you and learn of me; for my yoke is easy, and my burden is light."

XIV.

'CÆSAR AND GOD.

St Matthew xxii. 21.—"Render unto Cæsar the things which are Cæsar's, and unto God the things that are God's."

I HAVE protested in a recent sermon[1] against a current and plausible misinterpretation of this saying. But I am induced to ask your attention to a fuller exposition of the true meaning of it, because the public interest is especially engaged at the present moment by controversies in which this saying is adduced as an authoritative text, and the sense put upon the precept is, I may say, a demonstrably erroneous one. It is worth while, I feel assured, to try even by repetition to guard ourselves against this misapprehension, and to fasten to our minds the true sense of our Lord's profoundly edifying admonition.

The saying is supposed to refer to the provinces of the State and the Church, or of the civil authority and the religious authority, respectively, and to lay down the principle that these

[1] See page 113.

provinces should be kept carefully distinct. In this sense the text is invoked equally by the Roman Catholic and by the Protestant Dissenter, by Archbishop Manning and by Mr Miall. The Romanist alleges that when the State interferes with the province of the Church, this direct command of Christ is violated. "The province of the Church is that of faith and morals; within that province the Church ought to be supreme; it is sacrilege and blasphemy for the civil power to make regulations, except as the obedient servant of the Church, which have anything to do with faith and morals." Considering, as Mr Gladstone[1] is pointing out to us, that our whole life belongs in some sense to the sphere of faith and morals, we can only see in this doctrine a claim on the part of the Church, as distinct from the State, to rule the whole of human life. If we demur to what seems to involve such consequences, we are reminded that our Lord bade us render to Cæsar the things that are Cæsar's, and to God the things that are God's. The interference of the State with the Church is named "Cæsarism"; it is the presumption of a Cæsar taking to himself the things that belong to God.

[1] This sermon was preached on the Sunday after the publication of the "Vatican Decrees."

With a very different understanding of what "the Church" is, English voluntaryism equally appeals to this saying as affirming the separate independence of the civil power and of religion. It declares the sphere of the conscience to be one, and the sphere of the law to be another. In maintaining a State-Church, we render, it complains, to Cæsar things which belong to God only. In our own Church, established as it is by law, this command of Christ is continually quoted as guarding in some way the independence of the Church and of religion, though the interpretation put upon it by Romanist and by Dissenter may be thought too extreme. The Parliament, say not a few, must not pass any law affecting the Church or religion without the consent of the Church as represented by the Convocations of Clergy, because our Lord has solemnly said, "Render to Cæsar the things that are Cæsar's, and to God the things that are God's."

Now it only requires a careful reading of the narrative to see that when our Lord spoke these words he was not intending to make any distinction at all between the secular and the ecclesiastical provinces, between the claims of the State and the claims of the Church. The ecclesiastical organization of his country, or of any other country, was not in our Lord's mind, any more than it was in the minds of his questioners. When the words are used to prove that the Church has rights with which the State ought not to interfere, they are applied to a purpose with which they really have nothing to do. So we lose, on the one hand, the benefit of the true meaning of an important lesson ; whilst on the other hand Christ's sanction is given to an arbitrary and impracticable theory.

I need hardly remind you of the condition of Judæa in our Lord's day. The country had lost its independence. It was a part of the great dominion of Rome. The imperial authority of the Roman Cæsar was represented in the land of Israel by vassal princes and governors and garrisons and tribute-collectors. The land had gone through many vicissitudes since the times best known to us, —those of the kings and the prophets. But the national idea cherished by devout Jews in every generation was that of a "theocracy." This means a system of government in which the God of the national worship was regarded as ruling the nation through his appointed ministers. It is the very principle of a theocracy, that the civil and the ecclesiastical organizations are *not* kept distinct from one another. When you read the Prophets, is it religion or politics that you find in the pages of Isaiah or Jeremiah? One just as much as the other. It is all religion; it is all politics. The people of Israel are addressed as the people of their God Jehovah by prophets claiming to speak in his name; they are addressed with reference to their national faults, their national dangers, the national glory that was promised them. This entire blending of politics and religion in the life of the ancient Jews must be evident to all who read the Old Testament. When the people of Jehovah fell under the yoke of a heathen emperor, it seems hardly reasonable to assume that this degradation produced a happy separation of the temporal and the spiritual functions. Cæsar was a foreign despot, under whose sway it was impossible for Jews who cherished the traditions of Israel to live contented.

It was however a peculiar baseness in the Jews who persecuted the Lord Jesus and his followers, that they tried to bring them into collision with the Roman authorities. They would pay a homage of which they were bitterly ashamed, for 'the sake of destroying those whom they hated. They denounced Jesus to Pontius Pilate as a pretender inciting the people to insurrection; they afterwards denounced the preachers of the Gospel to the Roman authorities throughout the Empire as promoters of sedition.

The Pharisees took counsel, we are told, how they might entangle Jesus in his talk. They wanted to get him into a difficulty. So they sent emissaries to him, charging them to compliment him on his courage and his truthfulness, and then to propose to him a perplexing question. They addressed him thus; "Master, we know that thou art true, and teachest the way of God in truth, neither carest thou for any man; for thou regardest not the person of men. Tell us therefore, what thinkest thou? Is it lawful to give tribute to Cæsar or not?" Their object was to force Jesus into a dilemma. If he said, partly persuaded by their flattery, that it was *not* lawful, then they might accuse him to the Roman government. If he answered that it *was* lawful, they hoped to bring him into discredit with the people. For they regarded him as a man who wanted to make a party and gain a following, and who was seeking to accomplish these ends like other popular leaders by appealing to the old religious patriotism of his countrymen. And if Jesus had been what they supposed him to be, their plan would have been a very promising one. But Jesus perceived their wickedness, and instead of having recourse to any conciliatory evasion in his reply, he made *them* wince under his righteous indignation. "Why tempt ye me"—that is, Why are you making your experiments upon me—"ye hypocrites?" There was no honest purpose in their inquiry, he knew. Still, they should have their answer, and know that he was not afraid to answer them plainly. "Shew me the tribute-money." "Whose"—he asked, when they brought him a coin—"Whose is this image and superscription?" " Cæsar's." It was the Imperial coinage. And what did the currency of this coin imply? It implied that Cæsar was the actual accepted ruler of the land,—a foreign conqueror, it was true, but still, keeping the peace, administering justice, exercising the necessary functions of government. The ruler of the land might claim tribute. Our Lord leaves here untouched, I think, the questions, whether it was right that the Cæsar should have become the ruler of the land, whether the people would in any circumstances be justified in rising against him, how far they might plan resistance or indulge discontent. He knew, we may venture to say, that there was not the mind, the faith, in the people,—certainly not in these hypocritical questioners,—that would justify an appeal to arms in behalf of national independence. It was from the first the fixed resolution of the Lord Jesus, not to encourage any insurrectionary movement. In that day, and for the population of that land, it was needful and right to submit to the Roman government. There could be no question, if this were so, about the lawfulness of paying tribute. The Cæsar who was God's minister for keeping order and repressing crime and faction could claim the tribute as his due. "Render therefore to Cæsar what belongs to Cæsar." But there are other dues to render. Mark this, ye hypocrites, who are seeking to slay God's prophet because he speaks the truth to you. "Render *to God* what belongs to God."

And what then were those Pharisees and Herodians to think of as belonging to God?

You will perceive that at all events the claims of ecclesiastical as distinct from civil authority are foreign to the occasion. There is no question here about the authority of the priests or of the council. The one question had been, Ought we children of Abraham to pay tribute to a heathen conqueror? Yes, pay it, said Jesus, so long as it is God's just judgment on your fathers and you that you should be his conquered subjects. Render to Cæsar his dues; and render to *God his* dues.

Primarily, perhaps, this last command should be associated with our Lord's rebuke to the treacherous falseness of his questioners. They knew in their consciences that in cherishing this mind they were defrauding the God of truth and righteousness of the homage which was his due. He required truth in the inward parts. He required of them to do justly and to love mercy and to walk humbly with him. The demand, Render to God what belongs to God, was well aimed at the conscience of the Pharisee. As soon as he began to ask himself, What then does God require of us? answers would not be wanting. He could not stop till he had confessed that he had *himself* to render to God, his possessions, his powers, his heart.

And then perhaps it might occur to him there was an apt symbolism in the coin and its image and superscription. Was there anything *in himself* answering to that coin? Yes, he too bore an image stamped upon him. It was the faith handed down to him, that God made man in his own image. If Cæsar claimed the coin with his image upon it, so God claimed the man with *his* image upon him. Nay, the children of the covenant bore a superscription also, in the sign of the covenant, which legibly declared them to belong to their God. Render to God his dues, you that have given yourselves to be children of the spirit of lies and hatred: render to the righteous God what bears his image and superscription,—your own nature, made in the Divine image, having the Divine name and the call of the covenant written upon it.

It may be open to question whether this symbolism was in our Lord's primary meaning. It is enough to say that Jesus, penetrating with his Divine indignation to the conscience of the Pharisees, bade them consider what they owed to God, and how they were paying the debt. Most certainly it was not *a part* of themselves, not one province of life, which they owed to God, whilst the rest was reserved for Cæsar. If God could claim anything, he claimed the whole man, body, soul, and spirit. In paying tribute to Cæsar, they were rendering to God himself a part of his claim. This, as you will remember, is St Paul's doctrine. "For this cause ye pay tribute also; for rulers are God's ministers, attending continually upon this very thing." So that loyalty to rulers is comprehended in duty to God, and servants of God must be loyal subjects for conscience's sake.

Let us, Christian brethren, find a lesson in the rebuke and warning addressed to those hypocrites. The truth of it is not for them only. It turns the payment of earthly dues into a witness to our heavenly obligation. As you pay your tax loyally to the earthly government which, however imperfect, gives you benefits worth far more than your contribution, consider also the heavenly government under which you live, and what it requires of you. Render to God, the Father of our Lord Jesus Christ, what he claims of you. Are you not his? Were you not bought with a price? Have you not been sealed in your baptism with his Name? You bear God's image and superscription, you have no right to withhold *yourselves* from God. Render yourselves up to him, in sincerity, in trust, in loving obedience.

You will not allow, I hope, this acted parable to be displaced in your minds by that unfortunate misapprehension which takes Cæsar, the name of an alien despot, to represent civil government, which assumes that God is another name for an ecclesiastical assembly, and which implies that the civil ruler and God are two coordinate and independent powers. But when the relations of Church and State are occupying our minds, and troubling them, perhaps, as a perplexing problem, you may go on to ask, " If there is nothing in this passage which lays down any law about those relations, in what other parts of the New Testament shall we find maxims that will guide us either in making claims for the State or in asserting the independence of the Church ?" I believe we should look in vain for such maxims. Precepts are given in the New Testament with reference to the actual circumstances of those to whom they are addressed; and the circumstances of the New Testament Christians were extremely different from ours. They formed little new aggressive communities in the midst of a vast pagan empire; they were happy if they could escape persecution; their policy was to be as submissive and loyal as it was possible for them to be without denying Christ, and to avoid every needless occasion of offence, whilst they lived a secret life of their own, in which those around them could have no part. The wonder is that the Roman authorities are treated with so much respect in the Epistles, that St Paul, with a Caligula and a Nero in his mind, could say, " the powers that be are ordained of God." But it is obvious that the rules of conduct adjusted to the circumstances of the Christian Church in the first

century could hardly suit our circumstances in the
Christian England of to-day. Indeed it must soon
become clear to any who look back to history or
abroad upon the world, that the relations between
the Church and the State must vary with the circumstances of each time and country. At one
extreme you may see one Christian Communion
comprehending all the inhabitants of a country; at
the other you may see a nation split up into a
number of separate religious bodies of which none
can claim undisputed precedence. In either of
these cases the policy to be adopted would be
comparatively simple, determined without controversy by the facts themselves. We in England
have a much more complex state of things to deal
with, and we have great need to ask for wisdom
and grace to guide us in right action. We cannot.
shut our eyes to the fact that the majority of the
people in Scotland are Presbyterians, in Ireland
are Roman Catholics, and that in England and
Wales we have a most powerful minority of Nonconformists. The two questions will inevitably
arise, Is it fair that the Church of England should
be preserved as the public Church of so mixed a
population? Is it fair that the Church of England
should be regulated by a Parliament representing

that mixed population? On the one hand there is the possibility of injustice to the people; on the other hand there is the possibility of injustice to the Church. I repeat it, there are no propositions in the New Testament which can be made to serve, without forcing, as answers to these questions. We can only look for guidance to God himself teaching us through the facts of history and through the inspirations of his justice and love.

But the God to whom we look is the God of the New Testament, he who spoke to mankind in his Son Jesus Christ, he who began the building of the Church upon his Son through his holy Apostles and Prophets. We know that this our God claims earth for himself as well as heaven, that he leaves out no province of secular life from his dominion, that he taught the faithful to look forward to the future glory when the kingdoms of this world should become the kingdoms of our Lord and of his Christ. We know that there is nothing ungodly in civil government, no necessary godliness in religious assemblies. After Jesus had justified the payment of tribute to Cæsar, Cæsar through his officer put the Lord of glory to an unjust and cruel death. But those that delivered Jesus to Pilate had the greater sin, and they were

God's priests, who offered God's sacrifices in God's Temple. The State may be in the wrong, and the Church may be in the wrong; and both are likely to miss the more excellent way when their representatives boast of their rights and substitute arrogance for docility. Above the State and above the Church there is the one God over all, by whom kings reign and Parliaments legislate, by whose Spirit the whole body of the Church is governed and sanctified. In looking to him we shall see light, in surrendering ourselves to him, Church and nation, societies and individuals, we shall find safety and blessedness.

XV.

COMPETITION AND SELF-SURRENDER[1].

PHILIPPIANS II. 3, 4.—"Let nothing be done through strife or vainglory; but in lowliness of mind let each esteem other better than themselves. Look not every man on his own things, but every man also on the things of others."

LIKE all our English institutions, our great schools are being constantly brought under the criticism of the public opinion of the day. It is no unfriendly criticism, certainly, for we are all proud of our public schools, the like of which are not to be found in any other land; and there can hardly be an Englishman of the middle and upper classes who has not personal reasons for being interested in one or more of them. In the newspapers and in conversation, schools and school life are always a welcome subject of discussion. But when this anniversary brings you together in the place of your common worship, it is the office of the

[1] Preached in the Chapel of Marlborough College on Michaelmas Day, 1874.

preacher to remind you that schools like this are not only English but Christian schools. You have another judgment to think of than that of your countrymen; a standard to aim at which is not set by the tradition of English schools or by the best modern culture. Your presence here confesses that you are under law to Christ.

I am thankful that in these days we are not permitted to hold our Christianity lazily separate from our practical life. The keen and anxious spirit of inquiry which is abroad forbids it. It probes hollow profession, asking eagerly, "What is the Christianity you profess? Will it stand, will it live and work, in this modern age? Are you really acting upon it in the strain of life, or is your scheme of conduct framed according to other principles?" It is good for us, though it may be at the cost of pain and disturbance, to be thus called to account. We may well regard anything as a boon, which forces our faith and our life into closer contact, and which will help us to know the glory and power and hope of our calling.

Speaking then as a Christian to Christians, I shall ask you to-day to consider one very conspicuous feature of education as it is now, and to bring it honestly into comparison with a great law of our Christian calling. There is an apparent discord between the two, to which we ought not to be insensible. The principle of Competition has been introduced into every part of our educational system, and is impressed upon it beyond all former precedent; Suppression of self is the Christian principle to which it seems to be opposed. The age is exhorting you, "Strive incessantly in all things to be foremost;" the voice of Christ says to you, "Follow me, in lowliness and self-sacrifice; many that are first shall be last and the last first." Let us consider how far, and under what conditions, competition may be approved by those who would conform themselves sincerely, however imperfectly, to the mind of Christ.

Competition is no new thing in education, any more than in the business of life. Teachers have at all times endeavoured to stimulate their pupils by appealing to the desire of each to outdo his fellows. "Always to excel and to be superior to others" has been the motto of the trainers of youth in every generation. But there *is* something new in the prodigious development of the system and machinery of competition which has taken place within my own memory. From infancy upwards, boy is matched against boy, young man against young man, in every department of effort. Let a youth look before him along what line he will, he sees a prize tempting him. If he can beat his competitors, he may carry off something desirable, an honorary distinction, a book, an exhibition, a scholarship, an appointment for life. There never was anything like it before. Keen eyes seem to be perpetually ranging over the whole compass of human activity, in the hope of discovering some form of exertion to which prizes have not yet been offered, so that one more department, however insignificant or incongruous, may be added to the domain of formal competition. Nor is it only in serious pursuits that registered success is thus made the object of effort. It is so at least equally in games. Sports are pursued, not so much from love of the occupation or for the sake of refreshment from labour, as with a view to beating competitors. Cricket, one might fear, would lose half its charm, if scores were not kept and published. As in horse-racing no one thinks of the enjoyment of the sport by the horses, so in boating the pleasure of the exercise is completely subordinated to the necessity of coming in first. The shooter, I believe, is hardly less solicitous about the number of the lives he takes than the cricketer about his score. The climbing of mountains became a passion when it was made a form of racing as to height and time. That predominance of bodily exercise against which all educated good sense is now beginning to protest, and which will have to be in some way checked, is manifestly due, not to imitation of the Greeks or to theories of the moral value of muscular exertion, but to the fact that the honours and prizes which youths desire are to be won by athletics and boating and cricket.

I speak the more freely, perhaps, because it is not my purpose to denounce this all-subduing system of competition. It would be a serious attempt, indeed, to assail it,—one not to be undertaken with a light heart. Besides, I know not who could commence the attack with clean hands. No one thinks it a sin to accept the benefits of competition when they come in his way. Nor can any one easily resist the evidence of the good done by the stimulation of rivalry for prizes, in the promotion of really beneficial effort. This seems to me so unquestionable, that I should have no more scruple than others have in offering prizes and inviting the young or grown-up persons to compete for them, as, for example, with the aim of extending certain advantages to a poorer class. We may all justly lay on each other some share of responsibility for the system which has become so dominant in the England of our day.

But now let us recall to mind that we are Christians. It is true that even from the Christian point of view our calling has been described in terms borrowed from the splendid games of ancient Greece. We are reminded that we have a race to run, that we are engaged in a contest which demands all our energy. He whom we follow is said to have kept his prize in view. In looking to Jesus, we look to one who for the joy that was set before him endured the cross, despising the shame. But what was the joy set before him? That of saving his brethren. Nothing exclusive, nothing that could feed selfish pride or vanity. The mind that was in Christ Jesus was shewn in the emptying of self, in voluntary descent and humiliation. The Apostle says to us Christians, "Let this mind be in you." He proposes to us the glory of caring for others more than for ourselves, of putting self back, of willingly relinquishing the objects of human desire whenever the great end of building up the body in harmony and efficiency may thereby be promoted. It is because this suppression and sacrifice of self is so difficult to us that the language of the arena is applied to it. It is so natural to love pre-eminence, to love praise, to love pleasant and precious things, that we are reminded of the necessity of struggling against these desires as the wrestler struggled against his antagonist. To look round on our neighbours and say, "Here are competitors to be beaten," is to know them after the flesh; to know them after the spirit or after Christ is to say "Here are brothers to be served and helped." Those that would be Christians have the law of self-surrender unmistakably declared to them, the joy of ministration and sympathy and of pleasing the Father unmistakably held out to them as their prize.

What then is the attitude which we ought to take as loyal Christians towards the method which stimulates exertion by offering prizes to those who outstrip their fellows?

Let me endeavour to give some partial answer to this important question, in reflections which I hope may be practical for you who hear me.

1. I have intimated already that I do not think we are called upon, as a Christian community, to abolish the whole system of competition. We can see that it has certain good effects. These are

entitled to fair consideration. It is unlikely that a practice out of which good comes should be itself intrinsically and necessarily evil. We are warranted in taking into account all the bearings of the question. We are at liberty to inquire, with our best judgment, whether the system of competition does on the whole more good or harm. We must not rashly assume that if it were removed its place would instantly be taken by ideally perfect motives. Suppose, for example, that every prize and comparison of one boy with another were abolished in this school, and that no competition remained in either mental or bodily exercises; you would probably find school work and school life considerably flatter, and we have no reason to believe that by this simple process they would be made nobler or more Christian. Dullness and inertia form no natural soil for the highest qualities to grow in. Experience and analogy seem to prove that competition is an appointed condition of the merely natural order throughout all human existence. The struggle for the first place does not lose its usefulness until it is absorbed into higher motives. Some day, possibly, we may grow out of the competition of buying and selling; but if we ever issue from it, it must be by *growing* out of it ; we cannot decree that there shall be no competition. Nature would baffle us, and in attempting to accomplish our desire we should find ourselves throwing away a convenient and indispensable force without being able to put another in its place. So it is with regard to the play of competition in educational training. It is right, let us say, to recognize and to use it. We want very much any agency that promises to promote life and activity, if it is not an incurably unwholesome one. We want some means of *selection* also, in which the community can place confidence. And on the whole the plan of getting boys to exert themselves by inducing them to try to beat one another is found in practice to work better than that of leaving them without this stimulus.

2. But if we recognize and use competition as a natural—and therefore in a proper sense Divinely ordained—condition of human life, we are bound to take care that it does not usurp an undue predominance over the life of Christians. There are things which we are to use without abusing them, which we are to use as instruments without allowing them to become our masters.

And it will hardly be questioned,—in a vigorous school like this any more than in the outside world

—that we are in danger of having our minds too much engaged and possessed by incessant emulation, by incessant comparison of the producible work of one with that of another, by incessant anxiety to gain distinctions. It is not desirable, or at all events not the most desirable characteristic, in a boy-community, that the most energetic should be taught and compelled to be always thinking of gaining competitive victories. I gladly admit that the particular evil which would have been feared beforehand, that of spoiling goodwill and friendship between rivals, does not appear to have been produced in any painful amount by competition. I have no doubt it has been proved here, as it certainly has been elsewhere, that spirited competitors may be hearty and affectionate friends. If this were impossible, the system would be decisively stamped as unchristian. But to be matched against a friend for a highly valued prize, and still more to be defeated by a friend, can hardly fail to be now and then a severe trial of friendship. And the tone of mind produced by the tension of these contests is not the noblest any more than the happiest.

It is a great point, then, to see clearly that competition belongs to the lower—to what St Paul would probably have called the fleshly—order. It ought to be kept down in its lower place. It has no sacredness in it to the Christian mind, no high moral dignity. The real question of interest about man or boy is not whether he has beaten such or such competitors, but how well he has done the work committed to him, how high he has risen, not by comparison with certain other persons, but in the real Divine scale.

3. But, thirdly, let the strong pressure which this system is continually bringing to bear upon us be an argument for fixing our thoughts the more earnestly upon the mind that was in Christ. This is the best way to deal with anything questionable in the customs of that world of which we individually form so powerless a part. It is often difficult to make up our minds whether an existing custom has on the whole an influence for good or for evil; it is very difficult to reorganize society in any important respect according to our minds; it would be still more difficult to secure that nothing but good should come in with the change. But it is always possible, when there is anything in external order or method that does not look like a Christian form of life, to take this as a warning to cherish with more thorough devotion the essentially Chris-

tian mind. Take for example the distribution and employment of wealth amongst us. This must often strike us as painfully unlike the Christian ideal. Well, whatever it may be possible and right for any of us to do in the way of promoting change in the relations of the rich and the poor, every one of us may constantly remind himself of the supreme principles which Christ has laid down, as that each is the steward and not the absolute owner of what he possesses, that all possessions should be made available for the common good, that riches are dangerous to spirituality, that every poorer person has a kind of natural claim on every richer, that the weaker or less comely member ought to be the more honoured in the body of Christ. So, if the age is setting you to race and struggle with one another, it is the more necessary to take to heart those eternal principles of the Christian calling which ambition has at least the appearance of thwarting.

Let me name first the sentiment of generous goodwill. Our public schools have not been wanting in the power of cementing mutual attachment amongst those whom they have trained. Let the corporate spirit which lives in the atmosphere of a great school be exalted into Christian goodwill, and clothe itself with gentleness, with consideration for the weak, with refinement. Let all inclination towards grudging and jealousy, all impulse to pass unfair and detracting judgments, and still more, let the baseness which would take a mean or dishonest advantage, be shamed in disciples of Jesus Christ by the true Christian consciousness. Chivalrous feeling is a genuine element of the Christian mind. And there is something in competition, as in the generous rivalry of Arthur's knights, which may even stimulate it. But it is well that those who are thrown into the arena together should seek, not merely to breathe the conventional sentiment of honour, but to imbibe at its perennial fountain the more vital instinct of sympathy which joins member to member in the body of Christ.

There is another disposition which the Christian is plainly called to cultivate, and which the temptations of competition might naturally bring to our mind. It is the endeavour to abide in one's own place, and to do the duty of that place in contentment and modesty. We have the happiness of believing that we are objects of Divine care and providence, not coming into the world by chance to struggle for existence, but having each of us an assigned place, with work answering to it, and endowments which will enable us to perform the work. This faith is the basis of Christian patience, modesty, and sense of responsibility. St Paul teaches " Bear ye one another's burdens, and so fulfil the law of Christ ;" but he adds almost immediately, "Every man shall bear his own burden," and he exhorts therefore, " Let every man prove his own work." The probation of life may be said to consist in finding out with the help of experiments what our appointed work is, and then in trying how well we can do it. The temper of mind thus encouraged is a different one from the restless eagerness to be before others which constant struggling is apt to engender, and it is surely a most desirable one for both boys and men to cultivate. There is real lasting strength in it, and it is the safeguard of many virtues. Not only will our life be happier and more wholesome, but our work will in the end be more perfectly done, if we can say, "My business is not to get before others, but to do well what is given me to do. I must not waste my time, which is not indeed mine to waste. I must do the best I can to satisfy those for whom and under whom I work ; but it is not to them that I am ultimately responsible. Let me live and labour as ever in the great Taskmaster's eye. If God has not endowed me with faculties which enable me to be first in the race, let me not be discouraged or grudge to others their success. God above does not measure success by these external standards." If we could count upon Christian convictions like these in all who have been baptized into the name of Christ, we might throw to the winds the machinery of competitive rewards, and be well rid of it. Let us not be beguiled into any forgetfulness of the need, the blessedness, the practical value, of this faith.

Once more, it is the pride of the Christian to love and desire knowledge for its own sake, and not for the honours and prizes it will bring. Knowledge, as the Christian understands it, brings him nearer to God himself. The things that we know are the ways and works of God. It is true that all things are not equally good to know. It is important that a wise selection of studies be made, so that what is learnt may be best calculated to enrich, expand, and elevate the mind. But knowledge, I repeat, is sacred to the Christian. He looks upon it as a treasure compared with which gold is valueless. To lay out all the energy of our Divinely given faculties in acquiring knowledge, and to do this only or mainly for the sake of gaining a prize or of being declared before the world to have earned so many more marks than some other candidate, must seem to one who re-verences his calling an unworthy act. I know that there are motives far higher than covetousness or vanity which create an eager desire for success. The thought of the joy that others will feel in his triumph, of the pride he may put into the hearts of those who have taught him and of those who love him, is often the chief stimulus to the efforts of the aspiring student. There is nothing unworthy in working for such a reward. But even in such a case knowledge has missed its due honour. It is an unhappy sign when youths care for no know-ledge but that which will bring success. And it is to be regretted, I venture to say, when they are so urged by whatever pressure to competitive efforts as to have no time or energy left to push forward their reading or inquiry in channels of their own choice.

I have endeavoured thus briefly to indicate how the ancient teaching of the Gospel of Christ may nourish in the members of a community like this habits of mind that will control and correct the inferior influences which act upon them. Let us be thankful that we who call ourselves after the name of Christ are not ultimately subject to the traditions of a past age or to the opinion of the present. We have reason indeed to confess our deep obligations to the noble institutions and customs handed down to us, and to rejoice in the progress and achievements by which our own age is illustrated. But we have an eternal standard by which to measure ourselves, an unseen Teacher from whom to learn; a heavenly Father to honour and please. May God grant to this noble school, not only a continuance of its intellectual vigour and prosperity, but also the dignity and the happiness and the power of doing good beyond our estimate, which are the rewards of loyalty to Christ!

XVI.

DOGMA, SENTIMENT, AND RITUAL[1].

St John xx. 21.—"Then said Jesus to them again, Peace be unto you: as my Father hath sent me, even so send I you."

As the Lord Jesus had come from the Father to bring peace, so his envoys, the disciples whom he had trained for their office, were similarly to be messengers of peace to mankind. The whole Apostolic ministry was summed up in this word. There was enmity on the earth. Men were alienated from God, and made enemies to him by their wickedness. There was a separation, which bore the marks of God's own hand, between the chosen people and the nations whom God had not called. There was unnatural ill-feeling of every degree between neighbour and neighbour. Christ came to be the peace of the world,—peace between the Father and men, peace between Jew and Gentile, peace between man and man. His Apostles or envoys, in being heralds of their crucified and risen

[1] Preached at Banbury Church, Oct. 7th, 1874.

Master, were heralds of peace. It was their commission to proclaim the Divine forgiveness, and to beseech men to receive it.

I take this Divinely-ordained ministry of peace, my Christian brethren, as a starting-point for our reflections this evening. It is a subject which harmonizes well with the circumstances under which I am permitted to address you. Coming at the kind request of my valued friend your Vicar to bear a part in a ceremony so interesting to him and to you as this opening of your new Chancel, what can my first feeling be but to wish and pray that his ministry may be true and faithful, may be honoured and rewarded, amongst you? And I am sure that the work of a minister of Christ has the promise of being successful in the sight of God, whether in the sight of men or not, in proportion as priest and people realize together that Christ through his servants is still speaking peace to mankind.

There is something *elementary* in this original word of reconciliation as spoken by the Apostles of Jesus Christ, which may suggest questions like these. "Is it enough? Does it not require that a good deal should be added to it ? Or, have we not outgrown it ? Do we not want, in this advanced age, something more modern ?" My answer to any such questions would be, that the original commission of the Christian ministry can never become obsolete, that it must always be the kernel, the heart, the life-power, of a Church; but that, the more simply and purely the message of peace is carried on from age to age, the more freely and actively will it take up whatever is new, so as to organize modern life in harmony with itself. I say that the strength of the ministry of the Church of England would be found at the present day in a kind of severe loyalty to the commission which Christ first gave to his Galilean disciples.

There are two tendencies manifestly active in our religious life, one drawing towards comprehension, the other towards separation.

Those who are the most affected by the former are generally averse to dogma, and make much of Christian sentiment. They point out that all Christian communions agree in commending the great practical matters of Christian life, such as truth, goodwill, purity. They see, on the other hand, doctrines which one communion pronounces to be essential rejected as false and hurtful by another. They know that the history of the Christian Church has been deformed by the mutual contradictions of Catholics and Arians, of Romanists and Protestants, of Calvinists and Arminians, of Churchmen and Dissenters. The only deliverance, they say, from these barren and discreditable controversies is in preferring sentiment to dogma. Let it be understood that the important point is not what a man thinks, but how he feels. "He can't be wrong, whose life is in the right." Each denomination, each party in the Church, might learn to insist less and less on its distinctive dogmas, and then there would be a hope of all gradually drawing together.

Comprehension by the discouragement of dogma is a watch-word of considerable power amongst us. It appeals to very common experiences,—to the discoveries which the young soon make, that those of their own traditional way of thinking are not practically better than some upon whose opinions they have been taught to look with aversion and fear; to the veneration which noble lives excite in all generous minds; to the perplexities about belief by which many in days of inquiry are likely to be distressed. The more excellent way of charity has high sanctions, and offers itself persuasively to Christian hearts.

But on the other hand there is a strong instinctive conviction that sentiment cannot be healthy and vigorous unless it has a root in faith. Those who are called upon to be loving want to know whom or what they are to love, and why they are to love. Sentiment nourished for the sentiment's sake does not gain that powerful hold with which the conscience must be seized if a new life is to be led. Then, what are these statements which are to be discouraged under the name of dogmas? Are they not concerned with sin, with guilt, with forgiveness, with the motive powers of a new life, that is, with the very things about which an awakened soul is most in earnest? Could it be expected that a religious union, in which there should be an agreement of silence on such points as the offence of sin and the removal of the barrier which obstructs the approach of the sin-laden conscience to the holy presence of God, should be vital and durable? Can it possibly be a matter of indifference whether God has spoken to men or not, and if he has spoken, what the things are that he has said? There is an evident likelihood that a union in Christian sentiment without dogma would prove a lifeless and vapid fellowship, from which those who are stirred to the lower spiritual depths would turn away in disappointment. Look, it is urged, at the energy developed in those who hold together the same strictly defined faith concerning the ways and purposes of God. Who have been the people who have shewn religious zeal? Who have made sacrifices proving them to be heartily in earnest? History answers that it has been they who have believed that God has made known some way by which men may reach to him, and who have agreed one with another in their conceptions as to the manner and purport of that revelation. These have felt their religion to be a serious thing; these have sought to bring others over to what they have held to be saving truth. To ask men to subordinate doctrine to sentiment is in fact to ask them to admit that they know of nothing which they can firmly believe as to the ways of God; it is to ask them to give up the hope by which human life has been sustained at its best, and from time to time recovered and raised from its lowest.

So there is a disposition not uncommon amongst us to conclude that the best course is that persons who take the same views on religious subjects should form themselves through mutual attraction into separate religious communions. The Dissenting bodies in this country have attained considerable results by following this policy. An association of persons holding identical opinions works freely when compared with an association

the members of which differ much amongst themselves. The rivalry of religious bodies, each concerned to demonstrate that its own truth is the
real and absolute truth, often stirs them to great—
it may be to beneficial—activity. The National
Church of this country moves slowly. Earnest
members of it naturally fret and are impatient
under the obstructions which are caused principally
by the differences of opinion which it embraces
within its hospitable shelter. Some outside the
Church of England,—some within it,—are beginning to say, "How much freedom and force would
be gained, if this unwieldly State-system were
broken up, and the different schools in the Church
were made each a denomination by itself! Evan-
gelicals could then mould the Prayer-book more
exactly to their way of thinking, and could get rid
of the offence of acknowledging as fellow-members
of the same Church those High-Churchmen and
liberal Churchmen whose views they consider so
dangerous. High-Churchmen could advance with
no restraints from unwilling parishioners or dis-
approving bishops, with no fear of prosecutions
before their eyes. Liberal Churchmen might free
themselves from every superstition which the progress of knowledge appears to them to have made

untenable." The introduction of perfect freedom of voluntary association would lead, it is urged, to a sudden and remarkable development of religious energy.

Yes; I have little doubt that it would. But at what a cost! Do we want, can we patiently contemplate, an ever-increasing multiplication and subdivision of religious bodies? Do we not already see and deplore a tendency to make much of particular opinions for the very sake of having a distinction and a difference? Does not this put the great mass of simple Christians at the mercy of those who are opinionated and pertinacious? Considering what a Gospel we all profess to have received, is it not lamentable that we who read the same Bible should find it necessary to separate ourselves into so many folds?

But I must not dwell on the practical arguments against religious division, nor upon the loss which would seem to me as an Englishman an almost intolerable one, the loss of a national Church representing in an organic form the national Christianity. I must return to my point, namely, the strength which the Church of England may find in the simplest loyalty to the ministry of reconciliation.

If there is to be no confident declaration to mankind of forgiveness and redemption, then the Church of Christ ought to be expressly abolished, to make place for an institution of a different kind. Those who believe that in Christ God was reconciling the world to himself cannot possibly be willing to put this light under a bushel as a matter of mere personal opinion, or as an obsolete dogma. But this very declaration, dogmatic as it would be called, is a proclamation of unity and comprehension, a call to peace. It may indeed be met with enmity; the bringer of peace may in effect be sometimes the bringer of a sword. But the preacher of reconciliation assures men that there is a peace with God and with one another into which they may enter if they will. The Church which duly cherishes this testimony is pledged by its principal dogma to promote peace, to remove stumbling-blocks out of the way, to offer a welcome to all who are willing to be reconciled to God. The Church of England, as charged with the ministry of peace, ought to lay aside all exclusiveness, to cast out the spirit of self-complacence and scorn, to be considerate of prejudices and weaknesses, to count it a shame and reproach that its practical witness for comprehension has not been more earnest and effectual. If the entreaty, "We pray you in Christ's stead, be ye reconciled to God," were to become more genuinely the characteristic voice of the Church, can we doubt that a wider influence over the consciences of men would reward such faithfulness? Judge, my brethren, by what you know of yourselves, how the offer of forgiveness, if it only reach the conscience of any man, must work upon him. Think how the grace of God will soften the hard heart, and humble the pride which is the root of so much evil; how it engages a man to enter upon a lifelong struggle against the dominion of that sinfulness which is enmity against God and enmity amongst men; what a vital spring of endurance and effort there is in the consciousness of being brought near to God and having hope in him; how the man is practically saved from those impulses which hinder godly union and concord. Here surely, in the thankful acceptance of God's grace, is the seed of all spiritual life, the guarantee of all true fellowship.

If this ministry of reconciliation, ordained in the primary commission given by our Lord to his Apostles, is entitled to have the central and ruling place in our Christianity which the New Testament seems to assign to it, other doctrines and all the observances of religion will be best understood when they are referred to it and interpreted by it. We shall shew our faith in the great message of the Gospel by allowing it to work its own effects both upon our mental apprehensions and upon our practice. The peace into which it is our privilege to enter must have its fruit in a continued spiritual fellowship. We are not to stand still as Christians, however Divine be the foundation on which we are placed. It is appointed to us to go forward, to grow in knowledge, to be more energetic and efficient in action. There is a partnership in the Gospel, a fellowship in good works, a serving of the eternal purposes of God, to which we Christians are called. The design and hope of the Saviour will not be fulfilled without the most earnest cooperation of his disciples in the work which he finds for their hands to do.

It is sufficiently obvious that in our Church, as in any Church, Christian fellowship can only be carried out into Christian work by a close and hearty sympathy between the clergy and the laity. The clergy cannot do the work of the Church without the laity; the laity cannot do it without the clergy. In the Church of England, one of the faults we have to acknowledge,—I do not know on whom the blame should be laid,—is that we have had too little of this general partnership of all in Christian work. We may rejoice to confess this error, because in so doing we are putting the finger on a discovered cause of weakness. We have found one of the leaks in our noble vessel, and we can hasten to stop it. We are awakening, I trust, clergy and laity together, to a sense of our common responsibility. Clergymen are longing to call in more and more the help of the people, and are willing, if they are wise, that those who give their help should share the power and practical government of the Church. Laymen, feeling that they have their part in the Church, are not by this conviction drawn away from the clergy, but on the contrary, I believe, are drawn more closely to them, entering more heartily into their cares and responsibilities, sometimes, no doubt, restraining and checking them as well as urging them forward with their support, but in the one action as well as the other proving that all are members of one body, and that each organ has the liveliest interest in the healthy working of the rest.

Let us pray that these tendencies, by the grace of God, may go on and prosper. It may well fill us with anxious hope to think what a future is before us, if the members of our English Church were to be fully roused by the great ideas embodied in the constitution of our national Church. It is inspiring, surely, to think of England as a Christian country, built as a city that is at unity in itself, embracing all the various elements of national life, all the traditions of the past, all the knowledge and activity of the present, all the aims of the future, within the bonds of a worship which is grounded on the original ministry of Christ and his Apostles, and which has come down to us safely through all the vicissitudes and the sins of our history. May it be given to us to bear our humble part in working out such an ideal. Here, in this place, there are happy indications that there is no lack of Christian zeal and true Churchlike cooperation. You have been doing much; may it be the earnest of more yet to be done. It is the instinct of every awakened Christian body to take an interest and a pride even in the outward accessories of worship. It would be unnatural in Christian Englishmen at the present time to be satisfied with an inadequate house of God. The life within organizes and moulds that which is on the surface. But it should be steadily borne in mind by both priests and people that the outward is outward, and that the life of faith and love is what our Master desires and looks for.

On this point there ought to be no mistake. The Lord of the universe, whom we worship, is indeed the author of all beauty, physical as well as moral; it is he who has given us the faculties by which we choose and delight in beautiful things; and we cannot think of Divine or heavenly perfection without borrowing aid from some of the images of beauty which the outward world presents to us. But, if we had to compare together two assemblies, the one consisting of rude uncultivated persons, content with the unadorned necessities of existence, not sensitive to the grossest violations of artistic taste, but burning with love and devotion within and making it their supreme object to be in harmony, through faith and penitence, with the Divine will; the other worshipping in a sublime Gothic cathedral, trained to move in perfect harmony under the sway of the laws of reverence, singing exquisite music without a false note, but caring for Art more than for God, thinking more of a satisfactory "service" than of bearing the burdens of humanity, and wanting in those deepest affections which found their Divine utterance in a

Life—the life of the Son of God—totally un-adorned by Art; it would be folly and impiety to doubt on which of the two scenes God would look down with the most satisfaction. Whenever people, beginning with the honest intention of making the outward offering of their faith as worthy and perfect as they can, have gone on to fix their minds on the outward forms so as to neglect the inner reality, then he who rebuked the Pharisees for their bondage to tradition has found it necessary to rebuke the lovers of beauty also, and to complain, " Thus have ye made the word of God of none effect by your æsthetics."

That there is such a danger in the present day, it would be well for us to bear in mind. It is a time of reaction against a strange condition of the general mind, when through some unintended alliance between Puritan feeling and cold indifference the nation turned its back upon its noble inheritance of ecclesiastical form and beauty, and dulness and vulgarity became the accepted characteristics of our Anglican worship. We are now in the flush of a reaction against that state of mind; and quiet people are in many places fretted by the eagerness with which improvements in style and manner are being introduced into our Churches and services, not to speak of decorations and symbols of doubtful taste or alien to the spirit of our English Christianity. They do right who refuse to be dragged into excesses of decorative and symbolical worship.

But we do not effectually avoid this danger, by simply resolving to cling to what is old-fashioned and dull and bare. Our religious worship ought to participate, in a fit and proportionate manner, in any tendency which characterizes the general mind. It was a true instinct expressed in those words of David, "I will not offer to the Lord my God of that which costs me nothing." Religion is the more real when people clothe it in the forms which seem to them the worthiest. A rude community may worship rudely; a wealthy community, interesting itself in form and colour, studying the laws of Art, and seeking to possess beautiful things, would be less sincere towards God, if it made a rule of excluding Art from its worship. And on the other hand, it will be good for our secular life that Religion should not be divorced from Art. Art may be either high or low, either morally useful, or morally degraded. If people insist on regarding the delights of form and colour and sound as only proper to be associated with a kind of pleasure of which they are almost ashamed, a large part of their life becomes emptied of purpose and aspiration. When Art is thought worthy of being associated with the deepest convictions and with the most serious aims, then a healthier and purer breath is inspired into common pursuits and pleasures.

I would conclude then, Leave not the outward beauty of service uncared for,—leave not these other things undone; but the things you ought to *do*, with all your heart and soul and strength, are the great moral and spiritual acts of the inner life. These are acceptable to God; these are also useful to men. May our worship be truly spiritual, in order that our daily lives may be spiritual. Let us cherish the awe which the recollection of God's presence must inspire. Let us think of ourselves as gathered together before him who is holy, just, and good, before our Father and the Father of our wandering and neglected brethren. May God in his goodness make us thoughtful, earnest, spiritual Christians! Then he will teach us to rejoice in all his good gifts; then he will make us desire to shew forth our delight in his service.

XVII.

CHURCH-GOING: ITS DANGERS AND BENEFITS[1].

St Luke xviii. 10.—"Two men went up into the temple to pray, the one a Pharisee, the other a publican."

I am to speak to you to-night, dear brethren, both to those who are Church-goers and to those who are not, about going to Church.

It must seem to you very natural that I should wish every one to come to Church. It is to be expected that I should feel inclined to remonstrate urgently with those who stay away, to tell them of what they lose by their absence, to warn them of the danger into which they run by neglecting what God has ordained for their good. Generally, it is only in conversation or through print that there is a chance of addressing such remonstrances to those who are not in the habit of going to Church. To-night there may be some here, who have not been in Church for a long time before this Mission week,

[1] Preached at Christ Church, St Marylebone, in the week of the "London Mission," 1874.

and who have come now out of kindly feeling because they have been specially invited and perhaps entreated to come; so that I have an opportunity for once of saying something in Church to those who have hitherto neglected Church-going.

But two considerations constantly occur to me when I think of urging people to come to Church, which always have the effect of putting a bridle on the energy with which I might otherwise appeal to them.

1. Is it so certain, I cannot help asking, that every one is the better for coming to Church? I assure you that I do not wait to have that question put to me by some one who does not care about Church-going. We clergymen who have so much to do with services are reminded oftener than other people of the possibility of attending Divine Service Sunday after Sunday, and yet of remaining hard and worldly and frivolous. We cannot shut our eyes to this possibility. We feel the danger of it in our own hearts; we are saddened by the proofs of it that we see in the mass of the Church-going population.

When we look into our Bibles, we see the most vehement rebukes addressed not to the carelessly irreligious, but to the formally religious. The prophets of the Lord thundered against those who came with their sacrifices and prayers, but brought at the same time covetous, cruel, and deceitful hearts into the sanctuary. They declared that the worship of such men was hateful in God's sight, so that the more there was of it, the more was God displeased. And when the Son of man was upon the earth, who were they that moved him to indignant invective? Not the irreligious, but the religious. The Pharisees, who prayed and fasted and offered sacrifices and paid tithe of mint and anise and cummin, accused Jesus of irreligion, and were accused by him in turn of neglecting the weightier matters of the law, justice, mercy, and faith. You cannot imagine the Lord Jesus exhorting the careless multitudes to do as the Pharisees did and become as like them as they could.

It often seems to me, therefore, that if we are to follow in the steps of the prophets and of our blessed Lord and of his apostles, our duty with regard to Church-going is much more to point out to regular worshippers the danger of being hollow and formal, than to prescribe attendance at Church as a specific for spiritual maladies, and to urge all sinners to use it.

2. The other consideration to which I referred

was this,—that Church-going is so much a matter of course for those who have any genuine Christian convictions, that one would fancy it might be left to take care of itself. I do not mean to pass any judgment upon exceptional cases; but I think every one here would admit that if you suppose a man earnest in Christian belief and sentiment, he will not want urging to come to Church. He will not necessarily come to one of our Churches, but he will do something corresponding to Church-going; he will not go on living in careless neglect of public worship.

Is not that so? But then, if it is, the thing needed appears to be, not that people should be induced to come to Church whatever they are, but that they should be filled with the desires and instincts which would naturally bring them to Church.

I do not wish that these two considerations should have less weight with me or any one else to-night than they have had hitherto. With regard to the former, nothing ought to deter or dissuade us from declaring that the outside worship offered by godless hearts is hateful in the sight of God, and that all worshippers are in so great danger of a dead formalism that they need to be most carefully on their guard against it. The other,—that if people are Christians in heart they will want no pressing to go to Church,—is a thought to which I will ask you to give some further attention.

Mark the importance of such an admission. Those who are earnestly Christian, we say, are sure to come to Church. In the first place, they know that as Christians they ought to do so. When the Christian Church was brought into existence by the power of the Holy Ghost on the Day of Pentecost, the life led by the first believers is described as follows: "All that believed were together, and had all things common; and sold their possessions and goods, and parted them to all men, as every man had need. And they, continuing daily with one accord in the temple, and breaking bread from house to house, did eat their meat with gladness and singleness of heart, praising God, and having favour with all the people." You see what a completely social life, and what a life of worship, it was! And these two features have always remained characteristic of Christian life. Members of Christ have never felt it right to be shut up in themselves. Nor have they felt it possible to live without worship, as if they belonged to this world only. When faith and love began to grow cold, the believers were exhorted not to fall into the habit of forsaking the assembling of themselves together. The modes of assembling, and of offering worship, have varied considerably amongst Christians. It is quite possible that good Christians may not altogether like the ways of worship which they find offered to them. Some like more music, some less; some like a longer, some a shorter service; some prefer one kind of preaching, others another kind. But sincere Christians do not easily allow themselves to be so repelled by things which they do not like in a service as to give up Church-going altogether. They do, as a matter of fact, find comfort, support, and encouragement, in their ordinances of worship. Their minds are solemnized by the ancient and venerable forms of Divine service; their spirits ascend upwards in the common praise and prayer; they listen with advantage to the assurances of pardon, to the warnings, and to the instructions, which they hear given with authority from the Word of God. Those who are Church-goers in this congregation,—I know that I might confidently appeal to them,—would bear witness to those who are not, that they would shrink from the abandonment of public worship as from a spiritual loss and danger; that it would seem to them · like renouncing their Christian profession and rejecting Divine grace itself together with its appointed means.

I say this, without at all forgetting the possibility of a dead and hypocritical worship which would be an offence to God. I say it notwithstanding all that I know of the imperfections for which the clergy are responsible, and of the coldness which may partly be laid to the account of the people. It is because worship is in itself so good, that when it is spoilt and counterfeited it becomes so bad. The perfection of Christian life comprehends common employments and worship in one. There ought to be no separation, but the closest union, between what we do in the world and our joint communion in the Spirit with the Saviour and the Father. We have our lots appointed us, our tasks set us, our trials prepared for us, by the same Father to whom in Church we pray and give thanks. Without his grace we fail in our common duties, and bring misery upon ourselves and others through our sin. Our worship ought to be the living bond between the visible world in which we are and the invisible world to which we belong, connecting what we do with what we believe, and arming us with Divine strength for our work and our temptations.

I shall not speak expressly to-night of the Communion of the Body and Blood of Christ, because I can speak of that on any Sunday; but I desire that it should be borne in mind that this is the great Christian act of worship. In the first days, all Christians joined in it, and not a minority only; and it is from this act of fellowship with Christ and with one another, from this act of thanksgiving for the redemption given to sinners, that we learn the truest idea of Christian worship and of that Divine grace of which God would make us partakers.

Being so sure, then, that our common worship is a necessary part of Christian life, and that it has in it inexhaustible promises of Divine blessing for struggling sinners, how can we help longing that those multitudes of our people whom we miss in the houses of God should claim their rights of presence and fellowship there? It seems so strange, it is almost enough to make us suspicious of the genuine quality of our Christianity, that those who especially want the tenderness of comfort and the guidance of instruction, those who can least make up on week-days for what they deny to themselves on Sundays, should be indifferent to the ordinances which we find blessed and helpful.

It certainly is not that they are raised, in spirit or in circumstances, above the need of the means of grace which their Church-going fellow-countrymen value. They are not peculiarly strong against temptation, peculiarly free from sin, peculiarly happy and at their ease, peculiarly spiritual in mind. Nor do they themselves deliberately believe that they have chosen a better way. They never seem to think of saying to us who come to Church, "If you wish to be better and happier than you are, do as we do, give up going to Church."

We, on the contrary, do not doubt that it would be a great blessing to the whole land if those negligent multitudes of the common people were to come crowding once more into our Churches, with no preparation but that of humble and teachable hearts.

If I could speak to those absent multitudes,— and I may be speaking to a few representatives of them present here,—I would say, We want you, not for your own sake only, but also for ours. Do you know that, in leaving the comparatively well-to-do to worship by themselves, you are injuring *our* Christianity? Depend upon it that it is so. Why, the New Testament is a volume which could not possibly have been written as it is, which must have been something essentially different, had not Christ lived amongst the suffering multitudes, and had not the Apostles drawn poor and despised men into the equality of the Christian fold. No Christianity can be living and heavenly in its operation, which is that of upper classes exclusively. The motto of our churches ought to be, "The rich and the poor meet together, the Lord is the maker of all." It is a spiritual advantage to the rich man that his poorest neighbours should stand by his side claiming equality with him before God. Just as the Jewish belief in Christ could not have the largeness and depth and knowledge which it was intended to have, until the Gentiles claimed to be in the Church with as good right as the Jews, so we shall not inherit such a national or personal Christianity as God reserves for us, until we are constrained to think more reverently of the humanity which we share with every man, than of the distinctions which place some above others. It would come like a steady tide of inspiration to the clergy, in particular, stirring their hearts and opening their lips, if the common people were to demand their proportion of places in our Churches—places which God gives them, and which, thank God, the country and the Church guarantee to them. Then they would exert their natural influence. They could practically insist that the service and the teaching should be in part accommodated to their needs. But I rejoice to believe that the influence of the lower classes, when it has really made itself felt in our religious habits, will not stop there.   It will go on to deal with social life, and will tend in many ways to accomplish the blessed work of lifting up all those that are down.

But I would add with confidence, It will be directly good for you also. Yes, brethren, we are sure it will. You are in little danger, probably, of unrighteous formalism, at all events for some time to come.   What will you hear, in what will you be expected to join, when you come to Church? It will be taken for granted that you are sinners, sinners like the best of us. And does this fact never force itself upon you and trouble you? Does conscience never make you ashamed? You are not so blind as to deceive yourselves with the notion that you are blameless. Well then, being invited to confess yourselves the sinners that you are, you hear in the Church of God's wonderful forgiveness of sins, of the reconciliation he wrought through his Son who gave himself up on the Cross, of his constant readiness to receive as forgiven every sinner who repents. It is the *property* of God,—so the Church testifies,—it is his essential nature, always to have mercy and to forgive. And this is the substance of all our communion with God in worship, that he meets us as our reconciling Father, and we come to him as his offending but penitent children. But, as he has taught and continually inspires us to do, we offer him praises and thanksgivings and prayers, casting all our care upon him, committing the keeping of our souls to him as to a faithful Creator. And further, if you come to Church, you will hear chosen passages of Holy Scripture, now the thrilling words of an ancient prophet, now the story of some beneficent work of the Lord Jesus Christ, now the profound exhortation of an Apostle. Could you be the worse for this? And if the preacher is not all that you might wish and could imagine him to be, if he does not always speak so that his words go home with force to heart and mind and conscience alike, yet if you listen sympathizingly, you will hear him say something, at least, upon which your minds may dwell with profit, something in which the voice of God himself, encouraging, warning, or consoling, may be recognized.

Then you will go home again, to take up once

17—2

more the daily burden of cares and duties, to be husbands and wives, parents, sons and daughters, workpeople, and so on. Now will you tell me that any other way of spending the time,—say two hours and a half on Sunday,—would have done more to strengthen and animate you for the bearing of that burden, to lift your souls into a pure atmosphere, to give you gentleness and courage, to brace your energies together, to turn your affections from what is foul or mean? Hardly any one now wishes to make the Sunday a day of gloom, or to put a ban upon the enjoyment of the open air or of society on that day. But there are many hours in a day, and a portion given to the united worship of God will make the rest of the day and of the week the happier. I never like to assume that Sunday is the only day of common worship; it would be pleasant to imagine a daily consecration of our daily toil. But our modern customs present a very strong resistance to daily worship. And I have those now in my mind, who have to begin with regular Church-going on Sundays.

I hope I may venture to appeal to your experience of these Mission Services,—of this service to-night. Will you not say, with the Apostles who saw the glory on the mount, "It is good for us to be here"? Have not some precious recollections been awakened, have not some secret places of emotion been unlocked in your hearts, as the touching words of the hymns have gone up in sweet music to heaven? My brethren, I will believe that by God's grace it has been so. There has been much in the response given to the Mission call, to justify us in entertaining good hopes.

Don't let the heavenly impulse, the sincere purpose, be swept away from your hearts by unworthy causes. I know of several reasons commonly given for not coming to Church which ought to be as gossamer in the way of a strong spiritual conviction. If God enables you to think steadily of himself, and of heaven, and of the future, and of your duties to your families, and of the grand traditions of the Church, and of the well-being of the country,—then all excuses will be silenced. You can come to Church, if you are convinced that you ought. I am unwilling to think of want of courage as preventing any one from saying in simplicity, "I am going to Church to-day." But there is no harm in mutual support. Rather it is a good thing that neighbour should encourage neighbour. I remember once desiring to do an act which it was natural to shrink a little from doing ; and after some talk with a friend who also desired to do the same thing, I bound myself to him, and he bound himself to me, that we would break the ice at the same time. In that way the stronger may help the weaker, and the weak may help one another. Why should not many agree together to say, "We know it would be a good thing to go to Church ; let us promise each other that we will not fail without reasonable cause to be at Christ Church, or at St Barnabas, once at least on a Sunday."

But there is one reason for not coming to Church which deserves the most considerate respect. Not a few feel, "It would be inconsistent in me to go to Church, it would be no better than humbug, if I were to go on doing just as I do now, taking a little too much to drink sometimes, or using bad language which has become a habit to me, or buying or selling on Sundays. I will at least not be a hypocrite, as some poor wretches are." How am I to answer that ? I will say, Remember the publican, who went up into the Temple to pray. He had many things on his conscience, more than one bad habit to break ; but God's grace took hold of him, and he went up into the Temple to pray. Not as a hypocrite. No, that character belonged more truly to the respectable Pharisee who thanked God he was not as that publican. No: he went, in simplicity and sincerity, and what he said was, "God be merciful to me a sinner." He asked for pardon for the past, for help for the future. And because he thus threw himself on the mercy of God, he went down to his house justified rather than the Pharisee. Brethren, what God judges is the heart. If our heart condemn us, God is greater than our heart, and knows all things. You may be sure,—I venture to say it,—that God's eye sees many things in the hearts of the completely respectable, which offend him more than the outward irregularities which catch the world's eye. Only, let it be true to us all alike, that we come to Church, not to cover our sins, but to get rid of them. If we come with even a faint desire of pleasing God, he will help us to do whatever is right for us to do. Remember, you do not make an evil thing good by abstaining from a religious profession. If a habit is evil, it is hurting you, hurting your children, hurting your neighbours. You who are doing what you yourself think wrong, if you make no pretence of religion, will be beaten with fewer stripes than if you were a hypocritical professor. But you will be beaten. Safety, duty, credit, happiness, all lie in the path of confession and amendment. You should welcome therefore anything that engages that excellent principle, your hatred of hypocrisy, on the side of a change which is for your good.

If I have been speaking to but few of those who have yet to be drawn into the communion of our worship, I trust that the same thoughts are not without their lesson to us whose habit it already is to come to Church. These thoughts constrain us at all events to say within ourselves, If we are persuaded that others might derive so much benefit from Church-going, are we taking care that by teachableness and devotion and sincerity *we* are making the most of what we would commend to *them?*

XVIII.

SUPERNATURAL RELIGION.

St John iv. 48.—"Then said Jesus unto him, Except ye see signs and wonders, ye will not believe."

No one can fail to see that something of a reproach is intended in these words. Our Lord means to say that it would have been better if the Jews had been willing to believe without seeing signs and wonders. And this is a very important statement. The spirit of it, you will observe, is entirely in accordance with what is described to us as having been the general practice of the Lord Jesus. He never welcomed or desired the adhesion of those who believed in him because they saw the miracles which he did. He wrought mighty works, not to overpower disbelief, but to encourage and reward faith. In places where the people shewed no disposition to believe in him, he could not, we are told, do mighty works.

Now this way of regarding faith and miracles is

in very definite opposition to a certain mode of describing Christianity, which has prevailed amongst its defenders, but which is found to suit the purposes of its assailants, and which they therefore gladly employ. I will endeavour to put it into a few words.

Christianity, it is assumed, is a supernatural Revelation, the contents of which are exceedingly strange, but which we are required to believe because those who brought this revelation performed miracles in attestation of its truth. It is taken for granted that we should pay no attention to the professed Revelation, except for the miracles. It follows then, that in examining into our religion, our first business is with the miracles. These must be shewn to be so manifestly supernatural as to defy all attempts at explanation. But they are external occurrences, depending upon historical testimony. The evidence for things so extremely improbable in themselves, and which are to be the basis of a supernatural revelation still more extraordinary, ought in all reason to be irresistible. You can scarcely imagine, indeed, any evidence which would be sufficient to enforce conviction. At all events, it ought to be more conclusive than the proofs you would require of an apparently miraculous occurrence at the present day. This being the position held by Christianity, let us see—say the doubters and disbelievers—what the evidence is by which the Christian miracles are proved. It is very well, they observe, to allege that the miracles are astonishing enough to attest the Revelation ; but first of all, what is the testimony which attests the miracles? And then they set to work, as lawyers would, to cross-examine the witnesses, and to strip and shake the evidence.

But if you have been impressed at all by that language of Scripture to which I have referred, you will be little inclined to acquiesce in the primary account of Christianity from which this method starts. Christianity, it is said, is a supernatural Revelation, the contents of which could only be received on the strength of undeniable miracles. I have admitted that this sort of account has been given by defenders of Christianity and may be found in Christian books. But I am appealing now to Scripture, to the habitual language of Christ and of his Apostles. What did Christ mean, I ask, when he said, " Except ye see signs and wonders, ye will not believe"? You cannot imagine him who so spoke describing his mission in any terms such as these,—" I am going to tell

you something which you would of course not receive on my word by itself, and therefore I shall
first perform wonders among you which you will
be compelled to regard as entirely beyond human
power, and these will prove to you that what I tell
you, however incredible, must be accepted as true."
I am sure you will feel that our Lord's method of
approaching men was something quite different
from this.

1. The word "supernatural" is unknown in
the New Testament. And not only so, but the
attempted distinction between natural and supernatural is alien to the New Testament mind. You
may fancy, perhaps, that the distinction is a broad
and simple one; but you will find, if you try to
explain it, that it is not so. Well, only those who
make or use the distinction are bound to justify it.
So far as I am able to judge, it introduces confusion
into any subject to which it is applied. I do not
go so far as to say that either word, natural or
supernatural, may not be used reasonably. But I
do contend that you cannot divide life or creation
or history into two parts, distinguished from one
another by the condition that the one is natural
and the other supernatural.

The Lord Jesus was accustomed to insist very

strongly that he came from God, that he was sent by the Father; and if that is what is meant by calling Christianity a supernatural religion or revelation, every one must admit that he did make that claim, but we may prefer his own way of stating it. Most assuredly, the whole virtue of what he taught depended on its coming from God and being true. "If any one desires to do the will of God," said Jesus, "he will know of my teaching whether I speak from myself." Not, "if any one scrutinizes the miraculous character of my works, he will be forced to believe that I have Divine attestation to my teaching;" but, "if any wills or is minded to do God's will, he will recognize my teaching as not coming out of my own head, but as proceeding from God." Assuredly, I repeat, our Lord presented himself to his country-men as having come from heaven, as being commissioned and sealed by the Father, as doing acts and speaking words which were not his but the Father's. It is not his glory in the New Testament to have been the wisest of men, but to have spoken to men with authority from and concerning the heavenly Father. Rob Christianity of this its claim, and it becomes not somewhat less sacred and authoritative, but an imposture. Strike out from the New Testament all that implies this claim, and how much will be left?

2. Revelation is a word which occurs in the New Testament; but it is never used in such a way that you could join the word "contents" with it. People who now speak about Christianity as a supernatural Revelation will generally go on to allude to its contents; as if it were something which might be compared to a box, or at least as if it were a book. But revelation, which means unveiling, is always used by New Testament writers in the sense of unveiling; and we should not speak of the contents of an unveiling. Do not suppose that this is a mere verbal or grammatical criticism. The Scriptural theory of revelation is not that a book or a document has been communicated to mankind, containing certain propositions which we are bound to believe because they are in the Divine communication; but that the Divine nature and will have been manifested, as if by the removal of veils or coverings which hid them from the knowledge of men. Jesus Christ came to reveal his Father; no one, he said, knows the Father, but the Son, and he to whomsoever the Son will reveal him. Now mark the difference between one who says, "I am enabling you to see and know the

Father, in his justice and his goodness and his glorious purposes for mankind," and another who should say, "I have here in a document certain statements which I could not expect you to believe in themselves, but when you have seen the mighty works I can perform, you will feel that you have no alternative but to receive them." The latter method is not what Scripture calls revelation. The glory of God, which Christ reveals, commends itself without the compulsion of miracles to open eyes and willing hearts.

3. So that our faith as Christians, if we take the New Testament view of it, cannot properly be described as an assent, grounded upon miracles, to certain supernatural doctrines. It would seem that the highest and best faith was that which was rendered to the Lord Jesus without the evidence of mighty works at all. Let us endeavour to see clearly how this was, in the hope that we may be the better able to understand the true ground of our own faith.

We frequently read in the Gospels of persons believing and not believing. What kind of belief is it that is meant? Or, in other words, how did the Lord Jesus present himself to his countrymen? What was the teaching he offered them?

He proclaimed the kingdom of heaven as brought near to them; he spoke of the heavenly Father as offering them forgiveness, and calling them to repentance, through him. He spoke with authority not as an expositor or commentator, but as one who knew the truth of what he was announcing. His word was variously received; he himself has described, in the parable of the sower, its various fortunes as it fell on the ears of its many hearers. By some it was welcomed; these were they who received it into an honest and good heart. They were persons who felt the burden of sin and rejoiced to be set free from it through forgiveness; who were troubled by the miseries of their fellow-countrymen and the distractions of their country, and rejoiced to be assured that God was manifesting himself for deliverance. These believers did not ask for miracles to attest a supernatural revelation; their hearts leapt up in answer to the gracious words which proceeded out of the mouth of Jesus. This was the kind of faith which he approved. It is true that the Lord Jesus, whilst he proclaimed the kingdom of God, wrought mighty works; but he wrought them, one would say, rather as illustrations than as evidences. They were almost exclusively works of healing; acts of grace, accompanying and illustrating words of grace. To the sufferer whose mind was burdened by sin and whose body was fettered by disease, Jesus spoke with authority, "Thy sins are forgiven thee; arise and walk!" No doubt the cures which Jesus wrought made a great impression both on individual minds and on the general opinion of the multitude. Those who had welcomed for its own sake the word of the kingdom and of reconciliation became more thoroughly convinced of the reality and authenticity of it when they saw the Prophet of Nazareth acting as the Son of the Father, and wielding the powers of the Kingdom. Many, without caring for the word, were quite willing to make much of Jesus as a Divinely sent prophet on account of his miracles. But from supporters like these Jesus was accustomed to withdraw himself. He counted himself successful, if one may say so, when his word touched the heart of a hearer, commending itself by its own heavenly quality and drawing out the faith to which it appealed.

After a very short time, it was no longer Jesus himself in the flesh who was preaching, but his Apostles or .envoys. It was their mission to proclaim through him the forgiveness of sins. They bore witness that the Father had raised him from the dead, and called on men to believe in him that they might have life.   Mighty works were not wanting to the preaching of the Apostles; their word was confirmed by signs following.   But there was no logical presentation of miracles as the ground for accepting a supernatural revelation. In this sense, on the contrary, miracles were slighted and refused.   What can be plainer than St Paul's account of the method of his work as a preacher of the Gospel?   He was perfectly familiar with that craving for miracles of which our Lord speaks with disapproval.   "The Jews," he says, "require signs, and the Greeks seek after wisdom : but we proclaim Christ crucified, to the Jews a stumblingblock, and to the Greeks foolishness, but unto them which are called, both Jews and Greeks, Christ the power of God, and the wisdom of God." And again, "I determined not to know anything among you, save Jesus Christ, and him crucified. And I was with you in weakness, and in fear, and in much trembling.   And my speech and my preaching was not with enticing words of man's wisdom, but in demonstration of the Spirit and of power: that your faith should not stand in the wisdom of men, but in the power of God."   The power of God is not here wonder-working power;

it is spiritual power. It is the power with which the proclamation of a Son of God, who gave himself up to die and was raised again, is carried home to simple unworldly hearts. I do not know whether this action of the Gospel upon the heart should be called natural or supernatural. It belongs to the higher world, the world of God and of the soul ; it does not grow out of competition and survival of the fittest and social evolution. So it may be called supernatural. But on the other hand, it ought to be normal and universal ; it appeals to the common human affections; it is of a piece with all the higher and more precious influences of human life ; so that any one who was inclined to call it natural might find much justification for doing so.

If you carry your thoughts onwards along the course of the Church's history, you will see this same method illustrated over and over again. Whenever the Gospel has won substantial victories, they have been due, not to the exhibition of signs and wonders, nor to the presentation of irresistible evidence of former signs and wonders, but to the power of the Gospel itself upon the souls of men. Miracles and their evidence belong much more to the makers of systems than to the living growth of

Christianity or of the Church of Christ. Wherever Christianity spreads, or deepens, or revives, there you will be able to trace the operation of the Word and of the Spirit; of the Word of forgiveness and adoption commending itself to the needs and hopes and aspirations of sinful humanity; of the Spirit moving with its contagious warmth and vitality in the affections through which man is akin to God. From the day when John the Baptist stood forth, crying "Repent, for the Kingdom of heaven is at hand," to the present moment, the real force of the kingdom of God has always been spiritual, never relying upon signs and wonders, always seeking to awaken, to win, to carry captive, the souls of men in demonstration of the Spirit and of power.

How will these considerations tell on us, brethren, when we are visited by doubts or are desiring to strengthen ourselves in reasonable faith? Clearly, they will not send us to signs and wonders, or to demonstrative historical evidence of signs and wonders. They will keep us in mind of that poor craving of the Jews for signs; of the sorrowful complaint of our Lord, "Except ye see signs and wonders, ye will not believe." Our chief concern is with Jesus Christ, and him crucified.

Can we recognize in him a Divine wonder of love and goodness? When the soul is quickened by hope, and crushed into remorseful hatred of sin, and exalted by unselfish love, are we content to put all that aside as delusion and infectious fancy? Are we satisfied to turn a deaf ear to every voice that seems to speak to us from heaven, and to know nothing but that which grows and pushes from the earth? These are the sort of questions which real Christianity addresses to us. It does not, and it never did, profess to offer a system which argument cannot assail. The Christianity which has gloried for more than eighteen centuries in the demonstration of the Spirit, is not now going to change its nature, and to build itself upon signs and wonders. It is even idle to meet the appeals of the Gospel with a demand for signs or with a critical pursuit of wisdom. The Gospel will certainly not say, "Here then are the supernatural wonders which *you* ask for; here is the natural wisdom which will satisfy *you.*" Its business is to proclaim Christ, the Divine power, the Divine wisdom, to all them that believe. If Christ fails, it is time for Christianity to fail too, and to disappear before the wisdom of this world.

But Christ will not fail, dear brethren, in this

age more than in any former. He may find our hearts dull, and blinded by the god of this world, and hard to the soft touches of the Spirit, and so there may be great condemnation and loss both for ourselves and for the world. But he will have the old prevailing arguments and influences for all that are susceptible to them. Let us hope and pray that we and our age may not be so immersed in the things of this visible world as to be dead to the things of heaven. Let us beware of dictating to God how he should speak to us and call us. The question for us is whether God is not calling us, whether that which professes to be his voice is not indeed worthy of the God of heaven and earth. Let us ask in all humility and teachableness that our ears may be purged, and the vail may be taken from our hearts, and that we may know what the true heavenly glory is. It is a part of the mystery of that work which Christ is carrying on through the ages, that each Christian serves as evidence to his brethren. It is now as it was of old. Nothing is so practically convincing as the fruit of the Spirit in Christian lives. The princes of this world tried to crush out Christianity in its infancy by persecuting Christians; but their attempt was turned against themselves, because every sufferer whose patience and love were proved like gold in the fire, became a new argument of the Spirit to confirm the waverers and to win over the unbelieving. It is not necessarily a weak or a base thing to believe because others believe. It is so when the motive is simply to save trouble and avoid inconvenience by following the fashion of the world and doing as others do. But human lives visibly purified and raised and softened through spiritual loyalty to Christ are arguments which the Spirit uses, and by which men do right in allowing themselves to be persuaded.

XIX.

THE COST OF DISCIPLESHIP.

St Luke xiv. 26.—"If any man come to me, and hate not his father, and mother, and wife, and children, and brethren, and sisters, yea, and his own life also, he cannot be my disciple."

This is surely one of the "hard sayings" of our Lord's teaching.

He it was who said, "A new commandment I give unto you, that ye love one another; as I have loved you, that ye also love one another. By this shall all men know that ye are my disciples, if ye have love one to another." Is the same Lord so jealous, so exacting, so indifferent to the mutual affections of human beings, as to demand that men must hate all, for the more perfect following of himself? There is no one, you might have thought, less likely to have made such a demand than Jesus Christ, whose glory it was to humble and empty himself on behalf of his brethren, to give up his life for his sheep.

Yet, with a little more reflection, you might see in the *boldness* of this saying what is peculiarly characteristic of the Lord Jesus. This is, in truth, just what no other teacher, or master of disciples, could be imagined to say. There is more here than the ordinary exactingness of human egotism. The masters of schools and founders of religions have been tempted to set their pretensions very high, and have found it profitable to do so: such self-exaltation pleases, rather than repels, those who are inclined to become their followers. But one would not expect to find amongst the sayings reported and recorded by their disciples anything that would put their claims in so invidious and disturbing a light. But our Lord, we know, was not unwilling to surprise and perplex his hearers, by saying what would at the moment offend them and repel them from him, instead of attracting them to him.

We should remember that many sayings are best to be understood by the tone in which they are uttered. When we are reading written words, it is of course not easy to recover with certainty the speaker's tone. There must always be some doubt whether we interpret rightly the mood in which our Lord spoke any words of his which we may be studying. But it is beyond all doubt, I believe, that some of his sayings are misapprehended by us, and others are greatly weakened to our minds, through a common habit of taking for granted that Christ always spoke in a uniformly passionless mood, and of reading his utterances, therefore, as if delivered in a calm didactic tone. There are indications enough of deep and varied feeling, giving special significance to particular portions of our Lord's teaching. What the feeling was, is in part to be gathered from the circumstances of the history.

We can see that our Lord was not always able to be as gracious as he would have desired to be. In his own spirit, indeed, he was without intermission full of grace as of truth. But his manner was sometimes of necessity stern, rather than soft; repellent, rather than winning. And this was not only the case in his well-known dealings with the Pharisees, when his rebukes were full of fiery invectives and threatenings. At times he had to push back the common multitudes who thronged round him in cheap admiration. As he proclaimed the glad tidings of the Kingdom of heaven, and wrought the beneficent signs of it in acts of healing, the people, captivated by what they heard and saw, pressed as it were with violence into the Kingdom of heaven. But Jesus did not welcome this superficial enthusiasm. We have accounts like the following of his attitude towards it. "Many believed on his name, when they saw the miracles which he did. But Jesus did not commit himself unto them, because he knew all men, and needed not that any should testify of men." "When Jesus therefore perceived that they would come and take him by force, to make him a king, he departed again unto a mountain himself alone." When an eager multitude had taken great trouble to find him, Jesus said to them, "Verily, verily, I say unto you, Ye seek me, not because ye saw signs, but because ye did eat of the loaves and were filled." He would not let them suppose that the deliverance he proclaimed was to be found in laxity of conduct. "Think not that I am come to destroy the law or the prophets; I am not come to destroy, but to fulfil...I say unto you, That except your righteousness shall exceed the righteousness of the scribes and Pharisees, ye shall in no case enter into the kingdom of heaven." The pattern parable, that of the Sower, describes the various kinds of reception given to the word of the King-dom, and warns two classes of the worthlessness of the receiving of it into a shallow heart, or into one occupied with the cares and pleasures of this world. And in the same mind Jesus told his hearers that they must strive—make efforts—to enter in at the narrow gate, for many would seek to enter in, and would not be able.

These are examples of the *discouragement* which our Lord was accustomed to offer to the contagious enthusiasm which the sight of his wonderful works and the expression of his sympathy with the humbler classes inspired amongst the common people. He was full of grace; but he was also full of truth: and he must tell his hearers the truth, at the cost of appearing to neutralize the grace. The sympathies, the hopes, the promises, which touched the people and made them wonder at the gracious words which proceeded out of his mouth, were perfectly sincere and real; but our Lord knew that he was not opening a Paradise of easy delights to men. Not such was the Kingdom of heaven; nor was it to be entered and possessed by pleasure-seekers. The true bliss of it was to be attained through self-renunciation and sacrifice, through the testing fire of tribulation. The Lord Jesus must make this thoroughly understood; but it was impossible that he should bear this testimony to those who thronged about him *without pain and sadness.*

And we ought to see a feeling of most earnest sadness in that warning which we are specially considering to-day. We have examples in the preceding part of the chapter of the way in which our Lord made the cause of the suffering classes his own. The Kingdom of heaven, he had plainly taught, was for the poor rather than for the rich, for the despised rather than for the highly esteemed. In ver. 25 we read, "There went great multitudes with him." The champion and benefactor of the poor, he had the popularity which he might seem to have courted. But the sight of this following caused him sorrow rather than joy. He knew what was in man: and this sort of discipleship he perceived to be fallacious. There was not the stuff of the true disciple of the Son of man in these multitudes. They would have to be tried and exposed. His followers would have to endure all losses, all distresses. He was looking forward to a terrible baptism for himself, and those who would cling to him must be prepared for their share in it.

Expressing this knowledge, he turned to the multitudes, and said, "If any man come to me, and hate not his father, and mother, and wife, and children, and brothers, and sisters, yea, and his own life also, he cannot be my disciple." Such words were not *a direction* given in a mood of calm contentment; they were a prophetic warning, wrung out of one of the agonies of the Son of man. There is a tone—if one must not say of *bitterness*, at least of protest and horror, in this forecast of the contradictions which the following of him would evoke. You may trace it in the slow iteration of relationships. He will not spare himself or his hearers one painful detail. " Think not," he said, "that I am come to send peace on the earth." Surely this was what believers in him were taught to expect! No, he says: "think not I am come to send peace on the earth, I am not come to send peace, but a sword. I am not come,"—[think of the intensity of all but despair with which such a profession must have been uttered by the Son of man],—"to make families of one mind, to replace domestic jars and jealousies by the sweet harmony of mutual affection. Don't expect *this*. Any man who would follow me will have to hate his father, and his mother, and wife, and children, and brothers, and sisters, yea and his own life also, or he cannot be my disciple. This is the result of my coming and of my Gospel in such a world as this is. I cannot proclaim the goodness of my Father, and call men to be at peace with him as his reconciled children without introducing these terrible dissensions into societies and families. My disciples must be prepared for these consequences. They must look for not merely bodily privations, but moral tortures, stripes and wounds of the affections, conflicts which will make them sometimes wonder whether the following of me can be *right*, if they intend to be constant as my disciples and to walk in my steps."

It is, then, as a warning of misery that would have to be endured, and of the kind of misery which was most shocking and intolerable to the Son of man, and not as the recommendation of a course to be pursued, that we are to understand our Lord's saying. If you suppose him to be teaching, in the calmly didactic tone, that his followers must withdraw their warmest affections from their human relatives to give them more absolutely to him, you are attributing to him, I am persuaded, not only a *different* feeling from that which was in his mind, but the *very opposite* feeling. He uses the most painful expression,—to *hate*,—just because the thing he foresees, the apparent rending of closest ties, is so painful to him. His supreme desire is to promote love; and it is laid upon him and his followers to be apparently the causes of bitter and deadly strife.

Undoubtedly our Lord might have used more guarded and explanatory language. In what he did say, we shall be ready to believe, as reverent Christians, that he spoke from his own unerring sense of what was fittest. Very often, the best language is not that which is coldly calculated, but that which is suddenly fashioned by the heat of a worthy emotion. How are we to be aware of un-common feeling in the heart of a speaker, unless it shews its mark in some unexpected form of speech? Part of the value of speech is in its revealing emo-tion and character; and if we read our Lord's his-tory rightly, we shall see plainly enough that his nature did not differ from the natures of other men in being more even and placid, but that it was agitated more than others by joy and by grief, by indignation and by horror.

When he was thus moved by the prospect of the moral distresses which would attend the follow-ing of him, our Lord had in view primarily the circumstances of his own age, and the future of those whom he was immediately addressing. He was leading a "little flock" into the fire of perse-cution. The followers of the Nazarene were to be hated of all men. "The brother," as Jesus said on another occasion, "shall deliver up the brother to death, and the father the child: and the children shall rise up against their parents, and cause them to be put to death." The first days of the Kingdom of heaven were days of peculiar tribulation. What was said with reference to the trials of those days would not be exactly applicable to other times.

But although the saying we are considering is to be regarded as a warning of impending trials rather than as an exhortation, and those trials belong to a particular age, yet we may undoubtedly see in it a moral call or demand. The Lord Jesus, whilst he plainly warned his hearers what the following of him would cost, implied that to follow him was worth the cost. Though he apparently made no efforts to proselytize, and repelled many who offered themselves as adherents, he yet took the responsibility of forming a small band of followers, and he committed to them the charge of drawing others into the Kingdom, and spoke continually of the rewards of the Kingdom for those who could enter it through tribulation, and declared that as it was Divine so it must grow and triumph. Painful as was the prospect of inevitable strifes and hatreds, our Lord by no means exhorted his disciples to shrink from becoming the occasions of them. He does therefore in these words exalt the following of himself into the highest of duties. Whatever might be the consequences, moral as well as bodily, of following him, those who saw things in the true light would without hesitation cleave to him. The disciple such as Jesus desired must be ready to give up all,—possessions, friends, his life,—when the discipleship should require it.

So this warning as to the trials of a particular age hardly needs any translation to become an extremely exacting call addressed to all Christians. If it was right for the first followers of Christ to encounter even the rending of his family affections for his name's sake, what is there that we in this day could plead as having a title to qualify the same discipleship, and to turn it into a compromise? When Christ calls, neither father nor mother, neither wife nor child, neither brothers nor sisters, can rightly stand in the way of obedience to the summons.

What is it that can reconcile our consciences to the exactingness of a claim which thus overrides all that nature makes most binding upon us?—Only the true apprehension of what Christ is. For him it was perfectly safe to use such dangerous language. If men were utterly careless about his nature and mission and general teaching, they were not likely to turn that saying into a plea for neglecting natural duties; they would rather scoff at it as monstrous. If on the other hand they were attracted by him, they *could not* so abuse it.

Remember that the Lord Jesus declared himself to be sent by the Father; that he bore witness of the Father as infinitely gracious; that he affirmed the true enemy of mankind to be the spirit of hatred and deceit, from whom he was come to deliver men. He was himself the manifestation of the mind which he declared to be in the Father, seeking to bind men together by mutual love, setting forth love and unity as the glory to which the soul of man owes natural allegiance and for which it must endlessly crave. He had spent a blameless childhood and youth as one of a family, subject to his parents, growing in favour both with God and man. He protested against the love of riches and of honour, against oppression and hardness, against every form of selfishness, and bade men come to and love the God of love and truth.

This Son of the Father was put to death, and held up to odium as one who was disloyal to the Jewish religion. Christ crucified became to the

Jews a stumblingblock. When therefore a member of a Jewish household was drawn by the Father to him, and by him to the Father, and determined to profess himself a disciple of the Crucified, you can imagine that his determination would offend his relatives, that all sorts of reproaches would be cast upon him, that efforts would be made to induce him to give up the cause to which he was attaching himself; and that when he proved constant, he would be accused of breaking the family harmony, of disobeying and dishonouring his parents, of violating those natural obligations to which the God of his fathers had given his express sanction. Why then *should* he thus "hate" father and mother, wife and child? The reply of his conscience, no doubt, would be, that God himself was calling him. But then this God, whom he had learned to know and confess, was one who led him in the ways of truth and love. Allegiance to the Crucified implied a triumph over worldliness and self-seeking; it constrained him to care, not for his own interests, but for his brethren and for mankind.

Now what are the natural enemies of the family affections? Are they conscientiousness, devotion to truth, faith in God's love, self-conquest, desire of the universal well-being, zeal for the will of the just and gracious God? Impossible! Surely they are vanity, self-esteem, jealousy; indulgence of appetite and passion; the desire of shielding what is discreditable by deception; distrust and misconstruction. If only *these* could be conquered, how happy the life of households would be! how spontaneously would mutual affection thrive! how closely the ties of mutual dependence would be knit!— Nothing is more certain than that the following of the Crucified wars against the lusts which impair the natural affections, and supplies the atmosphere and the soil in which they are made to thrive.

Therefore that early follower of the Crucified would be involved in a most distressing conflict. He could not escape from pain and perplexity. He could not be happy in displeasing his nearest friends. He would probably love father and mother, wife and child, *all the more* for seeming to hate them. He would feel mastered by that greater vocation of the cause of God and of mankind, which bade him sacrifice his own present happiness to the greater gain of the world; and he would be sustained, no doubt, by faith and hope in him to whom he knew his kinsfolk to be as dear as to himself. So whatever he might suffer, and whatever might be said as to his hating those of his own house, he would cleave to his crucified master.

We may be unfeignedly thankful that the following of Jesus Christ does not for us involve such bitter trials. The lesson I would ask you to learn from the remembrance of them is, that we are called, at whatever cost of physical or mental or moral pain, to give ourselves up absolutely to the cause of goodness and truth, which is the cause of the Kingdom of heaven. There is a Master whose claim over us transcends all inferior obligations, and he is Truth and Love.

We are tempted, partly by reverence, to name *Religion* instead of God or Christ; but it is really unsafe to speak of the claims of *Religion* as being thus paramount. The Jews who persecuted our Lord and his followers were devotees of Religion, and it was in the name of Religion that they persecuted. The claims of Religion have often come into competition with domestic duty. But then Religion is not identical with the Son of man. We read, God is Love, God is Truth; but not, God is Religion. It would be most dangerous to say, that if any one would follow Religion, he must hate father and mother, wife and child. By such a doctrine a man may really be seduced into the neglect or disparagement of family affections. But let a man be a follower of the *Son of man,* or of *the heavenly Father,* and then I say he may try, if he pleases, to hate father and mother, wife and child ;—*he will not be able.*

I admit that there may be perplexities about the degree and manner in which it is right for any one to devote himself to his family when wider claims seem to be made upon him. Ought such a one to become a missionary and go out to preach the Gospel in heathen lands? Ought such another to allow the business of his profession to take him away for long or indefinite periods from his home? Ought fathers in general to resist the absorbing demands which their business is apt to make upon them? Such questions cause genuine anxiety to very many. We can hardly hope to solve them in particular cases to our perfect satisfaction; and the circumstances so vary in particular cases that it is not very helpful to lay down general rules about them. But I think I may venture to say, that such direct following of the Son of man as takes effect in the shape of voluntary endeavours to bring in and extend his Kingdom, hardly has its due consideration amongst us. The soldier or the sailor, the merchant, the engineer, the scientific explorer, take it for granted that domestic claims must be overruled. But domestic claims are much more easily allowed to dispute the obligation to do some voluntary work in promoting God's glory and bettering the future of the world. The difficulty no doubt is, that when a man has a secular occupation, he sees his work and knows that he can do it; he is not tormented by uncertainty whether he has a genuine call and is able to do the good he wishes to do; he is not giving up more definite duties for the more indefinite. Of course, if any one of us were able to be a St Paul, we should not doubt that home ought to be given up for such a career as much as for that of a soldier. But who knows that he could be a St Paul even according to his smaller measure? So, a man will ask whether he can persuade himself that if he were to give up time for such work as that of a Sunday School teacher or District Visitor, or for that of promoting any philanthropic movement, he would be sure to make the most valuable investment of the time. I admit the weight of such uncertainties. It is simpler and safer to do the nearest and plainest things than to give them up for more ambitious but more distant and difficult attempts. But I can hardly doubt that we should see our way more distinct, and the call more imperative, to voluntary efforts in the cause of the Son of man, if we were in the habit of contemplating that cause more steadily as the one comprehensive object for which we should live.

Of this however I am sure, that no devotion to the Son of man or his cause would on the whole weaken the natural ties of human life. If we give up our cares, our interests, our affections, to God who makes and who places us, he does not throw them away as worthless things; he returns them to us purified and consecrated. The earthly selfish temper which mingles with our best feelings and with the discharge of our most sacred duties is dross and alloy to be got rid of. It is well that it should be purged away in the fire of love to God and Christ. God will teach us to love more unselfishly, not less earnestly, all whom we learn to love *in him.*

XX.

HEAVEN AND THE WORLD.

St John xiv. 18.—"I will not leave you comfortless: I will come
to you."

ACCORDING to our Christian belief, and according
to the nearly universal belief of mankind, we are *in
two worlds*.

The one is that which we seem to know best,
this visible world. We see the sky over our heads,
the ground·under our feet. We are amongst objects which we see and feel and smell and taste.
We perceive one another and hold communication
with one another. We have our own bodies, sensitive to pleasure and pain, nourished by what we
eat and drink, growing and decaying. We appear
in this visible world at our birth, we disappear
from it at our death. We are all supposed to be
pretty well acquainted with this world; it takes
care that we shall not disregard it; we can none of
us treat it as if it did not exist, or as if we had
nothing to do with it.

It is true, at the same time, and it is a very curious fact, that when thinking persons gaze steadily at this visible world, it seems to them less and less *real.* Our sense of its reality is somewhat disturbed, when we see the most solid substances volatilized into invisible gases. But thought dissolves the outward world more effectually than chemistry. We know things about us by sensation: how do we know that it is not all sensation, and nothing else? If I become blind, the outward world, as a visible scene, does not exist for me; if all my senses perish, how do I know that anything external remains? A man dies, and the world is dead to him; when all die, may not the world, which had existed in their sensations, become non-existent?

So inquiry speculates, and these speculations are by no means frivolous. Nevertheless, for us, as we are now, this visible world is real enough, and no one, as I said, can ignore it, or practically treat it as non-existent.

The other world in which we believe is the invisible world. This is confessedly mysterious. It is difficult to describe and explain it, partly because the very language we use is taken from the operations of our senses. And men do not agree about its nature, so much as they do about that of the visible world.　They cannot investigate it by the same process.　Altogether there is much that is baffling about it.　Men cannot get it out of their heads ; their imaginations, their hopes, and their fears, insist upon penetrating into it.　By all that is highest and best in us, by all that is enduring, we seem to be related to an unseen world, as we are by what is lower and more transitory and mutable to the world of the senses.　Our nature is haunted even·in childhood by vague and shadowy apprehensions in which the poet has recognized intimations of another world to which we really belong.

> "Not in entire forgetfulness,
> And not in utter nakedness,
> But trailing clouds of glory do we come
> From God, who is our home."

And if this is true of childhood, it is more certainly true that the developed experiences of adult life, the witness of the conscience, and the workings of the affections, urge upon us in our more thoughtful moments the reality of the unseen world and of our relations to it.

There are some philosophers who would persuade us that this is a mere delusive enchantment. We are beguiled, they say, by a too active fancy, and we project images of our earthly life upon the curtain which effectually closes us in. They would have us shut our eyes resolutely to this imaginary unseen world, in which we suppose God and other invisible beings to dwell. We can know nothing about it, they assure us; our faculties are incompetent to apprehend it; our only wise course is to acquiesce in its being an absolute blank, and to turn our thoughts from it to the world which we can know and work in.

Against this conclusion, the irrepressible workings of human instinct will continue to rebel, and the Gospel utters its protesting witness.

We certainly have reason to be on our guard against the activity of the imagination, when it is stimulated by the darkness of the unseen world. Where the religious imagination has had free play, as in the heathen religions, with what various shapes, of power, of fear, of attraction, has it peopled that world! Sometimes it has aimed at creating graceful and pleasing forms and scenes; at other times it has revelled in horrors. And if we see this most glaringly displayed in heathen mythologies, we know very well that Christianity, in its course of eighteen centuries, has not been kept free from this source of corruption. We shall fare ill, if we are left at the mercy of the religious instinct, working in accordance with what the fears of guilt and the dreams of pleasure may suggest.

But our privilege, dear brethren, as Christians, is to hear the Gospel and be guided by the teachings of Christ. Our Master took pains to put his followers in the way of thinking rightly about the unseen world. Let us listen this morning to the lesson which he gave to his Apostles in the prospect of his approaching departure from this visible world.

The departure began with his death, and was completed by his ascension. Before his death the Lord Jesus had been living with his followers under the conditions of this world of the senses. As St John says, they heard him, they saw him with their eyes, they looked upon him, their hands touched and grasped him. He died upon the Cross the death of all men. Then the disciples, forgetting what he had taught them and the promises he had given them, were plunged in disappointment and grief. He was gone from them, and they had sorrow. Soon he shewed himself to them alive,—not continuously, but in mysterious interviews, enough to assure them that he had triumphed over death. He was seen by them at intervals during forty days, and spoke to them of things pertaining to the Kingdom of God. Their grief gave way to awe and hope. Having thus trained them, as it were, to think of him as alive, he brought this intermediate period to an end, and went up into heaven. So his departure from this visible world was consummated.

But the disciples were not again cast down. The force of that first terrible shock had spent itself. They now fed on the promises of their Master, and especially on one great promise which he had repeated to them over and over again. The promise was to be very quickly fulfilled. They had not long to wait; and they waited in patience and even joyfully.

This promise took two forms.

One of them we see in our text: "I will not leave you comfortless: *I will come to you.*" You are probably aware that the word rendered by "comfortless" might more accurately be translated "bereaved." Jesus had made himself more than parent or husband to the chosen few to whom he was speaking. He was their support and stay. His death was the greatest bereavement they could suffer. Jesus felt keenly, in his more than human sympathy, how his disciples would be affected by losing him. They would be like orphan children, like the widowed wife. But, he assured them, "I will not leave you thus bereaved." My absence will be but for a short time. "I will come to you." "*I will come to you;*" this was one form of the promise. "Yet a little while," he continues, "and the world seeth me no more; but ye see me, because I live, and ye shall live." (This is probably a truer rendering than that of our received version, "because I live, ye shall live also.") "Ye see me, because I live and you shall then live. At that day ye shall know that I am in my Father, and ye in me, and I in you." The disciples did not understand how it was to be that Jesus should be visible to the disciples and invisible to the world. One of them asked him, "Lord, how is it that thou wilt manifest thyself unto us, and not unto the world?" The explanation which Jesus gave was this: "If a man love me, he will keep my words, and my Father will love him, and we will come unto him, and make our abode with him." These words are enough to make us cautious in understanding the promise "I will come to you." It is evident that the coming was not to be a bodily one. It was not to be one which could be seen by the observation of the senses. It was to be what we call a *spiritual* coming.

And this promise was evidently identical with that of the sending of the Spirit. "I will pray the Father, and he will give you another Comforter, that he may abide with you for ever; even the Spirit of truth, whom the world cannot receive, because it seeth him not, neither knoweth him." I say the two promises are substantially the same. It is true that Jesus speaks as if the Comforter were to be a *substitute* for him. "I tell you the truth; it is expedient for you that I go away; for if I go not away, the Comforter will not come unto you; but if I depart, I will send him unto you." Is this, "I am going away, and I will send the Spirit to be with you," is this the same, it may be asked, as the other saying, "I am going away for a little while, and then I will come to you again"? Yes, brethren, it is. The two different statements do not really contradict each other; the one makes the other more likely to be understood in its true sense. The Spirit of truth would come to them, and unite them in a spiritual fellowship with their Lord; Jesus himself would come to them in the Spirit, and make the disciples feel and know that he was with them.

Now here was *heaven*, here was the unseen world, as the Son of God revealed it to his disciples.

They would be really and consciously *in it*, when they should know the Father to be near them and with them. "This is life eternal," said Jesus in his prayer to his Father, "that they might know thee, the only true God, and Jesus Christ whom thou hast sent." They who should be quickened with that life, would perceive Christ and the Father loving them and abiding with them. They would themselves have abiding-places in the home of the Father. And all this would depend on their keeping, in a loyal spirit, the words or commandments of Christ.

Other things may be said about the unseen world. It may be pictured with the aid of the imagery of the Revelation, with a great white throne, with a sea of glass, with myriads of angels, with elders and living creatures round about the throne. There may be some subordinate value in the suggestions of these images. But incomparably the highest, truest, and most precious teaching concerning the unseen world is that which our Lord gave in these promises. It makes no attempt to reduce within our conceptions what is beyond their capacity. But it raises us to the highest thought of which we are capable, when it says to us, "Heaven is, to be visited by the unseen God, to behold and love and know the Son and the Father in the Spirit." And if it seem to you for a moment that such a heaven is uninviting, beside a heaven of spacious courts above the sky, the heaven of harps and jewels and shining raiment, remember first whose words they are that we are studying; and then let your consciences tell you that the dazzling of the senses by dreams of oriental splendour is but a poor thing compared with the awakening of Divine life in the soul. What shall it profit a man, if he shall gain the whole world, and lose himself? Royal palaces and gorgeous entertainments, and the supreme achievements of art and wealth, make fine spectacles, and even descriptions of them find eager readers; and it may be natural that the many should idealize these in their endeavours to conceive of perfect happiness: but if you want to make Christ's idea of heaven your own, think rather of a childlike disciple, in poverty perhaps and suffering, lifting up the aspirations of a penitent and humble but grateful and trusting heart to One felt to be infinitely gracious and closely near. *There* Jesus has come; there the Father and the Son are loving the obedient disciple, and making their abode with him; there the disciple is occupying the place prepared for him in the great home of the Father.

Whatever else you may think about heaven, let these Divine ideas be *dominant* in your minds. We speak of Christ as having ascended into heaven; we pray, in full conformity with the words of the Lord himself and his Apostles, that we also may in heart and mind thither ascend, and with him continually dwell. What do we mean by this prayer?—That we, when we die, may rise through the air into an abode of perfect enjoyment? Certainly not; we are not referring to the time of death at all. We are praying that now, we, living in this visible world, may ascend and dwell with Christ. And how is that to be done? By loving him and keeping his words; because, in accordance with his promise, he has given his Spirit to men, and to them who receive the Spirit humbly Christ comes and the Father, and they manifest themselves to them and dwell with them.

In those truly heavenly conversations with his disciples on the night before his Passion, our Lord makes no allusion to the change wrought by death. He is referring indeed to his own approaching death and departure from the visible world; but in what he promises and bids his disciples look forward to, he speaks wholly of what was to come to them in their lifetime. It is not easy for us to believe this; but it is so, certainly and demonstrably. His return to them, that they might dwell with him, was to be within a few days. What the Spirit was to do for them was to be done on the Day of Pentecost and from that day forwards. The more you can fix this in your minds, the better. But we cannot forget Death. It is constantly forcing itself upon us. We know that we ourselves must die, and it is good that we should bear it in mind. But before that time, it may be we shall know, perhaps more than once or twice, the *bereaving* power of Death. It is not possible to make light of this. The Lord Jesus referred to it solemnly and tenderly. But was he not doing something by his promises to assuage that power, not only on the minds that were to be grieved by his departure, but on minds which should afterwards be overwhelmed by other sad separations? Suppose one of that company of disciples to have thoroughly learnt the lesson, to have received the Spirit, and to have lived with Christ and the Father in faith and love. Suppose that Death came, and took from him a parent or other loved one. Do you not feel sure that the habitual sense of living in the unseen world, even whilst active amongst things seen, must have greatly altered the feeling of that disciple towards death, and therefore greatly softened the pain and the shock of separation ? Death is the passage from the visible world into the invisible : well, but what we most surely know of the invisible world is that Christ is there and the Father, and that spiritual communion may link those who are yet in the flesh with invisible beings. No progress of civilization or of scientific knowledge can avail in the slightest degree to make bereavement more tolerable. The happier our lot is in this world, and the more closely we are drawn to others, the more grievous must it be, that the loved companion should become the prey of the enemy. And where in this world is consolation to be found ? But there is real consolation for those who have come to feel naturalized in the heavenly commonwealth. They may reasonably cherish thoughts of reunion with those who have gone before them ; or, if at times they cannot help admitting how vain it is to speculate with any precision about the conditions of so different a life, they can at least cast themselves confidingly on the grace of him who visits and is mindful of such unworthy creatures as the sons of men.

On Sunday next, dear brethren, we commemorate the primary historical fulfilment of the Saviour's promise,—that is to say, a remarkable linking together of the seen and unseen worlds. The Church that came into organized being on the Day of Pentecost was a permanent witness of that union. Then began that feeding together on the Body and Blood of Christ which was appointed as a ladder from earth to heaven, an outward and visible sign of an inward and spiritual grace. A vast multitude of Christians in all parts of the world will on Whitsunday observe this sacred tradition, and come together to feed by faith on him whom, if they see him at all, they can only see with the spiritual eye. O that for many this inward vision may be made more real and clear! O that the *world*, to which nothing heavenly is visible, may have less occupation of the hearts of Christians! Let it be our distinct endeavour, with the help of God's grace, so to open our hearts to the Spirit of faith and love that worldly and carnal affections may be mortified in us, and that we may know what it is to dwell with God through Christ! We greatly need to become as little children, in simplicity, and teachableness, and indifference to the world, that we may see the kingdom of God. May the Spirit of truth make us sincere, honest, and courageous in our following of Christ. We have no right to hope to be clear-sighted, if we are not single-minded. If, professing to be Christians, we harden ourselves against Christian affections, and make the things of the world our genuine interests, how can we expect Christ to manifest himself to us? The pure in heart, *they* shall see God. It is by being patient, loving, high-minded, in the common intercourse and affairs of this life, that we shall strengthen our hold upon the things that are not seen; it is by walking in the steps of Jesus Christ that we shall come nearer to him; it is only in *loving* God that we can really *know* him.

CAMBRIDGE: PRINTED BY C. J. CLAY, M.A. AT THE UNIVERSITY PRESS.

A CATALOGUE of THEOLOGICAL BOOKS,

with a Short Account of their Character and Aim,

Published by

MACMILLAN AND CO.

Bedford Street, Strand, London, W.C.

....

Abbott (Rev. E. A.)—Works by the Rev. E. A. ABBOTT, D.D., Head Master of the City of London School.

BIBLE LESSONS. Second Edition. Crown 8vo. 4*s.* 6*d.*

"*Wise, suggestive, and really profound initiation into religious thought.*" —Guardian. *The Bishop of St. David's, in his speech at the Education Conference at Abergwilly, says he thinks "nobody could read them without being the better for them himself, and being also able to see how this difficult duty of imparting a sound religious education may be effected.*"

THE GOOD VOICES: A Child's Guide to the Bible. With upwards of 50 Illustrations. Crown 8vo. cloth gilt. 5*s.*

"*It would not be easy to combine simplicity with fulness and depth of meaning more successfully than Mr. Abbott has done.*"—Spectator. *The* Times *says—"Mr. Abbott writes with clearness, simplicity, and the deepest religious feeling.*"

PARABLES FOR CHILDREN. Crown 8vo. cloth gilt. 3*s.* 6*d.*

"*They are simple and direct in meaning and told in plain language, and are therefore well adapted to their purpose.*"—Guardian.

I

Ainger (Rev. Alfred).—SERMONS PREACHED IN THE TEMPLE CHURCH. By the Rev. ALFRED AINGER, M.A. of Trinity Hall, Cambridge, Reader at the Temple Church. Extra fcap. 8vo. 6*s.*

This volume contains twenty-four Sermons preached at various times during the last few years in the Temple Church. "It is," the British Quarterly *says, "the fresh unconventional talk of a clear independent thinker, addressed to a congregation of thinkers .... Thoughtful men will be greatly charmed by this little volume."*

Alexander.—THE LEADING IDEAS of the GOSPELS. Five Sermons preached before the University of Oxford in 1870—71. By WILLIAM ALEXANDER, D.D., Brasenose College; Lord Bishop of Derry and Raphao; Select Preacher. Cr. 8vo. 4*s.* 6*d.*

"Eloquence and force of language, clearness of statement, and a hearty appreciation of the grandeur and importance of the topics upon which he writes characterize his sermons."—Record.

Arnold.—A BIBLE READING BOOK FOR SCHOOLS. THE GREAT PROPHECY OF ISRAEL'S RESTORATION (Isaiah, Chapters 40—66). Arranged and Edited for Young Learners. By MATTHEW ARNOLD, D.C.L., formerly Professor of Poetry in the University of Oxford, and Fellow of Oriel. Third Edition. 18mo. cloth. 1*s.*

The Times *says—"Whatever may be the fate of this little book in Government Schools, there can be no doubt that it will be found excellently calculated to further instruction in Biblical literature in any school into which it may be introduced.... We can safely say that whatever school uses this book, it will enable its pupils to understand Isaiah, a great advantage compared with other establishments which do not avail themselves of it."*

Baring-Gould.—LEGENDS OF OLD TESTAMENT CHARACTERS, from the Talmud and other sources. By the Rev. S. BARING-GOULD, M.A., Author of "Curious Myths of the Middle Ages," "The Origin and Development of Religious Belief," "In Exitu Israel," etc. In two vols. crown 8vo. 16*s.* Vol. I. Adam to Abraham. Vol. II. Melchizidek to Zechariah.

He has collected from the Talmud and other sources, Jewish and Mahommedan, a large number of curious and interesting legends concerning the principal characters of the Old Testament, comparing these frequently with similar legends current among many of the peoples, savage and civilised, all over the world. "These volumes contain much that is strange, and to the ordinary English reader, very novel."—Daily News.

Barry, Alfred, D.D.—The ATONEMENT of CHRIST. Six Lectures delivered in Hereford Cathedral during Holy Week, 1871. By ALFRED BARRY, D.D., D.C.L., Canon of Worcester, Principal of King's College, London. Fcap. 8vo. 2*s.* 6*d.*

In writing these Sermons, it has been the object of Canon Barry to set forth the deep practical importance of the doctrinal truths of the Atonement. "The one truth," says the Preface, "which, beyond all others, I desire that these may suggest, is the inseparable unity which must exist between Christian doctrine, even in its more mysterious forms, and Christian morality or devotion. They are a slight contribution to the plea of that connection of Religion and Theology, which in our own time is so frequently and, as it seems to me, so unreasonably denied." The Guardian *calls them "striking and eloquent lectures."*

Benham.—A COMPANION TO THE LECTIONARY, being a Commentary on the Proper Lessons for Sundays and Holydays. By the Rev. W. BENHAM, B.D., Vicar of Margate. Crown 8vo. 7s. 6d.

The Author's object is to give the reader a clear understanding of the Lessons of the Church, which he does by means of general and special introductions, and critical and explanatory notes on all words and passages presenting the least difficulty. "A very useful book. Mr. Benham has produced a good and welcome companion to our revised Lectionary. Its contents will, if not very original or profound, prove to be sensible and practical, and often suggestive to the preacher and the Sunday School teacher. They will also furnish some excellent Sunday reading for private hours."—Guardian.

Bernard.—THE PROGRESS OF DOCTRINE IN THE NEW TESTAMENT, considered in Eight Lectures before the University of Oxford in 1864. By THOMAS D. BERNARD, M.A., Rector of Walcot and Canon of Wells. Third and Cheaper Edition. Crown 8vo. 5s. (Bampton Lectures for 1864.)

"We lay down these lectures with a sense not only of being edified by sound teaching and careful thought, but also of being gratified by conciseness and clearness of expression and elegance of style."—Churchman.

Binney.—SERMONS PREACHED IN THE KING'S WEIGH HOUSE CHAPEL, 1829—69. By THOMAS BINNEY, D.D. New and Cheaper Edition. Extra fcap. 8vo. 4s. 6d.

"Full of robust intelligence, of reverent but independent thinking on the most profound and holy themes, and of earnest practical purpose."—London Quarterly Review.

Bradby.—SERMONS PREACHED AT HAILEYBURY. By E. H. BRADBY, M.A., Master. 8vo. 10s. 6d.

"He who claims a public hearing now, speaks to an audience accustomed to Cotton, Temple, Vaughan, Bradley, Butler, Farrar, and others...... Each has given us good work, several work of rare beauty, force, or originality; but we doubt whether any one of them has touched deeper chords, or brought more freshness and strength into his sermons, than the last of their number, the present Head Master of Haileybury."—Spectator.

Burgon.—A TREATISE on the PASTORAL OFFICE. Addressed chiefly to Candidates for Holy Orders, or to those who have recently undertaken the cure of souls. By the Rev. JOHN W. BURGON, M.A., Oxford. 8vo. 12s.

The object of this work is to expound the great ends to be accomplished by the Pastoral office, and to investigate the various means by which these ends may best be gained. Full directions are given as to preaching and sermon-writing, pastoral visitation, village education and catechising, and confirmation.—Spectator.

Butler (G.)—Works by the Rev. GEORGE BUTLER, M.A., Principal of Liverpool College :

FAMILY PRAYERS. Crown 8vo. 5s.

The prayers in this volume are all based on passages of Scripture—the morning prayers on Select Psalms, those for the evening on portions of the New Testament.

SERMONS PREACHED in CHELTENHAM COLLEGE CHAPEL. Crown 8vo. 7s. 6d.

Butler (Rev. H. M.)—SERMONS PREACHED in the CHAPEL OF HARROW SCHOOL. By H. MONTAGU BUTLER, Head Master. Crown 8vo. 7s. 6d.

"These sermons are adapted for every household. There is nothing more striking than the excellent good sense with which they are imbued." —Spectator.

A SECOND SERIES. Crown 8vo. 7s. 6d.

"Excellent specimens of what sermons should be,—plain, direct, practical, pervaded by the true spirit of the Gospel, and holding up lofty aims before the minds of the young."—Athenæum.

Butler (Rev. W. Archer).—Works by the Rev. WILLIAM ARCHER BUTLER, M.A., late Professor of Moral Philosophy in the University of Dublin :—

SERMONS, DOCTRINAL AND PRACTICAL. Edited, with a Memoir of the Author's Life, by THOMAS WOODWARD, Dean of Down. With Portrait. Ninth Edition. 8vo. 8s.

The Introductory Memoir narrates in considerable detail and with much interest, the events of Butler's brief life; and contains a few specimens of his poetry, and a few extracts from his addresses and essays, including a long and eloquent passage on the Province and Duty of the Preacher.

A SECOND SERIES OF SERMONS. Edited by J. A. JEREMIE, D.D., Dean of Lincoln. Seventh Edition. 8vo. 7s.

The North British Review *says, "Few sermons in our language exhibit the same rare combination of excellencies; imagery almost as rich as Taylor's; oratory as vigorous often as South's; judgment as sound as*

Butler (Rev. W. Archer.)—*continued.*

Barrow's; a style as attractive but more copious, original, and forcible than Atterbury's; piety as elevated as Howe's, and a fervour as intense at times as Baxter's. Mr. Butler's are the sermons of a true poet."

LETTERS ON ROMANISM, in reply to Dr. Newman's Essay on Development. Edited by the Dean of Down. Second Edition, revised by Archdeacon HARDWICK. 8vo. 10s. 6d.

These Letters contain an exhaustive criticism of Dr. Newman's famous "Essay on the Development of Christian Doctrine." "A work which ought to be in the Library of every student of Divinity."—BP. ST. DAVID'S.

LECTURES ON ANCIENT PHILOSOPHY. *See* SCIENTIFIC CATALOGUE.

Cambridge Lent Sermons. — SERMONS preached during Lent, 1864, in Great St. Mary's Church, Cambridge. By the BISHOP OF OXFORD, Revs. H. P. LIDDON, T. L. CLAUGHTON, J. R. WOODFORD, Dr. GOULBURN, J. W. BURGON, T. T. CARTER, Dr. PUSEY, Dean HOOK, W. J. BUTLER, Dean GOODWIN. Crown 8vo. 7s. 6d.

Campbell.—Works by JOHN M'LEOD CAMPBELL :—

THE NATURE OF THE ATONEMENT AND ITS RELATION TO REMISSION OF SINS AND ETERNAL LIFE. Fourth and Cheaper Edition, crown 8vo. 6s.

"Among the first theological treatises of this generation."—Guardian.
"One of the most remarkable theological books ever written."—Times.

CHRIST THE BREAD OF LIFE. An Attempt to give a profitable direction to the present occupation of Thought with Romanism. Second Edition, greatly enlarged. Crown 8vo. 4s. 6d.

"Deserves the most attentive study by all who interest themselves in the predominant religious controversy of the day."—Spectator.

RESPONSIBILITY FOR THE GIFT OF ETERNAL LIFE. Compiled by permission of the late J. M'LEOD CAMPBELL, D.D., from Sermons preached chiefly at Row in 1829—31. Crown 8vo. 5s.

"There is a healthy tone as well as a deep pathos not often seen in sermons. His words are weighty and the ideas they express tend to perfection of life."—Westminster Review.

REMINISCENCES AND REFLECTIONS, referring to his Early Ministry in the Parish of Row, 1825—31. Edited with an Introductory Narrative by his Son, DONALD CAMPBELL, M.A., Chaplain of King's College, London. Crown 8vo. 7s. 6d.

These 'Reminiscences and Reflections,' written during the last year of his life, were mainly intended to place on record thoughts which might prove helpful to others. "*We recommend this book cordially to all who are interested in the great cause of religious reformation.*"—Times. "*There is a thoroughness and depth, as well as a practical earnestness, in his grasp of each truth on which he dilates, which make his reflections very valuable.*"—Literary Churchman.

Canterbury.—THE PRESENT POSITION OF THE CHURCH OF ENGLAND. Seven Addresses delivered to the Clergy and Churchwardens of his Diocese, as his Charge, at his Primary Visitation, 1872. By ARCHIBALD CAMPBELL, Archbishop of Canterbury. Third Edition. 8vo. cloth. 3s. 6d.

The subjects of these Addresses are, I. Lay Co-operation. II. Cathedral Reform. III. and IV. Ecclesiastical Judicature. V. Ecclesiastical Legislation. VI. Missionary Work of the Church. VII. The Church of England in its relation to the Rest of Christendom. There are besides, a number of statistical and illustrative appendices.

Cheyne.—Works by T. K. CHEYNE, M.A., Fellow of Balliol College, Oxford :—

THE BOOK OF ISAIAH CHRONOLOGICALLY ARRANGED. An Amended Version, with Historical and Critical Introductions and Explanatory Notes. Crown 8vo. 7s. 6d.

The object of this edition is to restore the probable meaning of Isaiah, so far as can be expressed in appropriate English. The basis of the version is the revised translation of 1611, *but alterations have been introduced wherever the true sense of the prophecies appeared to require it. The* Westminster Review *speaks of it as* "*a piece of scholarly work, very carefully and considerately done.*" *The* Academy *calls it* "*a successful attempt to extend a right understanding of this important Old Testament writing.*"

NOTES AND CRITICISMS on the HEBREW TEXT OF ISAIAH. Crown 8vo. 2s. 6d.

This work is offered as a slight contribution to a more scientific study of the Old Testament Scriptures. The author aims at completeness, independence, and originality, and constantly endeavours to keep philology distinct from exegesis, to explain the form without pronouncing on the matter.

Choice Notes on the Four Gospels, drawn from Old and New Sources. Crown 8vo. 4s. 6d. each Vol. (St. Matthew and St. Mark in one Vol. price 9s.).

These Notes are selected from the Rev. Prebendary Ford's Illustrations of the Four Gospels, the choice being chiefly confined to those of a more simple and practical character.

Church.—Works by the Very Rev. R. W. CHURCH, M.A., Dean of St. Paul's.

SERMONS PREACHED BEFORE the UNIVERSITY OF OXFORD. By the Very Rev. R. W. CHURCH, M.A., Dean of St. Paul's. Second Edition. Crown 8vo. 4s. 6d.

Sermons on the relations between Christianity and the ideas and facts of modern civilized society. The subjects of the various discourses are:—" The Gifts of Civilization," " Christ's Words and Christian Society," " Christ's Example," and " Civilization and Religion." " Thoughtful and masterly... We regard these sermons as a landmark in religious thought. They help us to understand the latent strength of a Christianity that is assailed on all sides."—Spectator.

ON SOME INFLUENCES OF CHRISTIANITY UPON NATIONAL CHARACTER. Three Lectures delivered in St. Paul's Cathedral, Feb. 1873. Crown 8vo. 4s. 6d.

" Few books that we have met with have given us keener pleasure than this....... It would be a real pleasure to quote extensively, so wise and so true, so tender and so discriminating are Dean Church's judgments, but the limits of our space are inexorable. We hope the book will be bought."—Literary Churchman.

THE SACRED POETRY OF EARLY RELIGIONS. Two Lectures in St. Paul's Cathedral. 18mo. 1s. I. The Vedas. II. The Psalms.

Clay.—THE POWER OF THE KEYS. Sermons preached in Coventry. By the Rev. W. L. CLAY, M.A. Fcap. 8vo. 3s. 6d.

In this work an attempt is made to shew in what sense, and to what extent, the power of the Keys can be exercised by the layman, the Church, and the priest respectively. The Church Review *says the sermons are " in many respects of unusual merit."*

Clergyman's Self-Examination concerning the APOSTLES' CREED. Extra fcap. 8vo. 1s. 6d.

Collects of the Church of England. With a beautifully Coloured Floral Design to each Collect, and Illuminated Cover. Crown 8vo. 12s. Also kept in various styles of morocco.

The distinctive characteristic of this edition is the coloured floral design which accompanies each Collect, and which is generally emblematical of the character of the day or saint to which it is assigned; the flowers which have been selected are such as are likely to be in bloom on the day to which the Collect belongs. The Guardian *thinks it " a successful attempt to associate in a natural and unforced manner the flowers of our fields and gardens with the course of the Christian year."*

Cotton.—Works by the late GEORGE EDWARD LYNCH COTTON, D.D., Bishop of Calcutta :—

SERMONS PREACHED TO ENGLISH CONGREGATIONS IN INDIA. Crown 8vo. 7s. 6d.

"The sermons are models of what sermons should be, not only on account of their practical teachings, but also with regard to the singular felicity with which they are adapted to times, places, and circumstances."—Spectator.

EXPOSITORY SERMONS ON THE EPISTLES FOR THE SUNDAYS OF THE CHRISTIAN YEAR. Two Vols. Crown 8vo. 15s.

These two volumes contain in all fifty-seven Sermons. They were all preached at various stations throughout India.

Cure.—THE SEVEN WORDS OF CHRIST ON THE CROSS. Sermons preached at St. George's, Bloomsbury. By the Rev. E. CAPEL CURE, M.A. Fcap. 8vo. 3s. 6d.

Of these Sermons the John Bull *says, " They are earnest and practical;" the* Nonconformist, *" The Sermons are beautiful, tender, and instructive;" and the* Spectator *calls them "A set of really good Sermons."*

Curteis.—DISSENT in its RELATION to the CHURCH OF ENGLAND. Eight Lectures preached before the University of Oxford, in the year 1871, on the foundation of the late Rev. John Bampton, M.A., Canon of Salisbury. By GEORGE HERBERT CURTEIS, M.A., late Fellow and Sub-Rector of Exeter College; Principal of the Lichfield Theological College, and Prebendary of Lichfield Cathedral; Rector of Turweston, Bucks. Third and Cheaper Edition, crown 8vo. 7s. 6d.

"Mr. Curteis has done good service by maintaining in an eloquent, temperate, and practical manner, that discussion among Christians is really an evil, and that an intelligent basis can be found for at least a proximate union."—Saturday Review *"A well timed, learned, and thoughtful book."*

Davies.—Works by the Rev. J. LLEWELYN DAVIES, M.A., Rector of Christ Church, St. Marylebone, etc. :—

THE WORK OF CHRIST ; or, the World Reconciled to God. With a Preface on the Atonement Controversy. Fcap. 8vo. 6s.

SERMONS on the MANIFESTATION OF THE SON OF GOD. With a Preface addressed to Laymen on the present Position of the Clergy of the Church of England; and an Ap-

Davies (Rev. J. Llewelyn)—*continued.*

pendix on the Testimony of Scripture and the Church as to the possibility of Pardon in the Future State. Fcap. 8vo. 6s. 6d.

"This volume, both in its substance, prefix, and suffix, represents the noblest type of theology now preached in the English Church."—Spectator.

BAPTISM, CONFIRMATION, AND THE LORD'S SUPPER, as Interpreted by their Outward Signs. Three Expository Addresses for Parochial use. Fcap. 8vo., limp cloth. 1s. 6d.

The method adopted in these addresses is to set forth the natural and historical meaning of the signs of the two Sacraments and of Confirmation, and thus to arrive at the spiritual realities which they symbolize. The work touches on all the principal elements of a Christian man's faith.

THE EPISTLES of ST. PAUL TO THE EPHESIANS, THE COLOSSIANS, and PHILEMON. With Introductions and Notes, and an Essay on the Traces of Foreign Elements in the Theology of these Epistles. 8vo. 7s. 6d.

MORALITY ACCORDING TO THE SACRAMENT OF THE LORD'S SUPPER. Crown 8vo. 3s. 6d.

These discourses were preached before the University of Cambridge. They form a continuous exposition, and are directed mainly against the two-fold danger which at present threatens the Church—the tendency, on the one hand, to regard Morality as independent of Religion, and, on the other, to ignore the fact that Religion finds its proper sphere and criterion in the moral life.

THE GOSPEL and MODERN LIFE. Sermons on some of the Difficulties of the Present Day, with a Preface on a Recent Phase of Deism. Extra fcap. 8vo. 6s.

The "recent phase of Deism" examined in the preface to this volume is that professed by the "Pall Mall Gazette"—that in the sphere of Religion there are one or two "probable suppositions," but nothing more. Amongst other subjects examined are—"Christ and Modern Knowledge," "Humanity and the Trinity," "Nature," "Religion," "Conscience," "Human Corruption," and "Human Holiness."

WARNINGS AGAINST SUPERSTITION IN FOUR SERMONS FOR THE DAY. Extra fcap. 8vo. 2s. 6d

"We have seldom read a wiser little book. The Sermons are short, terse, and full of true spiritual wisdom, expressed with a lucidity and a moderation that must give them weight even with those who agree least with their author....... Of the volume as a whole it is hardly possible to speak with too cordial an appreciation."—Spectator.

De Teissier.—Works by G. F. DE TEISSIER, B.D.:—

VILLAGE SERMONS, FIRST SERIES. Crown 8vo. 9s.

This volume contains fifty-four short Sermons, embracing many subjects of practical importance to all Christians. The Guardian *says they are "a little too scholarlike in style for a country village, but sound and practical."*

VILLAGE SERMONS, SECOND SERIES. Crown 8vo. 8s. 6d.

"This second volume of Parochial Sermons is given to the public in the humble hope that it may afford many seasonable thoughts for such as are Mourners in Zion." There are in all fifty-two Sermons embracing a wide variety of subjects connected with Christian faith and practice.

Donaldson.—THE APOSTOLICAL FATHERS: a Critical Account of their Genuine Writings and of their Doctrines. By JAMES DONALDSON, LL.D. Crown 8vo. 7s. 6d.

This book was published in 1864 as the first volume of a 'Critical History of Christian Literature and Doctrine from the death of the Apostles to the Nicene Council.' The intention was to carry down the history continuously to the time of Eusebius, and this intention has not been abandoned. But as the writers can be sometimes grouped more easily according to subject or locality than according to time, it is deemed advisable to publish the history of each group separately. The Introduction to the present volume serves as an introduction to the whole period.

Ecce Homo. A SURVEY OF THE LIFE AND WORK OF JESUS CHRIST. Eleventh Edition. Crown 8vo. 6s.

"A very original and remarkable book, full of striking thought and delicate perception; a book which has realised with wonderful vigour and freshness the historical magnitude of Christ's work, and which here and there gives us readings of the finest kind of the probable motive of His individual words and actions."—Spectator. *"The best and most established believer will find it adding some fresh buttresses to his faith."*—Literary Churchman. *"If we have not misunderstood him, we have before us a writer who has a right to claim deference from those who think deepest and know most."*—Guardian.

Faber.—SERMONS AT A NEW SCHOOL. By the Rev. ARTHUR FABER, M.A., Head Master of Malvern College. Cr. 8vo. 6s.

"These are high-toned, earnest Sermons, orthodox and scholarlike, and laden with encouragement and warning, wisely adapted to the needs of school-life."—Literary Churchman. *"Admirably realizing that combination of fresh vigorous thought and simple expression of wise parental counsel, with brotherly sympathy and respect, which are essential to the success of such sermons, and to which so few attain."*—British Quarterly Review.

Farrar.—Works by the Rev. F. W. FARRAR, M.A., F.R.S., Head Master of Marlborough College, and Hon. Chaplain to the Queen :—

THE FALL OF MAN, AND OTHER SERMONS. Second and Cheaper Edition. Extra fcap. 8vo. 4s. 6d.

This volume contains twenty Sermons. No attempt is made in these Sermons to develope a system of doctrine. In each discourse some one aspect of truth is taken up, the chief object being to point out its bearings on practical religious life. The Nonconformist *says of these Sermons,—* "Mr. Farrar's Sermons are almost perfect specimens of one type of Sermons, which we may concisely call beautiful. The style of expression is beautiful—there is beauty in the thoughts, the illustrations, the allusions— they are expressive of genuinely beautiful perceptions and feelings." *The* British Quarterly *says,—*"Ability, eloquence, scholarship, and practical usefulness, are in these Sermons combined in a very unusual degree."

THE WITNESS OF HISTORY TO CHRIST. Being the Hulsean Lectures for 1870. New Edition. Crown 8vo. 5s.

The following are the subjects of the Five Lectures:—I. " The Antecedent Credibility of the Miraculous." II. " The Adequacy of the Gospel Records." III. "The Victories of Christianity." IV. "Christianity and the Individual." V. "Christianity and the Race." The subjects of the four Appendices are:—A. " The Diversity of Christian Evidences." B. "Confucius." C. "Buddha." D. "Comte."

SEEKERS AFTER GOD. The Lives of Seneca, Epictetus, and Marcus Aurelius. *See* SUNDAY LIBRARY at end of Catalogue.

THE SILENCE AND VOICES OF GOD : University and other Sermons. Crown 8vo. 6s.

"We can most cordially recommend Dr. Farrar's singularly beautiful volume of Sermons...... For beauty of diction, felicity of style, aptness of illustration and earnest loving exhortation, the volume is without its parallel."—John Bull. *" They are marked by great ability, by an honesty which does not hesitate to acknowledge difficulties and by an earnestness which commands respect."*—Pall Mall Gazette.

Fellowship : LETTERS ADDRESSED TO MY SISTER MOURNERS. Fcap. 8vo. cloth gilt. 3s. 6d.

"A beautiful little volume, written with genuine feeling, good taste, and a right appreciation of the teaching of Scripture relative to sorrow and suffering."—Nonconformist. *"A very touching, and at the same time a very sensible book. It breathes throughout the truest Christian spirit."*— Contemporary Review.

Forbes.—THE VOICE OF GOD IN THE PSALMS. By GRANVILLE FORBES, Rector of Broughton. Cr. 8vo. 6s. 6d.

Gifford.—THE GLORY OF GOD IN MAN. By E. H. GIFFORD, D.D. Fcap. 8vo., cloth. 3s. 6d.

Golden Treasury Psalter. *See* p. 27.

Hardwick.—Works by the Ven. ARCHDEACON HARDWICK:

CHRIST AND OTHER MASTERS. A Historical Inquiry into some of the Chief Parallelisms and Contrasts between Christianity and the Religious Systems of the Ancient World. New Edition, revised, and a Prefatory Memoir by the Rev. FRANCIS PROCTER, M.A. Two vols. crown 8vo. 15s.

After several introductory chapters dealing with the religious tendencies of the present age, the unity of the human race, and the characteristics of Religion under the Old Testament, the Author proceeds to consider the Religions of India, China, America, Oceanica, Egypt, and Medo-Persia. The history and characteristics of these Religions are examined, and an effort is made to bring out the points of difference and affinity between them and Christianity. The object is to establish the perfect adaptation of the latter faith to human nature in all its phases and at all times. "The plan of the work is boldly and almost nobly conceived. . . . . We commend the work to the perusal of all those who take interest in the study of ancient mythology, without losing their reverence for the supreme authority of the oracles of the living God."—Christian Observer.

A HISTORY OF THE CHRISTIAN CHURCH. Middle Age. From Gregory the Great to the Excommunication of Luther, Edited by WILLIAM STUBBS, M.A., Regius Professor of Modern History in the University of Oxford. With Four Maps constructed for this work by A. KEITH JOHNSTON. Third Edition. Crown 8vo. 10s. 6d.

For this edition Professor Stubbs has carefully revised both text and notes, making such corrections of facts, dates, and the like as the results of recent research warrant. The doctrinal, historical, and generally speculative views of the late author have been preserved intact. "As a Manual for the student of ecclesiastical history in the Middle Ages, we know no English work which can be compared to Mr. Hardwick's book."—Guardian.

A HISTORY of the CHRISTIAN CHURCH DURING THE REFORMATION. New Edition, revised by Professor STUBBS. Crown 8vo. 10s. 6d.

This volume is intended as a sequel and companion to the "History of the Christian Church during the Middle Age." The author's earnest wish has been to give the reader a trustworthy version of those stirring incidents which mark the Reformation period, without relinquishing his former claim to characterise peculiar systems, persons, and events according to the shades and colours they assume, when contemplated from an English point of view, and by a member of the Church of England.

Hervey.—THE GENEALOGIES OF OUR LORD AND SAVIOUR JESUS CHRIST, as contained in the Gospels of St. Matthew and St. Luke, reconciled with each other, and shown to be in harmony with the true Chronology of the Times. By Lord ARTHUR HERVEY, Bishop of Bath and Wells. 8vo. 10s. 6d.

Hymni Ecclesiæ.—Fcap. 8vo. 7s. 6d.

A selection of Latin Hymns of the Mediæval Church, containing selections from the Paris Breviary, and the Breviaries of Rome, Salisbury, and York. The selection is confined to such holy days and seasons as are recognised by the Church of England, and to special events or things recorded in Scripture. This collection was edited by Dr. Newman while he lived at Oxford.

Kempis, Thos. A.—DE IMITATIONE CHRISTI. LIBRI IV. Borders in the Ancient Style, after Holbein, Durer, and other Old Masters, containing Dances of Death, Acts of Mercy, Emblems, and a variety of curious ornamentations. In white cloth, extra gilt. 7s. 6d.

The original Latin text has been here faithfully reproduced. The Spectator *says of this edition, it "has many solid merits, and is perfect in its way." While the* Athenæum *says, "The whole work is admirable; some of the figure compositions have extraordinary merit."*

Kingsley.—Works by the Rev. CHARLES KINGSLEY, M.A., Rector of Eversley, and Canon of Westminster. (For other Works by the same author, *see* HISTORICAL and BELLES LETTRES CATALOGUES).

THE WATER OF LIFE, AND OTHER SERMONS. Second Edition. Fcap. 8vo. 3s. 6d.

This volume contains twenty-one Sermons preached at various places —Westminster Abbey, Chapel Royal, before the Queen at Windsor, etc.

VILLAGE SERMONS. Seventh Edition. Fcap. 8vo. 3s. 6d.

THE GOSPEL OF THE PENTATEUCH. Second Edition. Fcap. 8vo. 3s. 6d.

This volume consists of eighteen Sermons on passages taken from the Pentateuch. They are dedicated to Dean Stanley out of gratitude for his Lectures on the Jewish Church, *under the influence and in the spirit of which they were written.*

GOOD NEWS OF GOD. Fourth Edition. Fcap. 8vo. 3s. 6d.

This volume contains thirty-nine short Sermons, preached in the ordinary course of the author's parochial ministrations.

Kingsley (Rev. C.)—*continued.*

SERMONS FOR THE TIMES. Third. Edition. Fcap. 8vo. 3*s.* 6*d.*

Here are twenty-two Sermons, all bearing more or less on the every-day life of the present day, including such subjects as these:—"Fathers and Children;" "A Good Conscience;" "Names;" "Sponsorship;" "Duty and Superstition;" "England's Strength;" "The Lord's Prayer;" "Shame;" "Forgiveness;" "The True Gentleman;" "Public Spirit."

TOWN AND COUNTRY SERMONS. Second Edition. Extra fcap. 8vo. 3*s.* 6*d.*

Some of these Sermons were preached before the Queen, and some in the performance of the writer's ordinary parochial duty. Of these Sermons the Nonconformist *says, "They are warm with the fervour of the preacher's own heart, and strong from the force of his own convictions. There is nowhere an attempt at display, and the clearness and simplicity of the style make them suitable for the youngest or most unintelligent of his hearers."*

SERMONS on NATIONAL SUBJECTS. Second Edition. Fcap. 8vo. 3*s.* 6*d.*

THE KING OF THE EARTH, and other Sermons, a Second Series of Sermons on National Subjects. Second Edition. Fcap. 8vo. 3*s.* 6*d.*

The following extract from the Preface to the 2nd Series will explain the preacher's aim in these Sermons:—" I have tried......to proclaim the Lord Jesus Christ, as the Scriptures, both in their strictest letter and in their general method, from Genesis to Revelation, seem to me to proclaim Him; not merely as the Saviour of a few elect souls, but as the light and life of every human being who enters into the world; as the source of all reason, strength, and virtue in heathen or in Christian; as the King and Ruler of the whole universe, and of every nation, family, and man on earth; as the Redeemer of the whole earth and the whole human race... His death, as a full, perfect, and sufficient sacrifice, oblation, and satisfaction for the sins of the whole world, by which God is reconciled to the whole human race."

DISCIPLINE, AND OTHER SERMONS. Fcp. 8vo. 3*s.* 6*d.*

Twenty-four Sermons preached on various occasions, some of them of a public nature—at the Volunteer Camp, Wimbledon, before the Prince of Wales at Sandringham, at Wellington College, etc. The Guardian *says, —"There is much thought, tenderness, and devoutness of spirit in these Sermons, and some of them are models both in matter and expression."*

DAVID. FOUR SERMONS: David's Weakness—David's Strength—David's Anger—David's Deserts. Fcap. 8vo. 2*s.* 6*d.*

These four Sermons were preached before the University of Cambridge,

Kingsley (Rev. C.)—*continued.*

and are specially addressed to young men. Their titles are,—"David's Weakness;" "David's Strength;" "David's Anger;" "David's Deserts."

WESTMINSTER SERMONS. 8vo. 10s. 6d.

These Sermons were preached at Westminster Abbey or at one of the Chapels Royal. Their subjects are:—The Mystery of the Cross: The Perfect Love: The Spirit of Whitsuntide: Prayer: The Deaf and Dumb: The Fruits of the Spirit: Confusion: The Shaking of the Heavens and the Earth: The Kingdom of God: The Law of the Lord: God the Teacher: The Reasonable Prayer: The One Escape: The Word of God: I: The Cedars of Lebanon: Life: Death: Signs and Wonders: The Judgments of God: The War in Heaven: Noble Company: De Profundis: The Blessing and the Curse: The Silence of Faith: God and Mammon: The Beatific Vision.

Lightfoot.—Works by J. B. LIGHTFOOT, D.D., Hulsean Professor of Divinity in the University of Cambridge; Canon of St. Paul's.

ST. PAUL'S EPISTLE TO THE GALATIANS. A Revised Text, with Introduction, Notes, and Dissertations. Fourth Edition, revised. 8vo. cloth. 12s.

While the Author's object has been to make this commentary generally complete, he has paid special attention to everything relating to St. Paul's personal history and his intercourse with the Apostles and Church of the Circumcision, as it is this feature in the Epistle to the Galatians which has given it an overwhelming interest in recent theological controversy. The Spectator says "there is no commentator at once of sounder judgment and more liberal than Dr. Lightfoot."

ST. PAUL'S EPISTLE TO THE PHILIPPIANS. A Revised Text, with Introduction, Notes, and Dissertations. Third Edition. 8vo. 12s.

The plan of this volume is the same as that of " The Epistle to the Galatians." "No commentary in the English language can be compared with it in regard to fulness of information, exact scholarship, and laboured attempts to settle everything about the epistle on a solid foundation."—Athenæum.

ST. CLEMENT OF ROME, THE TWO EPISTLES TO THE CORINTHIANS. A Revised Text, with Introduction and Notes. 8vo. 8s. 6d.

This volume is the first part of a complete edition of the Apostolic Fathers. The Introductions deal with the questions of the genuineness and authenticity of the Epistles, discuss their date and character, and analyse their contents. An account is also given of all the different epistles which bear the name of Clement of Rome. "By far the most copiously annotated

Lightfoot (Dr. J. B.)—*continued.*

edition of St. Clement which we yet possess, and the most convenient in every way for the English reader."—Guardian.

ON A FRESH REVISION OF THE ENGLISH NEW TESTAMENT. Second Edition. Crown 8vo. 6s.

The Author shews in detail the necessity for a fresh revision of the authorized version on the following grounds:—1. False Readings. 2. Artificial distinctions created. 3. Real distinctions obliterated. 4. Faults of Grammar. 5. Faults of Lexicography. 6. Treatment of Proper Names, official titles, etc. 7. Archaisms, defects in the English, errors of the press, etc. "The book is marked by careful scholarship, familiarity with the subject, sobriety, and circumspection."—Athenæum.

Luckock.—THE TABLES OF STONE. A Course of Sermons preached in All Saints' Church, Cambridge, by H. M. LUCKOCK, M.A., Vicar. Fcap. 8vo. 3s. 6d.

Maclaren.—SERMONS PREACHED at MANCHESTER. By ALEXANDER MACLAREN. Third Edition. Fcap. 8vo. 4s. 6d.

These Sermons represent no special school, but deal with the broad principles of Christian truth, especially in their bearing on practical, every day life. A few of the titles are:—"The Stone of Stumbling," "Love and Forgiveness," "The Living Dead," "Memory in Another World," "Faith in Christ," "Love and Fear," "The Choice of Wisdom," "The Food of the World."

A SECOND SERIES OF SERMONS. Second Edition. Fcap. 8vo. 4s. 6d.

The Spectator *characterises them as "vigorous in style, full of thought, rich in illustration, and in an unusual degree interesting."*

A THIRD SERIES OF SERMONS. Second Edition. Fcap. 8vo. 4s. 6d.

Sermons more sober and yet more forcible, and with a certain wise and practical spirituality about them it would not be easy to find."—Spectator.

Maclear.—Works by G. F. MACLEAR, D.D., Head Master of King's College School:—

A CLASS-BOOK OF OLD TESTAMENT HISTORY. With Four Maps. Eighth Edition. 18mo. 4s. 6d.

"The present volume," says the Preface, "forms a Class-Book of Old Testament History from the Earliest Times to those of Ezra and Nehemiah. In its preparation the most recent authorities have been consulted, aud wherever it has appeared useful, Notes have been subjoined illustrative of the Text, and, for the sake of more advanced students, references added to larger works. The Index has been so arranged as to form a concise Dictionary of the Persons and Places mentioned in the course of the

Maclear (G. F.)—*continued.*

Narrative." The Maps, prepared by Stanford, materially add to the value and usefulness of the book. The British Quarterly Review *calls it "A careful and elaborate, though brief compendium of all that modern research has done for the illustration of the Old Testament. We know of no work which contains so much important information in so small a compass."*

A CLASS-BOOK OF NEW TESTAMENT HISTORY.
Including the Connexion of the Old and New Testament. Sixth Edition. 18mo. 5s. 6d.

The present volume forms a sequel to the Author's Class-Book of Old Testament History, and continues the narrative to the close of St. Paul's second imprisonment at Rome. The work is divided into three Books— I. The Connection between the Old and New Testaments. II. The Gospel History. III. The Apostolic History. In the Appendix are given Chronological Tables The Clerical Journal *says, "It is not often that such an amount of useful and interesting matter on biblical subjects, is found in so convenient and small a compass, as in this well-arranged volume."*

A CLASS-BOOK OF THE CATECHISM OF THE CHURCH OF ENGLAND. Third and Cheaper Edition.
18mo. 1s. 6d.

The present work is intended as a sequel to the two preceding books. "Like them, it is furnished with notes and references to larger works, and it is hoped that it may be found, especially in the higher forms of our Public Schools, to supply a suitable manual of instruction in the chief doctrines of our Church, and a useful help in the preparation of Candidates for Confirmation." The Literary Churchman *says, "It is indeed the work of a scholar and divine, and as such, though extremely simple, it is also extremely instructive. There are few clergy who would not find it useful in preparing candidates for Confirmation; and there are not a few who would find it useful to themselves as well."*

A FIRST CLASS-BOOK OF THE CATECHISM OF THE CHURCH OF ENGLAND, with Scripture Proofs for
Junior Classes and Schools. New Edition. 18mo. 6d.

This is an epitome of the larger Class-book, meant for junior students and elementary classes. The book has been carefully condensed, so as to contain clearly and fully, the most important part of the contents of the larger book.

A SHILLING-BOOK of OLD TESTAMENT HISTORY.
New Edition. 18mo. cloth limp. 1s.

This Manual bears the same relation to the larger Old Testament History, that the book just mentioned does to the larger work on the Catechism. It consists of Ten Books, divided into short chapters, and subdivided into

Maclear (G. F.)—*continued.*

sections, each section treating of a single episode in the history, the title of which is given in bold type.

A SHILLING-BOOK of NEW TESTAMENT HISTORY. New Edition. 18mo. cloth limp. 1*s.*

This bears the same relation to the larger New Testament History that the work just mentioned has to the large Old Testament History, and is marked by similar characteristics.

A MANUAL OF INSTRUCTION FOR CONFIRMA-TION AND FIRST COMMUNION, with Prayers and Devotions. 32mo. cloth extra, red edges. 2*s.*

This is an enlarged and improved edition of 'The Order of Confirmation.' To it have been added the Communion Office, with Notes and Explanations, together with a brief form of Self Examination and Devotions selected from the works of Cosin, Ken, Wilson, and others.

Macmillan.—Works by the Rev. HUGH MACMILLAN, LL.D., F.R.S.E. (For other Works by the same Author, see CATALOGUE OF TRAVELS and SCIENTIFIC CATALOGUE).

THE TRUE VINE; or, the Analogies of our Lord's Allegory. Second Edition. Globe 8vo. 6*s.*

This work is not merely an exposition of the fifteenth chapter of St. John's Gospel, but also a general parable of spiritual truth from the world of plants. It describes a few of the points in which the varied realm of vegetable life comes into contact with the higher spiritual realm, and shews how rich a field of promise lies before the analogical mind in this direction. The Nonconformist *says, "It abounds in exquisite bits of description, and in striking facts clearly stated." The* British Quarterly *says, "Readers and preachers who are unscientific will find many of his illustrations as valuable as they are beautiful."*

BIBLE TEACHINGS IN NATURE. Eighth Edition. Globe 8vo. 6*s.*

*In this volume the author has endeavoured to shew that the teaching of nature and the teaching of the Bible are directed to the same great end; that the Bible contains the spiritual truths which are necessary to make us wise unto salvation, and the objects and scenes of nature are the pictures by which these truths are illustrated. "He has made the world more beautiful to us, and unsealed our ears to voices of praise and messages of love that might otherwise have been unheard."—*British Quarterly Review. *"Mr. Macmillan has produced a book which may be fitly described as one of the happiest efforts for enlisting physical science in the direct service of religion."—*Guardian.

Macmillan (H.)—*continued.*

THE MINISTRY OF NATURE. Second Edition. Globe 8vo. 6*s.*

*In this volume the Author attempts to interpret Nature on her religious side in accordance with the most recent discoveries of physical science, and to shew how much greater significance is imparted to many passages of Scripture and many doctrines of Christianity when looked at in the light of these discoveries. Instead of regarding Physical Science as antagonistic to Christianity, the Author believes and seeks to shew that every new discovery tends more strongly to prove that Nature and the Bible have One Author. " Whether the reader agree or not with his conclusions, he will acknowledge he is in the presence of an original and thoughtful writer."—*Pall Mall Gazette. *" There is no class of educated men and women that will not profit by these essays."*—Standard.

M‘Cosh.—For Works by JAMES McCOSH, LL.D., President of Princeton College, New Jersey, U.S., *see* PHILOSOPHICAL CATALOGUE.

Maurice.—Works by the late Rev. F. DENISON MAURICE, M.A., Professor of Moral Philosophy in the University of Cambridge.

Professor Maurice's Works are recognized as having made a deep impression on modern theology. With whatever subject he dealt he tried to look at it in its bearing on living men and their every-day surroundings, and faced unshrinkingly the difficulties which occur to ordinary earnest thinkers in a manner that showed he had intense sympathy with all that concerns humanity. By all who wish to understand the various drifts of thought during the present century, Mr. Maurice's works must be studied. An intimate friend of Mr. Maurice's, one who has carefully studied all his works, and had besides many opportunities of knowing the Author's opinions, in speaking of his so-called "obscurity," ascribes it to "the never-failing assumption that God is really moving, teaching and acting; and that the writer's business is not so much to state something for the reader's benefit, as to apprehend what God is saying or doing." The Spectator *says—"Few of those of our own generation whose names will live in English history or literature have exerted so profound and so permanent an influence as Mr. Maurice."*

THE PATRIARCHS AND LAWGIVERS OF THE OLD TESTAMENT. Third and Cheaper Edition. Crown 8vo. 5*s.*

The Nineteen Discourses contained in this volume were preached in the chapel of Lincoln's Inn during the year 1851. The texts are taken from the books of Genesis, Exodus, Numbers, Deuteronomy, Joshua, Judges, and Samuel, and involve some of the most interesting biblical topics discussed in recent times.

Maurice (F. D.)—*continued.*

THE PROPHETS AND KINGS OF THE OLD TESTAMENT. Third Edition, with new Preface. Crown 8vo. 10s. 6d.

Mr. Maurice, in the spirit which animated the compilers of the Church Lessons, has in these Sermons regarded the Prophets more as preachers of righteousness than as mere predictors—an aspect of their lives which, he thinks, has been greatly overlooked in our day, and than which, there is none we have more need to contemplate. He has found that the Old Testament Prophets, taken in their simple natural sense, clear up many of the difficulties which beset us in the daily work of life; make the past intelligible, the present endurable, and the future real and hopeful.

THE GOSPEL OF THE KINGDOM OF HEAVEN. A Series of Lectures on the Gospel of St. Luke. Crown 8vo. 9s.

Mr. Maurice, in his Preface to these Twenty-eight Lectures, says,— "In these Lectures I have endeavoured to ascertain what is told us respecting the life of Jesus by one of those Evangelists who proclaim Him to be the Christ, who says that He did come from a Father, that He did baptize with the Holy Spirit, that He did rise from the dead. I have chosen the one who is most directly connected with the later history of the Church, who was not an Apostle, who professedly wrote for the use of a man already instructed in the faith of the Apostles. I have followed the course of the writer's narrative, not changing it under any pretext. I have adhered to his phraseology, striving to avoid the substitution of any other for his."

THE GOSPEL OF ST. JOHN. A Series of Discourses. Third and Cheaper Edition. Crown 8vo. 6s.

These Discourses, twenty-eight in number, are of a nature similar to those on the Gospel of St. Luke, and will be found to render valuable assistance to any one anxious to understand the Gospel of the beloved disciple, so different in many respects from those of the other three Evangelists. Appended are eleven notes illustrating various points which occur throughout the discourses. The Literary Churchman *thus speaks of this volume: —"Thorough honesty, reverence, and deep thought pervade the work, which is every way solid and philosophical, as well as theological, and abounding with suggestions which the patient student may draw out more at length for himself."*

THE EPISTLES OF ST. JOHN. A Series of Lectures on Christian Ethics. Second and Cheaper Edition. Cr. 8vo. 6s.

These Lectures on Christian Ethics were delivered to the students of the Working Men's College, Great Ormond Street, London, on a series of Sunday mornings. Mr. Maurice believes that the question in which we are most interested, the question which most affects our studies and our daily lives, is the question, whether there is a foundation for human morality,

Maurice (F. D.)—*continued.*

or whether it is dependent upon the opinions and fashions of different ages and countries. This important question will be found amply and fairly discussed in this volume, which the National Review *calls " Mr. Maurice's most effective and instructive work. He is peculiarly fitted by the constitution of his mind, to throw light on St. John's writings." Appended is a note on " Positivism and its Teacher."*

EXPOSITORY SERMONS ON THE PRAYER-BOOK. The Prayer-book considered especially in reference to the Romish System. Second Edition. Fcap. 8vo. 5*s.* 6*d.*

After an Introductory Sermon, Mr. Maurice goes over the various parts of the Church Service, expounds in eighteen Sermons, their intention and significance, and shews how appropriate they are as expressions of the deepest longings and wants of all classes of men.

LECTURES ON THE APOCALYPSE, or Book of the Revelation of St. John the Divine. Crown 8vo. 10*s.* 6*d.*

Mr. Maurice, instead of trying to find far-fetched allusions to great historical events in the distant future, endeavours to discover the plain, literal, obvious meaning of the words of the writer, and shews that as a rule these refer to events contemporaneous with or immediately succeeding the time when the book was written. At the same time he shews the applicability of the contents of the book to the circumstances of the present day and of all times. " Never," says the Nonconformist, *" has Mr. Maurice been more reverent, more careful for the letter of the Scripture, more discerning of the purpose of the Spirit, or more sober and practical in his teaching, than in this volume on the Apocalypse."*

WHAT IS REVELATION? A Series of Sermons on the Epiphany; to which are added, Letters to a Theological Student on the Bampton Lectures of Mr. Mansel. Crown 8vo. 10*s.* 6*d.*

Both Sermons and Letters were called forth by the doctrine maintained by Mr. Mansel in his Bampton Lectures, that Revelation cannot be a direct Manifestation of the Infinite Nature of God. Mr. Maurice maintains the opposite doctrine, and in his Sermons explains why, in spite of the high authorities on the other side, he must still assert the principle which he discovers in the Services of the Church and throughout the Bible.

SEQUEL TO THE INQUIRY, "WHAT IS REVELA-TION?" Letters in Reply to Mr. Mansel's Examination of " Strictures on the Bampton Lectures." Crown 8vo. 6*s.*

This, as the title indicates, was called forth by Mr. Mansel's Examination of Mr. Maurice's Strictures on his doctrine of the Infinite.

THEOLOGICAL ESSAYS. Third Edition. Crown 8vo. 10*s.* 6*d.*

" The book," says Mr. Maurice, " expresses thoughts which have been

Maurice (F. D.)—*continued.*

working in my mind for years; the method of it has not been adopted carelessly; even the composition has undergone frequent revision." There are seventeen Essays in all, and although meant primarily for Unitarians, to quote the words of the Clerical Journal, *"it leaves untouched scarcely any topic which is in agitation in the religious world; scarcely a moot point between our various sects; scarcely a plot of debateable ground between Christians and Infidels, between Romanists and Protestants, between Socinians and other Christians, between English Churchmen and Dissenters on both sides. Scarce is there a misgiving, a difficulty, an aspiration stirring amongst us now,—now, when men seem in earnest as hardly ever before about religion, and ask and demand satisfaction with a fearlessness which seems almost awful when one thinks what is at stake—which is not recognised and grappled with by Mr. Maurice."*

THE DOCTRINE OF SACRIFICE DEDUCED FROM THE SCRIPTURES. Crown 8vo. 7s. 6d.

Throughout the Nineteen Sermons contained in this volume, Mr. Maurice expounds the ideas which he has formed of the Doctrine of Sacrifice, as it is set forth in various parts of the Bible.

THE RELIGIONS OF THE WORLD, AND THEIR RELATIONS TO CHRISTIANITY. Fourth Edition. Fcap. 8vo. 5s.

These Eight Boyle Lectures are divided into two parts, of four Lectures each. In the first part Mr. Maurice examines the great Religious systems which present themselves in the history of the world, with the purpose of inquiring what is their main characteristic principle. The second four Lectures are occupied with a discussion of the questions, "In what relation does Christianity stand to these different faiths? If there be a faith which is meant for mankind, is this the one, or must we look for another?"

ON THE LORD'S PRAYER. Fourth Edition. Fcap. 8vo. 2s. 6d.

In these Nine Sermons the successive petitions of the Lord's Prayer are taken up by Mr. Maurice, their significance expounded, and, as was usual with him, connected with the every-day lives, feelings, and aspirations of the men of the present time.

ON THE SABBATH DAY; the Character of the Warrior, and on the Interpretation of History. Fcap. 8vo. 2s. 6d.

THE GROUND AND OBJECT OF HOPE FOR MANKIND. Four Sermons preached before the University of Cambridge. Crown 8vo. 3s. 6d.

In these Four Sermons Mr. Maurice views the subject in four aspects: —I. The Hope of the Missionary. II. The Hope of the Patriot. III. The Hope of the Churchman. IV. The Hope of Man. The Spectator

Maurice (F. D.)—*continued.*

says, " It is impossible to find anywhere deeper teaching than this ;" and the Nonconformist, *" We thank him for the manly, noble, stirring words in these Sermons—words fitted to quicken thoughts, to awaken high aspiration, to stimulate to lives of goodness."*

THE LORD'S PRAYER, THE CREED, AND THE COMMANDMENTS. A Manual for Parents and Schoolmasters. To which is added the Order of the Scriptures. 18mo. cloth limp. 1*s.*

This book is not written for clergymen, as such, but for parents and teachers, who are often either prejudiced against the contents of the Catechism, or regard it peculiarly as the clergyman's book, but, at the same time, have a general notion that a habit of prayer ought to be cultivated, that there are some things which ought to be believed, and some things which ought to be done. It will be found to be peculiarly valuable at the present time, when the question of religious education is occupying so much attention.

THE CLAIMS OF THE BIBLE AND OF SCIENCE. A Correspondence on some Questions respecting the Pentateuch. Crown 8vo. 4*s.* 6*d.*

This volume consists of a series of Fifteen Letters, the first and last addressed by a ' Layman' to Mr. Maurice, the intervening thirteen written by Mr. Maurice himself.

DIALOGUES ON FAMILY WORSHIP. Crown 8vo. 6*s.*

" The parties in these Dialogues," says the Preface, "are a Clergyman who accepts the doctrines of the Church, and a Layman whose faith in them is nearly gone. The object of the Dialogues is not confutation, but the discovery of a ground on which two Englishmen and two fathers may stand, and on which their country and their children may stand when their places know them no more."

THE COMMANDMENTS CONSIDERED AS IN-STRUMENTS OF NATIONAL REFORMATION. Crown 8vo. 4*s.* 6*d.*

The author endeavours to shew that the Commandments are now, and ever have been, the great protesters against Presbyteral and Prelatical assumptions, and that if we do not receive them as Commandments of the Lord God spoken to Israel, and spoken to every people under heaven now, we lose the greatest witnesses we possess for national morality and civil freedom.

MORAL AND METAPHYSICAL PHILOSOPHY. Vol. I. Ancient Philosophy from the First to the Thirteenth Centuries. Vol. II. Fourteenth Century and the French Revolution, with a Glimpse into the Nineteenth Century. Two Vols. 8vo. 25*s.*

This is an edition in two volumes of Professor Maurice's History of

Maurice (F. D.)—*continued.*

Philosophy from the earliest period to the present time. It was formerly issued in a number of separate volumes, and it is believed that all admirers of the author and all students of philosophy will welcome this compact edition. In a long introduction to this edition, in the form of a dialogue, Professor Maurice justifies his own views, and touches upon some of the most important topics of the time.

SOCIAL MORALITY. Twenty-one Lectures delivered in the University of Cambridge. New and Cheaper Edition. Cr. 8vo. 10s. 6d.

"Whilst reading it we are charmed by the freedom from exclusiveness and prejudice, the large charity, the loftiness of thought, the eagerness to recognise and appreciate whatever there is of real worth extant in the world, which animates it from one end to the other. We gain new thoughts and new ways of viewing things, even more, perhaps, from being brought for a time under the influence of so noble and spiritual a mind." —Athenæum.

THE CONSCIENCE: Lectures on Casuistry, delivered in the University of Cambridge. Second and Cheaper Edition. Crown 8vo. 5s.

In this series of nine Lectures, Professor Maurice, endeavours to settle what is meant by the word "Conscience," and discusses the most important questions immediately connected with the subject. Taking "Casuistry" in its old sense as being the "study of cases of Conscience," he endeavours to show in what way it may be brought to bear at the present day upon the acts and thoughts of our ordinary existence. He shows that Conscience asks for laws, not rules; for freedom, not chains; for education, not suppression. He has abstained from the use of philosophical terms, and has touched on philosophical systems only when he fancied "they were interfering with the rights and duties of wayfarers." The Saturday Review *says: "We rise from the perusal of these lectures with a detestation of all that is selfish and mean, and with a living impression that there is such a thing as goodness after all."*

LECTURES ON THE ECCLESIASTICAL HISTORY OF THE FIRST AND SECOND CENTURIES. 8vo. 10s. 6d.

In the first chapter on "The Jewish Calling," besides expounding his idea of the true nature of a "Church," the author gives a brief sketch of the position and economy of the Jews; while in the second he points out their relation to "the other Nations." Chapter Third contains a succinct account of the various Jewish Sects, while in Chapter Fourth are briefly set forth Mr. Maurice's ideas of the character of Christ and the nature of His mission, and a sketch of events is given up to the Day of Pentecost. The remaining Chapters, extending from the Apostles' personal Ministry to the end of the Second Century, contain sketches of the character and

Maurice (F. D.)—*continued.*

work of all the prominent men in any way connected with the Early Church, accounts of the origin and nature of the various doctrines orthodox and heretical which had their birth during the period, as well as of the planting and early history of the Chief Churches in Asia, Africa and Europe.

LEARNING AND WORKING. Six Lectures delivered in Willis's Rooms, London, in June and July, 1854.—THE RELIGION OF ROME, and its Influence on Modern Civilisation. Four Lectures delivered in the Philosophical Institution of Edinburgh, in December, 1854. Crown 8vo. 5s.

SERMONS PREACHED IN COUNTRY CHURCHES. Crown 8vo. 10s. 6d.

"Earnest, practical, and extremely simple."—Literary Churchman. *"Good specimens of his simple and earnest eloquence. The Gospel incidents are realized with a vividness which we can well believe made the common people hear him gladly. Moreover they are sermons which must have done the hearers good."*—John Bull.

Moorhouse.—Works by JAMES MOORHOUSE, M.A., Vicar of Paddington :—

SOME MODERN DIFFICULTIES RESPECTING the FACTS OF NATURE AND REVELATION. Fcap. 8vo. 2s. 6d.

The first of these Four Discourses is a systematic reply to the Essay of the Rev. Baden Powell on Christian Evidences in "Essays and Reviews." The fourth Sermon, on "The Resurrection," is in some measure complementary to this, and the two together are intended to furnish a tolerably complete view of modern objections to Revelation. In the second and third Sermons, on the "Temptation" and "Passion," the author has endeavoured "to exhibit the power and wonder of those great facts within the spiritual sphere, which modern theorists have especially sought to discredit."

JACOB. Three Sermons preached before the University of Cambridge in Lent 1870. Extra fcap. 8vo. 3s. 6d.

THE HULSEAN LECTURES FOR 1865. Cr. 8vo. 5s.

"Few more valuable works have come into our hands for many years... a most fruitful and welcome volume."—Church Review.

O'Brien.—AN ATTEMPT TO EXPLAIN and ESTABLISH THE DOCTRINE OF JUSTIFICATION by FAITH ONLY. By JAMES THOMAS O'BRIEN, D.D., Bishop of Ossory. Third Edition. 8vo. 12s.

This work consists of Ten Sermons. The first four treat of the nature and mutual relations of Faith and Justification; the fifth and sixth examine the corruptions of the doctrine of Justification by Faith only, and the objections which have been urged against it. The four concluding sermons deal with the moral effects of Faith. Various Notes are added explanatory of the Author's reasoning.

Palgrave.—HYMNS. By FRANCIS TURNER PALGRAVE. Third Edition, enlarged. 18mo. 1s. 6d.

This is a collection of twenty original Hymns, which the Literary Churchman *speaks of as "so choice, so perfect, and so refined,—so tender in feeling, and so scholarly in expression."*

Paul of Tarsus. An Inquiry into the Times and the Gospel of the Apostle of the Gentiles. By a GRADUATE. 8vo. 10s. 6d.

The Author of this work has attempted, out of the materials which were at his disposal, to construct for himself a sketch of the time in which St. Paul lived, of the religious systems with which he was brought in contact, of the doctrine which he taught, and of the work which he ultimately achieved. "Turn where we will throughout the volume, we find the best fruit of patient inquiry, sound scholarship, logical argument, and fairness of conclusion. No thoughtful reader will rise from its perusal without a real and lasting profit to himself, and a sense of permanent addition to the cause of truth."—Standard.

Picton.—THE MYSTERY OF MATTER; and other Essays. By J. ALLANSON PICTON, Author of "New Theories and the Old Faith." Crown 8vo. 10s. 6d.

Contents—The Mystery of Matter: The Philosophy of Ignorance: The Antithesis of Faith and Sight: The Essential Nature of Religion: Christian Pantheism.

Prescott.—THE THREEFOLD CORD. Sermons preached before the University of Cambridge. By J. E. PRESCOTT, B.D. Fcap. 8vo. 3s. 6d.

Procter.—A HISTORY OF THE BOOK OF COMMON PRAYER: With a Rationale of its Offices. By FRANCIS PROCTER, M.A. Eleventh Edition, revised and enlarged. Crown 8vo. 10s. 6d.

The Athenæum *says:—"The origin of every part of the Prayer-book has been diligently investigated,—and there are few questions or facts connected with it which are not either sufficiently explained, or so referred to, that persons interested may work out the truth for themselves."*

Procter and Maclear.—AN ELEMENTARY INTRODUCTION TO THE BOOK OF COMMON PRAYER. Re-arranged and Supplemented by an Explanation of the Morning and Evening Prayer and the Litany. By F. PROCTER, M.A. and G. F. MACLEAR, D.D. New Edition. 18mo. 2s. 6d.

This book has the same object and follows the same plan as the Manuals already noticed under Mr. Maclear's name. Each book is subdivided into chapters and sections. In Book I. is given a detailed History of the Book of Common Prayer down to the Attempted Revision in the Reign of William III. Book II., consisting of four Parts, treats in order the various parts of the Prayer Book. Notes, etymological, historical, and critical, are given throughout the book, while the Appendix contains several articles of much interest and importance. Appended is a General Index and an Index of Words explained in the Notes. The Literary Churchman *characterizes it as "by far the completest and most satisfactory book of its kind we know. We wish it were in the hands of every schoolboy and every schoolmaster in the kingdom."*

Psalms of David CHRONOLOGICALLY ARRANGED.

An Amended Version, with Historical Introductions and Explanatory Notes. By FOUR FRIENDS. Second and Cheaper Edition, much enlarged. Crown 8vo. 8s. 6d.

One of the chief designs of the Editors, in preparing this volume, was to restore the Psalter as far as possible to the order in which the Psalms were written. They give the division of each Psalm into strophes, and of each strophe into the lines which composed it, and amend the errors of translation. The Spectator *calls it "One of the most instructive and valuable books that have been published for many years."*

Golden Treasury Psalter.—THE STUDENT'S EDITION.

Being an Edition with briefer Notes of the above. 18mo. 3s. 6d.

This volume will be found to meet the requirements of those who wish for a smaller edition of the larger work, at a lower price for family use, and for the use of younger pupils in Public Schools. The short notes which are appended to the volume will, it is hoped, suffice to make the meaning intelligible throughout. The aim of this edition is simply to put the reader as far as possible in possession of the plain meaning of the writer. "It is a gem," the Nonconformist *says.*

Ramsay.—THE CATECHISER'S MANUAL; or, the

Church Catechism Illustrated and Explained, for the Use of Clergymen, Schoolmasters, and Teachers. By ARTHUR RAMSAY, M.A. Second Edition. 18mo. 1s. 6d.

Rays of Sunlight for Dark Days. A Book of Selec-

tions for the Suffering. With a Preface by C. J. VAUGHAN, D.D. 18mo. New Edition. 3s. 6d. Also in morocco, old style.

Dr. Vaughan says in the Preface, after speaking of the general run of Books of Comfort for Mourners, "It is because I think that the little volume now offered to the Christian sufferer is one of greater wisdom and of deeper experience, that I have readily consented to the request that I would introduce it by a few words of Preface." The book consists of a series of very brief extracts from a great variety of authors, in prose and poetry, suited to the many moods of a mourning or suffering mind. "Mostly gems of the first water."—Clerical Journal.

Reynolds.—NOTES OF THE CHRISTIAN LIFE. A Selection of Sermons by HENRY ROBERT REYNOLDS, B.A., President of Cheshunt College, and Fellow of University College, London. Crown 8vo. 7s. 6d.

This work may be taken as representative of the mode of thought and feeling which is most popular amongst the freer and more cultivated Nonconformists. "It is long," says the Nonconformist, *"since we have met with any published sermons better calculated than these to stimulate devout thought, and to bring home to the soul the reality of a spiritual life."*

Roberts.—DISCUSSIONS ON THE GOSPELS. By the Rev. ALEXANDER ROBERTS, D.D. Second Edition, revised and enlarged. 8vo. 16s.

This volume is divided into two parts. Part I. "On the Language employed by our Lord and His Disciples," in which the author endeavours to prove that Greek was the language usually employed by Christ Himself, in opposition to the common belief that Our Lord spoke Aramæan. Part II. is occupied with a discussion "On the Original Language of St. Matthew's Gospel," and on "The Origin and Authenticity of the Gospels." "The author brings the valuable qualifications of learning, temper, and an independent judgment."—Daily News.

Robertson.—PASTORAL COUNSELS. Being Chapters on Practical and Devotional Subjects. By the late JOHN ROBERTSON, D.D. Third Edition, with a Preface by the Author of "The Recreations of a Country Parson." Extra fcap. 8vo. 6s.

These Sermons are the free utterances of a strong and independent thinker. He does not depart from the essential doctrines of his Church, but he expounds them in a spirit of the widest charity, and always having most prominently in view the requirements of practical life. "The sermons are admirable specimens of a practical, earnest, and instructive style of pulpit teaching."—Nonconformist.

Rowsell.—MAN'S LABOUR AND GOD'S HARVEST. Sermons preached before the University of Cambridge in Lent, 1861. Fcap. 8vo. 3s.

"We strongly recommend this little volume to young men, and especially to those who are contemplating working for Christ in Holy Orders."—Literary Churchman.

Salmon.—THE REIGN OF LAW, and other Sermons, preached in the Chapel of Trinity College, Dublin. By the Rev. GEORGE SALMON, D.D., Regius Professor of Divinity in the University of Dublin. Crown 8vo. 6s.

"Well considered, learned, and powerful discourses."--Spectator.

Sanday.—THE AUTHORSHIP AND HISTORICAL CHARACTER OF THE FOURTH GOSPEL, considered in reference to the Contents of the Gospel itself. A Critical Essay. By WILLIAM SANDAY, M.A., Fellow of Trinity College, Oxford. Crown 8vo. 8s. 6d.

The object of this Essay is critical and nothing more. The Author attempts to apply faithfully and persistently to the contents of the much disputed fourth Gospel that scientific method which has been so successful in other directions. " The facts of religion," the Author believes, "(i. e. the documents, the history of religious bodies, &c.) are as much facts as the lie of a coal-bed or the formation of a coral-reef." " The Essay is not only most valuable in itself, but full of promise for the future."— Canon Westcott in the *Academy.*

Selborne.—THE BOOK OF PRAISE : From the Best English Hymn Writers. Selected and arranged by Lord SELBORNE. With Vignette by WOOLNER. 18mo. 4s. 6d.

The present is an attempt to present, under a convenient arrangement, a collection of such examples of a copious and interesting branch of popular literature, as, after several years' study of the subject, have seemed to the Editor most worthy of being separated from the mass to which they belong. It has been the Editor's desire and aim to adhere strictly, in all cases in which it could be ascertained, to the genuine uncorrupted text of the authors themselves. The names of the authors and date of composition of the hymns, when known, are affixed, while notes are added to the volume, giving further details. The Hymns are arranged according to subjects. " There is not room for two opinions as to the value of the 'Book of Praise.'" —Guardian. *"Approaches as nearly as one can conceive to perfection."* —Nonconformist.

BOOK OF PRAISE HYMNAL. *See* end of this Catalogue.

Sergeant.—SERMONS. By the Rev. E. W. SERGEANT, M.A., Balliol College, Oxford ; Assistant Master at Westminster College. Fcap. 8vo. 2s. 6d.

Smith.—PROPHECY A PREPARATION FOR CHRIST. Eight Lectures preached before the University of Oxford, being the Bampton Lectures for 1869. By R. PAYNE SMITH, D.D., Dean of Canterbury. Second and Cheaper Edition. Crown 8vo. 6s.

*The author's object in these Lectures is to shew that there exists in the Old Testament an element, which no criticism on naturalistic principles can either account for or explain away: that element is Prophecy. The author endeavours to prove that its force does not consist merely in its predictions. "These Lectures overflow with solid learning."—*Record.

Smith.—CHRISTIAN FAITH. Sermons preached before the University of Cambridge. By W. SAUMAREZ SMITH, M.A., Principal of St. Aidan's College, Birkenhead. Fcap. 8vo. 3s. 6d.

"Appropriate and earnest sermons, suited to the practical exhortation of an educated congregation."—Guardian.

Stanley.—Works by the Very Rev. A. P. STANLEY, D.D., Dean of Westminster.

THE ATHANASIAN CREED, with a Preface on the General Recommendations of the RITUAL COMMISSION. Cr. 8vo. 2s.

The object of the work is not so much to urge the omission or change of the Athanasian Creed, as to shew that such a relaxation ought to give offence to no reasonable or religious mind. With this view, the Dean of Westminster discusses in succession—(1) *the Authorship of the Creed,* (2) *its Internal Characteristics,* (3) *the Peculiarities of its Use in the Church of England,* (4) *its Advantages and Disadvantages,* (5) *its various Interpretations, and* (6) *the Judgment passed upon it by the Ritual Commission. In conclusion, Dr. Stanley maintains that the use of the Athanasian Creed should no longer be made compulsory. "Dr. Stanley puts with admirable force the objections which may be made to the Creed; equally admirable, we think, in his statement of its advantages."*—Spectator.

THE NATIONAL THANKSGIVING. Sermons preached in Westminster Abbey. Second Edition. Crown 8vo. 2s. 6d.

These Sermons are (1) *"Death and Life," preached December* 10, 1871 ; (2) *"The Trumpet of Patmos," December* 17, 1871 ; (3) *"The Day of Thanksgiving," March* 3, 1872. *"In point of fervour and polish by far the best specimens in print of Dean Stanley's eloquent style."*—Standard.

Sunday Library.   See end of this Catalogue.

Swainson.—Works by C. A. SWAINSON, D.D., Canon of Chichester :—

THE CREEDS OF THE CHURCH IN THEIR RE- LATIONS TO HOLY SCRIPTURE and the CONSCIENCE OF THE CHRISTIAN. 8vo. cloth. 9s.

The Lectures which compose this volume discuss, amongst others, the following subjects : "Faith in God," "Exercise of our Reason," "Origin and Authority of Creeds," and "Private Judgment, its use and exercise." "Treating of abstruse points of Scripture, he applies them so forcibly to Christian duty and practice as to prove eminently serviceable to the Church."—John Bull.

Swainson (C. A.)—*continued.*

THE AUTHORITY OF THE NEW TESTAMENT, and other LECTURES, delivered before the University of Cambridge. 8vo. cloth. 12s.

The first series of Lectures in this work is on " The Words spoken by the Apostles of Jesus," " The Inspiration of God's Servants," " The Human Character of the Inspired Writers," and " The Divine Character of the Word written." The second embraces Lectures on " Sin as Imperfection," " Sin as Self-will," " Whatsoever is not of Faith is Sin," " Christ the Saviour," and " The Blood of the New Covenant." The third is on "Christians One Body in Christ," " The One Body the Spouse of Christ," " Christ's Prayer for Unity," " Our Reconciliation should be manifested in common Worship," and " Ambassadors for Christ."

Taylor.—THE RESTORATION OF BELIEF. New and Revised Edition. By ISAAC TAYLOR, Esq. Crown 8vo. 8s. 6d.

The earlier chapters are occupied with an examination of the primitive history of the Christian Religion, and its relation to the Roman government; and here, as well as in the remainder of the work, the author shews the bearing of that history on some of the difficult and interesting questions which have recently been claiming the attention of all earnest men. The last chapter of this New Edition treats of " The Present Position of the Argument concerning Christianity," with special reference to M. Renan's Vie de Jésus.

Temple.—SERMONS PREACHED IN THE CHAPEL of RUGBY SCHOOL. By F. TEMPLE, D.D., Bishop of Exeter. New and Cheaper Edition. Extra fcap. 8vo. 4s. 6d.

This volume contains Thirty-five Sermons on topics more or less intimately connected with every-day life. The following are a few of the subjects discoursed upon:—"Love and Duty;" "Coming to Christ;" "Great Men;" "Faith;" " Doubts;" " Scruples;" "Original Sin;" "Friendship;" "Helping Others;" " The Discipline of Temptation;" "Strength a Duty;" "Worldliness;" "Ill Temper;" " The Burial of the Past."

A SECOND SERIES OF SERMONS PREACHED IN THE CHAPEL OF RUGBY SCHOOL. Second Edition. Extra fcap. 8vo. 6s.

This Second Series of Forty-two brief, pointed, practical Sermons, on topics intimately connected with the every-day life of young and old, will be acceptable to all who are acquainted with the First Series. The following are a few of the subjects treated of:—"Disobedience," "Almsgiving," " The Unknown Guidance of God," "Apathy one of our Trials," "High Aims in Leaders," "Doing our Best," " The Use of Knowledge," "Use of Observances," "Martha and Mary," "John the Baptist," "Severity

Temple (F., D.D.)—*continued.*

before Mercy," "Even Mistakes Punished," "Morality and Religion," "Children," "Action the Test of Spiritual Life," "Self-Respect," "Too Late," "The Tercentenary."

A THIRD SERIES OF SERMONS PREACHED IN RUGBY SCHOOL CHAPEL IN 1867—1869.　Extra fcap. 8vo.　6s.

This third series of Bishop Temple's Rugby Sermons, contains thirty-six brief discourses, including the " Good-bye" sermon preached on his leaving Rugby to enter on the office he now holds.

Thring.—Works by Rev. EDWARD THRING, M.A.

SERMONS DELIVERED AT UPPINGHAM SCHOOL.　Crown 8vo.　5s.

In this volume are contained Forty-seven brief Sermons, all on subjects more or less intimately connected with Public-school life.　"We desire very highly to commend these capital Sermons which treat of a boy's life and trials in a thoroughly practical way and with great simplicity and impressiveness.　They deserve to be classed with the best of their kind."—
Literary Churchman.

THOUGHTS ON LIFE-SCIENCE.　New Edition, enlarged and revised.　Crown 8vo.　7s. 6d.

In this volume are discussed in a familiar manner some of the most interesting problems between Science and Religion, Reason and Feeling.

Tracts for Priests and People.　By VARIOUS WRITERS.

THE FIRST SERIES.　Crown 8vo.　8s.

THE SECOND SERIES.　Crown 8vo.　8s.

The whole Series of Fifteen Tracts may be had separately, price One Shilling each.

Trench.—Works by R. CHENEVIX TRENCH, D.D., Archbishop of Dublin.　(For other Works by the same author, *see* BIOGRAPHICAL, BELLES LETTRES, and LINGUISTIC CATALOGUES).

NOTES ON THE PARABLES OF OUR LORD.　Twelfth Edition.　8vo.　12s.

This work has taken its place as a standard exposition and interpretation of Christ's Parables.　The book is prefaced by an Introductory Essay in four chapters:—I. On the definition of the Parable.　II. On Teaching by Parables.　III. On the Interpretation of the Parables.　IV. On other Parables besides those in the Scriptures.　The author then proceeds to take up the Parables one by one, and by the aid of philology, history,

Trench—*continued.*

antiquities, and the researches of travellers, shews forth the significance, beauty, and applicability of each, concluding with what he deems its true moral interpretation. In the numerous Notes are many valuable references, illustrative quotations, critical and philological annotations, etc., and appended to the volume is a classified list of fifty-six works on the Parables.

NOTES ON THE MIRACLES OF OUR LORD.
Ninth Edition. 8vo. 12s.

In the 'Preliminary Essay' to this work, all the momentous and interesting questions that have been raised in connection with Miracles, are discussed with considerable fulness. The Essay consists of six chapters:— I. On the Names of Miracles, i. e. the Greek words by which they are designated in the New Testament. II. The Miracles and Nature—What is the difference between a Miracle and any event in the ordinary course of Nature? III. The Authority of Miracles—Is the Miracle to command absolute obedience? IV. The Evangelical, compared with the other cycles of Miracles. V. The Assaults on the Miracles—1. The Jewish. 2. The Heathen (Celsus etc.). 3. The Pantheistic (Spinosa etc.). 4. The Sceptical (Hume). 5. The Miracles only relatively miraculous (Schleiermacher). 6. The Rationalistic (Paulus). 7. The Historico-Critical (Woolston, Strauss). VI. The Apologetic Worth of the Miracles. The author then treats the separate Miracles as he does the Parables.

SYNONYMS OF THE NEW TESTAMENT. New
Edition, enlarged. 8vo. cloth. 12s.

The study of synonyms in any language is valuable as a discipline for training the mind to close and accurate habits of thought; more especially is this the case in Greek—" a language spoken by a people of the finest and subtlest intellect; who saw distinctions where others saw none; who divided out to different words what others often were content to huddle confusedly under a common term. . . . Where is it so desirable that we should miss nothing, that we should lose no finer intention of the writer, as in those words which are the vehicles of the very mind of God Himself?" This Edition has been carefully revised, and a considerable number of new synonyms added. Appended is an Index to the Synonyms, and an Index to many other words alluded to or explained throughout the work. "He is," the Athenæum *says, " a guide in this department of knowledge to whom his readers may intrust themselves with confidence. His sober judgment and sound sense are barriers against the misleading influence of arbitrary hypotheses."*

ON THE AUTHORIZED VERSION OF THE NEW
TESTAMENT. Second Edition. 8vo. 7s.

After some Introductory Remarks, in which the propriety of a revision is briefly discussed, the whole question of the merits of the present version is gone into in detail, in eleven chapters. Appended is a chronological list

Trench—*continued.*

of works bearing on the subject, an Index of the principal Texts considered, an Index of Greek Words, and an Index of other Words referred to throughout the book.

STUDIES IN THE GOSPELS. Third Edition. 8vo. 10s. 6d.

This book is published under the conviction that the assertion often made is untrue,—viz. that the Gospels are in the main plain and easy, and that all the chief difficulties of the New Testament are to be found in the Epistles. These "Studies," sixteen in number, are the fruit of a much larger scheme, and each Study deals with some important episode mentioned in the Gospels, in a critical, philosophical, and practical manner. Many references and quotations are added to the Notes. Among the subjects treated are:—The Temptation; Christ and the Samaritan Woman; The Three Aspirants; The Transfiguration; Zacchæus; The True Vine; The Penitent Malefactor; Christ and the Two Disciples on the way to Emmaus.

COMMENTARY ON THE EPISTLES to the SEVEN CHURCHES IN ASIA. Third Edition, revised. 8vo. 8s. 6d.

The present work consists of an Introduction, being a commentary on Rev. i. 4—20, a detailed examination of each of the Seven Epistles, in all its bearings, and an Excursus on the Historico-Prophetical Interpretation of the Epistles.

THE SERMON ON THE MOUNT. An Exposition drawn from the writings of St. Augustine, with an Essay on his merits as an Interpreter of Holy Scripture. Third Edition, enlarged. 8vo. 10s. 6d.

The first half of the present work consists of a dissertation in eight chapters on "Augustine as an Interpreter of Scripture," the titles of the several chapters being as follow:—I. Augustine's General Views of Scripture and its Interpretation. II. The External Helps for the Interpretation of Scripture possessed by Augustine. III. Augustine's Principles and Canons of Interpretation. IV. Augustine's Allegorical Interpretation of Scripture. V. Illustrations of Augustine's Skill as an Interpreter of Scripture. VI. Augustine on John the Baptist and on St. Stephen. VII. Augustine on the Epistle to the Romans. VIII. Miscellaneous Examples of Augustine's Interpretation of Scripture. The latter half of the work consists of Augustine's Exposition of the Sermon on the Mount, not however a mere series of quotations from Augustine, but a connected account of his sentiments on the various passages of that Sermon, interspersed with criticisms by Archbishop Trench.

SERMONS PREACHED in WESTMINSTER ABBEY. Second Edition. 8vo. 10s. 6d.

These Sermons embrace a wide variety of topics, and are thoroughly

Trench—*continued.*

practical, earnest, and evangelical, and simple in style. The following are a few of the subjects:—"Tercentenary Celebration of Queen Elizabeth's Accession;" "Conviction and Conversion;" "The Incredulity of Thomas;" "The Angels' Hymn;" "Counting the Cost;" "The Holy Trinity in Relation to our Prayers;" "On the Death of General Havelock;" "Christ Weeping over Jerusalem;" "Walking with Christ in White."

SHIPWRECKS OF FAITH. Three Sermons preached before the University of Cambridge in May, 1867. Fcap. 8vo. 2s. 6d.

These Sermons are especially addressed to young men. The subjects are "Balaam," "Saul," and "Judas Iscariot." These lives are set forth as beacon-lights, "to warn us off from perilous reefs and quicksands, which have been the destruction of many, and which might only too easily be ours." The John Bull *says, "they are, like all he writes, affectionate and earnest discourses."*

SERMONS Preached for the most part in Ireland. 8vo. 10s. 6d.

This volume consists of Thirty-two Sermons, the greater part of which were preached in Ireland ; the subjects are as follows:—Jacob, a Prince with God and with Men—Agrippa—The Woman that was a Sinner—Secret Faults—The Seven Worse Spirits—Freedom in the Truth—Joseph and his Brethren—Bearing one another's Burdens—Christ's Challenge to the World—The Love of Money—The Salt of the Earth—The Armour of God—Light in the Lord—The Jailer of Philippi—The Thorn in the Flesh—Isaiah's Vision—Selfishness—Abraham interceding for Sodom—Vain Thoughts—Pontius Pilate—The Brazen Serpent—The Death and Burial of Moses—A Word from the Cross—The Church's Worship in the Beauty of Holiness—Every Good Gift from Above—On the Hearing of Prayer—The Kingdom which cometh not with Observation—Pressing towards the Mark—Saul—The Good Shepherd—The Valley of Dry Bones—All Saints.

Tudor.—The DECALOGUE VIEWED as the CHRISTIAN'S LAW. With Special Reference to the Questions and Wants of the Times. By the Rev. RICH. TUDOR, B.A. Crown 8vo. 10s. 6d.

The author's aim is to bring out the Christian sense of the Decalogue in its application to existing needs and questions. The work will be found to occupy ground which no other single work has hitherto filled. It is divided into Two Parts, the First Part consisting of three lectures on "Duty," and the Second Part of twelve lectures on the Ten Commandments. The Guardian *says of it, "His volume throughout is an outspoken and sound exposition of Christian morality, based deeply upon true foundations, set forth systematically, and forcibly and plainly expressed—as good la specimen of what pulpit lectures ought to be as is often to be found."*

Tulloch.—THE CHRIST OF THE GOSPELS AND THE CHRIST OF MODERN CRITICISM. Lectures on M. RENAN's "Vie de Jésus." By JOHN TULLOCH, D.D., Principal of the College of St. Mary, in the University of St. Andrew's. Extra fcap. 8vo. 4*s.* 6*d.*

Vaughan.—Works by CHARLES J. VAUGHAN, D.D., Master of the Temple :—

CHRIST SATISFYING THE INSTINCTS OF HU-MANITY. Eight Lectures delivered in the Temple Church. New Edition. Extra fcp. 8vo. 3*s.* 6*d.*

The object of these Sermons is to exhibit the spiritual wants of human nature, and to prove that all of them receive full satisfaction in Christ. The various instincts which He is shewn to meet are those of Truth, Reverence, Perfection, Liberty, Courage, Sympathy, Sacrifice, and Unity. "We are convinced that there are congregations, in number unmistakeably increasing, to whom such Essays as these, full of thought and learning, are infinitely more beneficial, for they are more acceptable, than the recognised type of sermons."—John Bull.

MEMORIALS OF HARROW SUNDAYS. A Selection of Sermons preached in Harrow School Chapel. With a View of the Chapel. Fourth Edition. Crown 8vo. 10*s.* 6*d.*

"Discussing," says the John Bull, *" those forms of evil and impediments to duty which peculiarly beset the young, Dr. Vaughan has, with singular tact, blended deep thought and analytical investigation of principles with interesting earnestness and eloquent simplicity."* The Nonconformist *says " the volume is a precious one for family reading, and for the hand of the thoughtful boy or young man entering life."*

THE BOOK AND THE LIFE, and other Sermons, preached before the University of Cambridge. New Edition. Fcap. 8vo. 4*s.* 6*d.*

These Sermons are all of a thoroughly practical nature, and some of them are especially adapted to those who are in a state of anxious doubt.

TWELVE DISCOURSES on SUBJECTS CONNECTED WITH THE LITURGY and WORSHIP of the CHURCH OF ENGLAND. Fcap. 8vo. 6*s.*

Four of these discourses were published in 1860, *in a work entitled* Revision of the Liturgy ; *four others have appeared in the form of separate sermons, delivered on various occasions, and published at the time by request ; and four are new. The Appendix contains two articles,—one on "Subscription and Scruples," the other on the "Rubric and the Burial Service."* The Press *characterises the volume as " eminently wise and temperate."*

Vaughan (Dr. C. J.)—*continued.*

LESSONS OF LIFE AND GODLINESS. A Selection of Sermons preached in the Parish Church of Doncaster. Fourth and Cheaper Edition. Fcap. 8vo. 3*s.* 6*d.*

This volume consists of Nineteen Sermons, mostly on subjects connected with the every-day walk and conversation of Christians. They bear such titles as "The Talebearer," "Features of Charity," "The Danger of Relapse," "The Secret Life and the Outward," "Family Prayer," "Zeal without Consistency," "The Gospel an Incentive to Industry in Business," "Use and Abuse of the World." The Spectator *styles them "earnest and human. They are adapted to every class and order in the social system, and will be read with wakeful interest by all who seek to amend whatever may be amiss in their natural disposition or in their acquired habits."*

WORDS FROM THE GOSPELS. A Second Selection of Sermons preached in the Parish Church of Doncaster. Second Edition. Fcap. 8vo. 4*s.* 6*d.*

The Nonconformist *characterises these Sermons as "of practical earnestness, of a thoughtfulness that penetrates the common conditions and experiences of life, and brings the truths and examples of Scripture to bear on them with singular force, and of a style that owes its real elegance to the simplicity and directness which have fine culture for their roots.*

LESSONS OF THE CROSS AND PASSION. Six Lectures delivered in Hereford Cathedral during the Week before Easter, 1869. Fcap. 8vo. 2*s.* 6*d.*

The titles of the Sermons are:—I. "Too Late" (Matt. xxvi. 45). II. "The Divine Sacrifice and the Human Priesthood." III. "Love not the World." IV. "The Moral Glory of Christ." V. "Christ made perfect through Suffering." VI. "Death the Remedy of Christ's Loneliness." "This little volume," the Nonconformist *says, "exhibits all his best characteristics. Elevated, calm, and clear, the Sermons owe much to their force, and yet they seem literally to owe nothing to it. They are studied, but their grace is the grace of perfect simplicity."*

LIFE'S WORK AND GOD'S DISCIPLINE. Three Sermons. New Edition. Fcap. 8vo. 2*s.* 6*d.*

The Three Sermons are on the following subjects:—I. "The Work burned and the Workmen saved." II. "The Individual Hiring." III. "The Remedial Discipline of Disease and Death."

THE WHOLESOME WORDS OF JESUS CHRIST. Four Sermons preached before the University of Cambridge in November 1866. Second Edition. Fcap. 8vo. cloth. 3*s.* 6*d.*

Dr. Vaughan uses the word "Wholesome" here in its literal and original sense, the sense in which St. Paul uses it, as meaning healthy,

Vaughan (Dr. C. J.)—*continued.*

sound, conducing to right living ; *and in these Sermons he points out and illustrates several of the "wholesome" characteristics of the Gospel,—the Words of Christ. The* John Bull *says this volume is "replete with all the author's well-known vigour of thought and richness of expression."*

FOES OF FAITH. Sermons preached before the University of Cambridge in November 1868. Fcap. 8vo. 3s. 6d.

The "Foes of Faith" preached against in these Four Sermons are:—I. "Unreality." II. "Indolence." III. "Irreverence." IV. "Inconsistency." "They are written," the London Review *says, "with culture and elegance, and exhibit the thoughtful earnestness, piety, and good sense of their author."*

LECTURES ON THE EPISTLE to the PHILIPPIANS. Third and Cheaper Edition. Extra fcap. 8vo. 5s.

Each Lecture is prefaced by a literal translation from the Greek of the paragraph which forms its subject, contains first a minute explanation of the passage on which it is based, and then a practical application of the verse or clause selected as its text.

LECTURES ON THE REVELATION OF ST. JOHN. Third and Cheaper Edition. Two Vols. Extra fcap. 8vo. 9s.

In this Edition of these Lectures, the literal translations of the passages expounded will be found interwoven in the body of the Lectures themselves. In attempting to expound this most-hard-to-understand Book, Dr. Vaughan, while taking from others what assistance he required, has not adhered to any particular school of interpretation, but has endeavoured to shew forth the significance of this Revelation by the help of his strong common sense, critical acumen, scholarship, and reverent spirit. "Dr. Vaughan's Sermons," the Spectator *says, "are the most practical discourses on the Apocalypse with which we are acquainted." Prefixed is a Synopsis of the Book of Revelation, and appended is an Index of passages illustrating the language of the Book.*

EPIPHANY, LENT, AND EASTER. A Selection of Expository Sermons. Third Edition. Crown 8vo. 10s. 6d.

The first eighteen of these Sermons were preached during the seasons of 1860, indicated in the title, and are practical expositions of passages taken from the lessons of the days on which they were delivered. Each Lecture is prefaced with a careful and literal rendering of the original of the passage of which the Lecture is an exposition. The Nonconformist *says that "in simplicity, dignity, close adherence to the words of Scripture, insight into ' the mind of the Spirit,' and practical thoughtfulness, they are models of that species of pulpit instruction to which they belong."*

THE EPISTLES OF ST. PAUL. For English Readers. Part I., containing the First Epistle to the Thessalonians. Second Edition. 8vo. 1s. 6d.

Vaughan (Dr. C. J.)—*continued.*

It is the object of this work to enable English readers, unacquainted with Greek, to enter with intelligence into the meaning, connection, and phraseology of the writings of the great Apostle.

ST. PAUL'S EPISTLE TO THE ROMANS. The Greek Text, with English Notes. Fourth Edition. Crown 8vo. 7s. 6d.

This volume contains the Greek Text of the Epistle to the Romans as settled by the Rev. B. F. Westcott, D.D., for his complete recension of the Text of the New Testament. Appended to the text are copious critical and exegetical Notes, the result of almost eighteen years' study on the part of the author. The "Index of Words illustrated or explained in the Notes" will be found, in some considerable degree, an Index to the Epistles as a whole. Prefixed to the volume is a discourse on "St. Paul's Conversion and Doctrine," suggested by some recent publications on St. Paul's theological standing. The Guardian *says of the work,—"For educated young men his commentary seems to fill a gap hitherto unfilled. . . . As a whole, Dr. Vaughan appears to us to have given to the world a valuable book of original and careful and earnest thought bestowed on the accomplishment of a work which will be of much service and which is much needed."*

THE CHURCH OF THE FIRST DAYS.

Series I. The Church of Jerusalem. Third Edition.
" II. The Church of the Gentiles. Second Edition.
" III. The Church of the World. Second Edition.
Fcap. 8vo. cloth. 4s. 6d. each.

Where necessary, the Authorized Version has been departed from, and a new literal translation taken as the basis of exposition. All possible topographical and historical light has been brought to bear on the subject; and while thoroughly practical in their aim, these Lectures will be found to afford a fair notion of the history and condition of the Primitive Church. The British Quarterly *says,—"These Sermons are worthy of all praise, and are models of pulpit teaching."*

COUNSELS for YOUNG STUDENTS. Three Sermons preached before the University of Cambridge at the Opening of the Academical Year 1870-71. Fcap. 8vo. 2s. 6d.

The titles of the Three Sermons contained in this volume are:—I. "The Great Decision." II. "The House and the Builder." III. "The Prayer and the Counter-Prayer." They all bear pointedly, earnestly, and sympathisingly upon the conduct and pursuits of young students and young men generally.

NOTES FOR LECTURES ON CONFIRMATION, with suitable Prayers. Eighth Edition. Fcap. 8vo. 1s. 6d.

In preparation for the Confirmation held in Harrow School Chapel, Dr. Vaughan was in the habit of printing week by week, and distributing among the Candidates, somewhat full notes of the Lecture he purposed to

Vaughan (Dr. C. J.)—*continued.*

deliver to them, together with a form of Prayer adapted to the particular subject.   He has collected these weekly Notes and Prayers into this little volume, in the hope that it may assist the labours of those who are engaged in preparing Candidates for Confirmation, and who find it difficult to lay their hand upon any one book of suitable instruction.

THE TWO GREAT TEMPTATIONS.   The Temptation of Man, and the Temptation of Christ.   Lectures delivered in the Temple Church, Lent 1872.   Extra fcap. 8vo.   3*s.* 6*d.*

Vaughan.—Works by DAVID J. VAUGHAN, M.A., Vicar of St. Martin's, Leicester :—

SERMONS PREACHED IN ST. JOHN'S CHURCH, LEICESTER, during the Years 1855 and 1856.   Cr. 8vo.   5*s.* 6*d.*

CHRISTIAN EVIDENCES AND THE BIBLE.   New Edition, revised and enlarged.   Fcap. 8vo. cloth.   5*s.* 6*d.*

"This little volume," the Spectator *says, "is a model of that honest and reverent criticism of the Bible which is not only right, but the duty of English clergymen in such times as these to put forth from the pulpit."*

Venn.—ON SOME OF THE CHARACTERISTICS OF BELIEF, Scientific and Religious.   Being the Hulsean Lectures for 1869.   By the Rev. J. VENN, M.A.   8vo.   6*s.* 6*d.*

These discourses are intended to illustrate, explain, and work out into some of their consequences, certain characteristics by which the attainment of religious belief is prominently distinguished from the attainment of belief upon most other subjects.

Warington.—THE WEEK OF CREATION; OR, THE COSMOGONY OF GENESIS CONSIDERED IN ITS RELATION TO MODERN SCIENCE.   By GEORGE WARINGTON, Author of "The Historic Character of the Pentateuch Vindicated."   Crown 8vo.   4*s.* 6*d.*

*The greater part of this work is taken up with the teaching of the Cosmogony.   Its purpose is also investigated, and a chapter is devoted to the consideration of the passage in which the difficulties occur.   "A very able vindication of the Mosaic Cosmogony by a writer who unites the advantages of a critical knowledge of the Hebrew text and of distinguished scientific attainments."—*Spectator.

Westcott.—Works by BROOKE FOSS WESTCOTT, D.D., Regius Professor of Divinity in the University of Cambridge; Canon of Peterborough :—

The London Quarterly, *speaking of Mr. Westcott, says,—"To a learning and accuracy which command respect and confidence, he unites what are not always to be found in union with these qualities, the no less valuable faculties of lucid arrangement and graceful and facile expression."*

Westcott (Dr. B. F.)—*continued.*

AN INTRODUCTION TO THE STUDY OF THE GOSPELS. Fourth Edition. Crown 8vo. 10s. 6d.

The author's chief object in this work has been to shew that there is a true mean between the idea of a formal harmonization of the Gospels and the abandonment of their absolute truth. After an Introduction on the General Effects of the course of Modern Philosophy on the popular views of Christianity, he proceeds to determine in what way the principles therein indicated may be applied to the study of the Gospels. The treatise is divided into eight Chapters:—I. The Preparation for the Gospel. II. The Jewish Doctrine of the Messiah. III. The Origin of the Gospels. IV. The Characteristics of the Gospels. V. The Gospel of St. John. VI. and VII. The Differences in detail and of arrangement in the Synoptic Evangelists. VIII. The Difficulties of the Gospels. The Appendices contain much valuable subsidiary matter.

A GENERAL SURVEY OF THE HISTORY OF THE CANON OF THE NEW TESTAMENT DURING THE FIRST FOUR CENTURIES. Third Edition, revised. Crown 8vo. 10s. 6d.

The object of this treatise is to deal with the New Testament as a whole, and that on purely historical grounds. The separate books of which it is composed are considered not individually, but as claiming to be parts of the apostolic heritage of Christians. The Author has thus endeavoured to connect the history of the New Testament Canon with the growth and consolidation of the Catholic Church, and to point out the relation existing between the amount of evidence for the authenticity of its component parts and the whole mass of Christian literature. "The treatise," says the British Quarterly, *"is a scholarly performance, learned, dispassionate, discriminating, worthy of his subject and of the present state of Christian literature in relation to it."*

THE BIBLE IN THE CHURCH. A Popular Account of the Collection and Reception of the Holy Scriptures in the Christian Churches. New Edition. 18mo. 4s. 6d.

The present volume has been written under the impression that a History of the whole Bible, and not of the New Testament only, would be required, if those unfamiliar with the subject were to be enabled to learn in what manner and with what consent the collection of Holy Scriptures was first made and then enlarged and finally closed by the Church. Though the work is intended to be simple and popular in its method, the author, for this very reason, has aimed at the strictest accuracy.

A GENERAL VIEW OF THE HISTORY OF THE ENGLISH BIBLE. Second Edition. Crown 8vo. 10s. 6d.

In the Introduction the author notices briefly the earliest vernacular versions of the Bible, especially those in Anglo-Saxon. Chapter I. is oc-

Westcott (Dr. B. F.)—*continued.*

cupied with an account of the Manuscript English Bible from the 14th century downwards; and in Chapter II. is narrated, with many interesting personal and other details, the External History of the Printed Bible. In Chapter III. is set forth the Internal History of the English Bible, shewing to what extent the various English Translations were independent, and to what extent the translators were indebted to earlier English and foreign versions. In the Appendices, among other interesting and valuable matter, will be found "Specimens of the Earlier and Later Wycliffite Versions;" "Chronological List of Bibles;" "An Examination of Mr. Froude's History of the English Bible." The Pall Mall Gazette *calls the work "A brief, scholarly, and, to a great extent, an original contribution to theological literature."*

THE CHRISTIAN LIFE, MANIFOLD AND ONE. Six Sermons preached in Peterborough Cathedral. Crown 8vo. 2s. 6d.

The Six Sermons contained in this volume are the first preached by the author as a Canon of Peterborough Cathedral. The subjects are:— I. "Life consecrated by the Ascension." II. "Many Gifts, One Spirit." III. "The Gospel of the Resurrection." IV. "Sufficiency of God." V. "Action the Test of Faith." VI. "Progress from the Confession of God." The Nonconformist *calls them "Beautiful discourses, singularly devout and tender."*

THE GOSPEL OF THE RESURRECTION. Thoughts on its Relation to Reason and History. Third Edition. Fcap. 8vo. 4s. 6d.

The present Essay is an endeavour to consider some of the elementary truths of Christianity, as a miraculous Revelation, from the side of History and Reason. The author endeavours to shew that a devout belief in the Life of Christ is quite compatible with a broad view of the course of human progress and a frank trust in the laws of our own minds. In the third edition the author has carefully reconsidered the whole argument, and by the help of several kind critics has been enabled to correct some faults and to remove some ambiguities, which had been overlooked before. He has not however made any attempt to alter the general character of the book.

ON THE RELIGIOUS OFFICE OF THE UNIVERSITIES. Crown 8vo. 4s. 6d.

"There is certainly, no man of our time—no man at least who has obtained the command of the public ear—whose utterances can compare with those of Professor Westcott for largeness of views and comprehensiveness of grasp...... There is wisdom, and truth, and thought enough, and a harmony and mutual connection running through them all, which makes the collection of more real value than many an ambitious treatise."— Literary Churchman.

Wilkins.—THE LIGHT OF THE WORLD. An Essay, by A. S. WILKINS, M.A., Professor of Latin in Owens College, Manchester. Second Edition. Crown 8vo. 3*s.* 6*d.*

This is the Hulsean Prize Essay for 1869. *The subject proposed by the Trustees was, "The Distinctive Features of Christian as compared with Pagan Ethics." The author has tried to show that the Christian ethics so far transcend the ethics of any or all of the Pagan systems in method, in purity and in power, as to compel us to assume for them an origin, differing in kind from the origin of any purely human system. "It would be difficult to praise too highly the spirit, the burden, the conclusions, or the scholarly finish of this beautiful Essay."*—British Quarterly Review.

Wilson.—RELIGIO CHEMICI. With a Vignette beautifully engraved after a Design by Sir NOEL PATON. By GEORGE WILSON, M.D. Crown 8vo. 8*s.* 6*d.*

"George Wilson," says the Preface to this volume, "had it in his heart for many years to write a book corresponding to the Religio Medici *of Sir Thomas Browne, with the title* Religio Chemici. *Several of the Essays in this volume were intended to form chapters of it, but the health and leisure necessary to carry out his plans were never attainable, and thus fragments only of the designed work exist. These fragments, however, being in most cases like finished gems waiting to be set, some of them are now given in a collected form to his friends and the public."—"A more fascinating volume," the* Spectator *says, "has seldom fallen into our hands."*

Wilson.—THE BIBLE STUDENT'S GUIDE TO THE MORE CORRECT UNDERSTANDING of the ENGLISH TRANSLATION OF THE OLD TESTAMENT, BY REFERENCE TO THE ORIGINAL HEBREW. By WILLIAM WILSON, D.D., Canon of Winchester. Second Edition, carefully revised. 4to. 25*s.*

"The author believes that the present work is the nearest approach to a complete Concordance of every word in the original that has yet been made: and as a Concordance, it may be found of great use to the Bible student, while at the same time it serves the important object of furnishing the means of comparing synonymous words, and of eliciting their precise and distinctive meaning. The knowledge of the Hebrew language is not absolutely necessary to the profitable use of the work. The plan of the work is simple: every word occurring in the English Version is arranged alphabetically, and under it is given the Hebrew word or words, with a full explanation of their meaning, of which it is meant to be a translation, and a complete list of the passages where it occurs. Following the general work is a complete Hebrew and English Index, which is, in effect, a Hebrew-English Dictionary.

Worship (The) of God and Fellowship among Men. Sermons on Public Worship. By Professor MAURICE, and others. Fcap. 8vo. 3*s.* 6*d.*

This volume consists of Six Sermons preached by various clergymen, and although not addressed specially to any class, were suggested by recent efforts to bring the members of the Working Class to our Churches. The preachers were—Professor Maurice, Rev. T. J. Rowsell, Rev. J. Ll. Davies, Rev. D. J. Vaughan.

Yonge (Charlotte M.)—SCRIPTURE READINGS for SCHOOLS AND FAMILIES. By CHARLOTTE M. YONGE, Author of "The Heir of Redclyffe." Globe 8vo. 1*s.* 6*d.* With Comments. 3*s.* 6*d.*

SECOND SERIES. From Joshua to Solomon. Extra fcap. 8vo. 1*s.* 6*d.* With Comments. 3*s.* 6*d.*

THIRD SERIES. The Kings and Prophets. Extra fcap. 8vo., 1*s.* 6*d.*, with Comments, 3*s.* 6*d.*

*Actual need has led the author to endeavour to prepare a reading book convenient for study with children, containing the very words of the Bible, with only a few expedient omissions, and arranged in Lessons of such length as by experience she has found to suit with children's ordinary power of accurate attentive interest. The verse form has been retained because of its convenience for children reading in class, and as more resembling their Bibles; but the poetical portions have been given in their lines. Professor Huxley at a meeting of the London School-board, particularly mentioned the Selection made by Miss Yonge, as an example of how selections might be made for School reading. "Her Comments are models of their kind."—*Literary Churchman.

....

In crown 8vo. cloth extra, Illustrated, price 4*s.* 6*d.* each Volume; also kept in morocco and calf bindings at moderate prices, and in Ornamental Boxes containing Four Vols., 21*s.* each.

MACMILLAN'S SUNDAY LIBRARY.

A SERIES OF ORIGINAL WORKS BY EMINENT AUTHORS.

The Guardian *says—"All Christian households owe a debt of gratitude to Mr. Macmillan for that useful ' Sunday Library.'"*

THE FOLLOWING VOLUMES ARE NOW READY:—

The Pupils of St. John the Divine.—By CHARLOTTE M. YONGE, Author of "The Heir of Redclyffe."

The author first gives a full sketch of the life and work of the Apostle himself, drawing the material from all the most trustworthy authorities, sacred and profane; then follow the lives of his immediate disciples, Ignatius,

Quadratus, Polycarp, and others; which are succeeded by the lives of many of their pupils. She then proceeds to sketch from their foundation the history of the many churches planted or superintended by St. John and his pupils, both in the East and West. In the last chapter is given an account of the present aspect of the Churches of St. John,—the Seven Churches of Asia mentioned in Revelations; *also those of Athens, of Nîmes, of Lyons, and others in the West. "Young and old will be equally refreshed and taught by these pages, in which nothing is dull, and nothing is far-fetched."*—Churchman.

The Hermits.—By Canon Kingsley.

The volume contains the lives of some of the most remarkable early Egyptian, Syrian, Persian, and Western hermits. The lives are mostly translations from the original biographies. "It is from first to last a production full of interest, written with a liberal appreciation of what is memorable for good in the lives of the Hermits, and with a wise forbearance towards legends which may be due to the ignorance, and, no doubt, also to the strong faith of the early chroniclers."—London Review.

Seekers after God.—Lives of Seneca, Epictetus, and Marcus Aurelius. By the Rev. F. W. Farrar, M.A., F.R.S., Head Master of Marlborough College.

In this volume the author seeks to record the lives, and gives copious samples of the almost Christ-like utterances of, with perhaps the exception of Socrates, "the best and holiest characters presented to us in the records of antiquity." The volume contains portraits of Aurelius, Seneca, and Antoninus Pius. "We can heartily recommend it as healthy in tone, instructive, interesting, mentally and spiritually stimulating and nutritious."—Nonconformist.

England's Antiphon.—By George Macdonald.

This volume deals chiefly with the lyric or song-form of English religious poetry, other kinds, however, being not infrequently introduced. The author has sought to trace the course of our religious poetry from the 13th to the 19th centuries, from before Chaucer to Tennyson. He endeavours to accomplish his object by selecting the men who have produced the finest religious poetry, setting forth the circumstances in which they were placed, characterising the men themselves, critically estimating their productions, and giving ample specimens of their best religious lyrics, and quotations from larger poems, illustrating the religious feeling of the poets or their times. "Dr. Macdonald has very successfully endeavoured to bring together in his little book a whole series of the sweet singers of England, and makes them raise, one after the other, their voices in praise of God."—Guardian.

Great Christians of France: St. Louis and Calvin. By M. Guizot.

From among French Catholics, M. Guizot has, in this volume, selected

Louis, King of France in the 13*th century, and among Protestants, Calvin the Reformer in the* 16*th century, "as two earnest and illustrious representatives of the Christian faith and life, as well as of the loftiest thought and purest morality of their country and generation." In setting forth with considerable fulness the lives of these prominent and representative Christian men, M. Guizot necessarily introduces much of the political and religious history of the periods during which they lived. "A very interesting book," says the* Guardian.

Christian Singers of Germany. — By CATHERINE WINKWORTH.

In this volume the authoress gives an account of the principal hymn-writers of Germany from the 9*th to the* 19*th century, introducing ample specimens from their best productions. In the translations, while the English is perfectly idiomatic and harmonious, the characteristic differences of the poems have been carefully imitated, and the general style and metre retained. "Miss Winkworth's volume of this series is, according to our view, the choicest production of her pen."—*British Quarterly Review.

Apostles of Mediæval Europe.—By the Rev. G. F. MACLEAR, D.D., Head Master of King's College School, London.

In two Introductory Chapters the author notices some of the chief characteristics of the mediæval period itself; gives a graphic sketch of the devastated state of Europe at the beginning of that period, and an interesting account of the religions of the three great groups of vigorous barbarians— the Celts, the Teutons, and the Sclaves—who had, wave after wave, overflowed its surface. He then proceeds to sketch the lives and work of the chief of the courageous men who devoted themselves to the stupendous task of their conversion and civilization, during a period extending from the 5*th to the* 13*th century; such as St. Patrick, St. Columba, St. Columbanus, St. Augustine of Canterbury, St. Boniface, St. Olaf, St. Cyril, Raymond Sull, and others. "Mr. Maclear will have done a great work if his admirable little volume shall help to break up the dense ignorance which is still prevailing among people at large."—*Literary Churchman.

Alfred the Great.—By THOMAS HUGHES, Author of "Tom Brown's School Days." Third Edition.

"The time is come when we English can no longer stand by as interested spectators only, but in which every one of our institutions will be sifted with rigour, and will have to shew cause for its existence..... As a help in this search, this life of the typical English King is here offered." Besides other illustrations in the volume, a Map of England is prefixed, shewing its divisions about 1000 A.D., *as well as at the present time. "Mr. Hughes has indeed written a good book, bright and readable we need hardly say, and of a very considerable historical value."—* Spectator.

Nations Around.—By Miss A. KEARY.

This volume contains many details concerning the social and political life, the religion, the superstitions, the literature, the architecture, the commerce, the industry, of the Nations around Palestine, an acquaintance with which is necessary in order to a clear and full understanding of the history of the Hebrew people.   The authoress has brought to her aid all the most recent investigations into the early history of these nations, referring frequently to the fruitful excavations which have brought to light the ruins and hieroglyphic writings of many of their buried cities.   "Miss Keary has skilfully availed herself of the opportunity to write a pleasing and instructive book."—Guardian.   *"A valuable and interesting volume."*—Illustrated Times.

St. Anselm.—By the Very Rev. R. W. CHURCH, M.A., Dean of St. Paul's.   Second Edition.

In this biography of St. Anselm, while the story of his life as a man, a Christian, a clergyman, and a politician, is told impartially and fully, much light is shed on the ecclesiastical and political history of the time during which he lived, and on the internal economy of the monastic establishments of the period.   The author has drawn his materials from contemporary biographers and chroniclers, while at the same time he has consulted the best recent authors who have treated of the man and his time.   "It is a sketch by the hand of a master, with every line marked by taste, learning, and real apprehension of the subject."—Pall Mall Gazette.

Francis of Assisi.—By Mrs. OLIPHANT.

The life of this saint, the founder of the Franciscan order, and one of the most remarkable men of his time, illustrates some of the chief characteristics of the religious life of the Middle Ages.   Much information is given concerning the missionary labours of the saint and his companions, as well as concerning the religious and monastic life of the time.   Many graphic details are introduced from the saint's contemporary biographers, which shew forth the prevalent beliefs of the period; and abundant samples are given of St. Francis's own sayings, as well as a few specimens of his simple tender hymns.   "We are grateful to Mrs. Oliphant for a book of much interest and pathetic beauty, a book which none can read without being the better for it."—John Bull.

Pioneers and Founders; or, Recent Workers in the Mission Field.   By CHARLOTTE M. YONGE, Author of "The Heir of Redclyffe."   With Frontispiece, and Vignette Portrait of BISHOP HEBER.

The missionaries whose biographies are here given, are—John Eliot, the Apostle of the Red Indians; David Brainerd, the Enthusiast; Christian F. Schwartz, the Councillor of Tanjore; Henry Martyn, the Scholar-Missionary; William Carey and Joshua Marshman, the Serampore Missionaries; the Judson Family; the Bishops of Calcutta,— Thomas Middleton, Reginald Heber, Daniel Wilson; Samuel Marsden, the Australian Chaplain and Friend of the Maori; John Williams, the Martyr of Erromango; Allen Gardener, the Sailor Martyr; Charles Frederick Mackenzie, the Martyr of Zambesi. "Likely to be one of the most popular of the 'Sunday Library' volumes."—Literary Churchman.

Angelique Arnauld, Abbess of Port Royal. By

FRANCES MARTIN.　Crown 8vo.　4s. 6d.

This new volume of the 'Sunday Library' contains the life of a very remarkable woman founded on the best authorities. She was a Roman Catholic Abbess who lived more than 200 years ago, whose life contained much struggle and suffering. But if we look beneath the surface, we find that sublime virtues are associated with her errors, there is something admirable in everything she does, and the study of her history leads to a continual enlargement of our own range of thought and sympathy.

THE "BOOK OF PRAISE" HYMNAL,

COMPILED AND ARRANGED BY

LORD SELBORNE.

In the following four forms :—

A. Beautifully printed in Royal 32mo., limp cloth, price 6d.
B. 　　　,,　　　　,,　　Small 18mo., larger type, cloth limp, 1s.
C. Same edition on fine paper, cloth, 1s. 6d.
Also an edition with Music, selected, harmonized, and composed
　　by JOHN HULLAH, in square 18mo., cloth, 3s. 6d.

The large acceptance which has been given to " The Book of Praise" by all classes of Christian people encourages the Publishers in entertaining the hope that this Hymnal, which is mainly selected from it, may be extensively used in Congregations, and in some degree at least meet the desires of those who seek uniformity in common worship as a means towards that unity which pious souls yearn after, and which our Lord prayed for in behalf of his Church. "The office of a hymn is not to teach controversial Theology, but to give the voice of song to practical religion. No doubt, to do this, it must embody sound doctrine; but it ought to do so, not after the manner of the schools, but with the breadth, freedom, and simplicity of the Fountain-head." On this principle has Sir R. Palmer proceeded in the preparation of this book.

The arrangement adopted is the following :—

　　PART I. *consists of Hymns arranged according to the subjects of the Creed—"God the Creator," "Christ Incarnate," "Christ Crucified," "Christ Risen," "Christ Ascended," "Christ's Kingdom and Judgment," etc.*

　　PART II. *comprises Hymns arranged according to the subjects of the Lord's Prayer.*

　　PART III. *Hymns for natural and sacred seasons.*

There are 320 Hymns in all.

CAMBRIDGE :—PRINTED BY J. PALMER.